SAVAGE BETRAYAL

A DARK MAFIA AGE GAP ROMANCE

DARK REDEMPTION
BOOK 1

IVY THORN

PNK PUBLISHING

1

TIA

"We must put an end to this Moretti scourge," Don Valencia states, slamming his fist down onto the table, his fork held like a sword he would like to spear through Leonardo Moretti's heart right about now.

His plate of pasta jumps with the force of his displeasure, the china clinking as it finds the surface of the dinner table once more. Next to him, his grown son, Tony, remains focused on his food, tearing off a large chunk from the garlic roll served with his meal.

Father doesn't even seem to notice as he studies our dinner guests with dignified understanding. "That's one of the reasons I invited you all here tonight," he confesses, scanning the table of prominent families that haven't collapsed under the Morettis' pressure. Yet.

The numbers are dwindling from just a few months ago, when my father last hosted a dinner to assess the potential of forming alliances while we still can—and how marriage is the best way to do so.

"My daughter Tia comes of age in just over a month, and I think each of the eligible men in this room would make a fine match for her."

Next to my father, my mother looks on with patient resolve, her face neutral and accepting. Their marriage was arranged, she often reminds me. So, why wouldn't I be as happy in my marriage as she has been in hers? It might not be a fairy tale romance, but it's more pragmatic.

"Joining the great Guerra household with another family that's rooted in Piovosa's rich history," Don Fiore observes, placing his utensils on his plate and leaning back in his chair.

"Indeed," my father says.

Don Fiore's eyes scan down the length of the table to land on me.

My heart skips a beat at his scrutinizing gaze, the way he seems to consider me like he would a prized horse he's considering adding to his stable. Never mind the fact that the widower is well over twice my age and supposed to still be in mourning—or at least he would be if he cared at all for his wife of twenty years, whom he lost just months ago.

"With your daughters' reputations of refinement and modesty, I'm sure it would be an honor to take Tia as a wife," he says, his voice dripping with lecherous pleasure.

Beside me, my sister Maria makes a not-so-subtle gagging noise, and I bite the inside of my cheek to stop myself from smiling. Only after Don Fiore returns his attention to the head of the table do I dare glance Maria's way.

At age sixteen, she's probably the only one of my four younger sisters who can fully comprehend what's coming for each of us eventually. And it's coming to me far sooner than the rest. Marriage—likely to some gross old man like Don Fiore. Because that's the only thing a houseful of Guerra daughters is good for. Our family name.

Seeing as Don Guerra was cursed with five daughters and not a single son, an alliance made through marriage is the only way my father can protect his legacy. Especially now, with the Moretti family's seemingly insatiable appetite to conquer and rule our thriving Italian settlement sequestered in the Allegheny Mountains.

We need help.

And marriage is the perfect way to guarantee it.

"It would establish an unbreakable bond between two families who might not be capable of stopping the Morettis on their own but, when joined together, could send them running with their tails between their legs," Father says.

"Yes, I would like to see that arrogant bastard brought down a few pegs," Don Valencia states.

"I'm ready to wipe the smug smile off Leonardo's face," Don Russo growls. "It's as if he thinks he's already won the town. The way he's throwing parties nearly every other week, pretending like we're not at war."

"So low class." Don Amici scoffs.

"I've heard the balls he hosts are a new level of sophistication," Lorenzo Valencia says, a hint of awe in his voice.

His statement triggers in me a curiosity, a thirst to understand, that's been growing inside for weeks now. I want to know what it is about the Morettis that drives people to such extreme emotions. Love them or hate them, it seems everybody's talking about the Morettis, and I want nothing more than to know what all the fuss is about.

Which is why I intend to sneak out. Tonight. After our dinner guests leave. I plan to go to a party hosted by Leonardo Moretti—the leader of the Moretti family, in all but title, and the rabble-rouser that my father speaks of as if he were the Boogeyman himself. From the way my father makes it sound, the Morettis are capable of unspeakable atrocities, and with Leonardo at their head, they have become all but an unstoppable force.

But as much as my father hates Leonardo Moretti, my cousins don't seem to think it's too dangerous to crash his house parties. Apparently, the guy rarely even makes an appearance at them. *So, why can't I?*

Just this once.

My sisters and I live such sheltered lives, being home-schooled, residing on the family estate, and only entering the town with escorts. It's a comfortable life, and one that's so entirely dull. I don't think I can stand another evening of reading by the fire. I want to see some of the world before my father marries me off to some gross old perv like Don Fiore.

I glance sideways at the three Valencia men in attendance just in time to catch Don Valencia giving his younger son a thunderous scowl. This is not the household to be handing out compliments to the Morettis. Even a harmless one like Lorenzo's.

But the older Valencia son seems too preoccupied with the meal to have noticed the tension in the room. "This tagliatelle is delicious," Tony Valencia says around his mouthful of pasta.

I try not to cringe as the stray noodles hanging from his lips are sucked into his maw with such force that sauce splatters across his chin and the napkin tucked into his shirt.

"Of course, I'm open to negotiations and would like to ensure the match with my daughter would be... agreeable on both sides," my father says.

I sincerely hope the hint of disgust in his tone means he's less inclined to marry me off to Tony. The sloppy eating, I could probably learn to live with. *But the gluttony of gambling debts the Valencia heir has accrued?* He's well on his way to spending every last penny of his inheritance before his father's even in his grave.

No, I don't think I could stomach living with a man so willingly a victim to his vices. And while his brother Lorenzo might not be nearly so bad, he's not much better.

"My son Valentine would make an excellent match for your daughter," Don Russo states with a sure grin.

"But isn't Valentine just twelve?" I ask, boldly meeting the don's eyes. "He can't possibly be ready for marriage."

"I hardly think you should concern yourself with matters you clearly don't understand. Obviously, he would grow into his role as your husband. And I would think you should consider yourself lucky not to be strapped with someone... older," Don Russo states dismissively, giving Don Fiore a sidelong glance before turning his eyes to my father.

The silent look states that Don Guerra should get his unruly daughter under control before I embarrass him further.

"Tia."

That's all my father needs to say. I know that hint of warning too well. If I don't hold my tongue, I will very much regret provoking the punishment that will follow our guests' departure.

I bristle at the perfunctory way they discuss my nuptials as if I were nothing more than a piece of dining room furniture to be traded away. But as I'm little more than a pawn to these *great* men, no one cares to tiptoe around my feelings.

The end game—the victory over the Morettis—is all that matters.

Still, I'll count my gentle scolding as a small blessing. Because it's given me a window of opportunity to bow out of the stifling negotiations.

"Pardon my ignorance, Don Russo. Of course, you would know better about the workings of these types of arrangements. If I might be excused, father? I'll leave the conversation to those who understand such things."

"Take your sisters with you," he agrees, sending me off with a wave of his hand.

Delicately wiping my lips, I set aside my napkin, then take Maria by the wrist and pull her out of her chair and toward the dining room door. Anna, Vienna, and little Sofia follow without a word.

"Blech," Maria says as soon as we're out of earshot. "I'm dreading the day father decides who to marry you off to."

I cringe internally. "Me too."

"I mean, don't get me wrong. I feel terrible for you. But just think, if that's what the options are, and you have first pick, who might I get stuck with as the leftovers?" Maria shudders visibly.

"Maybe you'll be lucky enough to land Valentine Russo," I tease.

Maria gives me a playful shove with her shoulder. "I'm not really interested in babysitting. Thanks."

I laugh, appreciating that I have at least one person to commiserate with.

Still, I haven't even told Maria about my plans for tonight...

It's well past sunset, and the house lights have already started to darken as I ease my bedroom window open. Not daring to breathe, I watch and listen to see if any of my family's guards made note of the soft shuffling noise, but if they're in the vicinity, none seem to be drawn my way.

Slowly releasing my breath, I ease my shoulders through the window and look to my left. The ivy-covered lattice that creeps up the side of our oversized home looked a lot less intimidating to climb down in the daylight—when I was concocting my elaborate escape.

Now, I just hope the wood hasn't started rotting after the century's worth of plant growth that creeps up the side of the picturesque New England mansion. But I'm not about to chicken out now.

I have been hearing about the extravagant Moretti house parties for months now. And tonight, I intend to see what the fuss is all about. After having spent my entire childhood following the rules, I am determined to have at least one good adventure.

A shiver races down my spine at the wood's agonized groan beneath my weight as I scale the siding. But I press on, clinging to the vines even as they scrape my palms and snag the skirt of my flirtiest dress. I'm more than a little grateful when I've climbed down far enough to drop the last few feet onto solid ground.

Crouching, I turn quickly to make sure no one saw me.

Looks like I'm in the clear.

Keeping low and moving fast, I head for the trees that line either side of our long drive.

The air is crisp for a night in late April, but I don't mind. My destination is a bit of a walk, which will keep me warm. As soon as I'm safe from view, I hunker into my fleece-lined Italian leather coat, cram my fingers into its pockets, and pick up a nice pace.

Giddy excitement bubbles in my veins as I head toward the historic downtown of Piovosa. I make it into town on rare occasions and never unsupervised—like we're some family out of the Dark Ages.

But I know it's because, in Piovosa, our family name is worth its weight in gold, and my father is only looking out for our safety. I just wish he weren't quite so overprotective. It's not like kidnappers are waiting around every corner to snatch up a Guerra girl and ransom her off for some exorbitant amount of money.

Against all odds—or so it would seem based on my father's extensive warnings not to leave the house unaccompanied—I arrive safely at my destination without a single abduction attempt.

It's not hard to find the party. Not when fancy cars line the pavement all the way from the street to the far end of the Morettis' winding drive. The flashy Corvettes and sleek Porsches accompany me all the way up to the backlit fountain at the center of the circular courtyard.

Few houses in Piovosa can rival mine. But as I stare up at the striking gothic architecture of Don Moretti's home, I think we might have met our match. The towering monstrosity is something between a mansion and a castle in both size and shape, with countless spires and haunting gargoyles protecting the corners of each eave.

Music spills through the grand double doors at the top of the front steps, and lights illuminate the windows with a golden glow that accentuates the structure's silent dignity. The elegant display of warmth somehow makes my mission all the more exciting.

Here, there appear to be no rules saying I must wait for an invitation. The atmosphere says all are welcome. And the thrill of meeting new people not preapproved by my father's stuffy expectations fills me with a sense of giddy anticipation. This promises to be a night of adventure.

Taking a deep, steadying breath, I comb my fingers through my thick mahogany locks, checking to make sure they're in place after my rather brisk night stroll. Then I square my shoulders and climb up the sweeping front steps and into the home of my family's sworn enemy.

The grand entry steals my breath away as I take in the open space with a marble staircase curving down either side. The back wall is made entirely of gilded mirrors that catch and reflect the sparkling lights bouncing off the decadent crystal chandelier.

Like an ornate version of a disco ball, the fixture dripping with jewels occupies the very center of the vaulted room. Visually, it's stunning, with so many rainbow refractions glimmering from its countless angles that I can't tell where the light starts or ends.

But what really catches my attention is the sheer number of bodies that fill the space, some dancing, some laughing, some standing close together in deep conversation.

Pulse quickening with the lively energy that envelops me, I stop to take it all in. I don't quite know where to begin. I'm party crashing—there's no doubt about that. But the distinct lack of bouncers or guards makes me think it doesn't matter to anyone here.

"Has he spoken to you?" one girl asks to my left, her tone almost dreamy in its breathlessness.

"Leo Moretti? I wish," her friend adds.

I glance in their direction to see three girls clustered together, their hair perfectly coiffed, dresses about as short as they can get without being scandalous, eyes scanning the room hungrily.

"I don't need him to speak with me. I just want him to look my way."

"Screw that. I want him to take me to bed. The man looks like a god, and I've heard he fucks like one too."

My cheeks heat at the lewd topic of conversation the girls are holding right there in the middle of the crowded room. And I can't help the juvenile giggle that bubbles up my throat. My father would never allow me to keep company with girls who would even *think* something like that, let alone say it.

And though I have no experience when it comes to men or the activities that go on between two people in a bedroom, it exhilarates me to think that I'm stepping outside of my safe little world to get a better understanding of this side of society.

Even if I have no clue where to go from here.

Stealing myself, I take several tentative steps toward the center of the room, hoping I don't look too out of place. But I can't help keeping my head on a swivel as I take in the luxurious decor and the lavish partygoers—it really does scream a sophistication my father has never once mentioned when talking about the Moretti heir.

"Are you lost?" someone asks in a sinfully smooth, masculine voice.

My heart skips a beat, and I turn to meet a pair of intelligent hazel eyes. The man before me is tall, well over six feet, with a sharp jawline darkened by the perfect amount of five-o'clock shadow.

Possibly the bouncer I was looking for, who stops gate crashers before they get too far into the hall?

But that's not what wipes my usually quick words from my mind. It's the fact that he might just be the most gorgeous man I've ever laid eyes on.

His black curls fall across his forehead in chaotic perfection. His broad shoulders fill out the mint-green dress shirt he's rolled up to his elbows in a casual display of comfort. And his collar is unbuttoned just enough to show the hint of dark chest hair that tells me he's several years my senior.

Dressed in only the finest brand names, his Italian leather shoes and black slacks crisp, clean, and tailored to perfection, he looks worthy of the front page of a magazine. And all together, the package gives him an air of silent confidence that says, without a doubt, he has the authority to end my night of fun before it's even begun.

He looks down his proud nose, and a slow, subtle grin tells me he knows I shouldn't be here. One dark eyebrow forms a sharp and artistic arch as I continue to stare at him, open-mouthed, at an utter loss for words.

"Did you come here with someone tonight?" His deep baritone makes my stomach quiver as his eyes shift to the door behind me.

"Oh, uh, no. I was invited," I say quickly.

My immediate blush gives me away, I'm sure, and his eyebrow creeps higher up his forehead, indicating he sees straight through me.

"By whom?"

Now what do I say? I have no idea who might have the power to invite me aside from the Morettis themselves. All I can do is hope that giving a name with authority will minimize his questions. Trying not to panic, I swallow hard and smile. "Don Moretti, of course."

"Really? Marco Moretti invited you to this party?" Both eyebrows rise now.

Oh, dear god. I am so busted. "Yes? Well, I mean, no. Just in a manner of speaking. It was more like his son."

"Leonardo Moretti sent an invitation to your house?"

It's just a hint of challenge that gives away his skepticism, and I can feel myself buckling under the pressure.

"Mm-hmm," I agree, flashing him my most winning smile.

Laser intelligence cuts through me, asking a hundred questions in the silence that follows. *I should not have come. What was I thinking?* He knows I don't belong, and I'm definitely about to get kicked out. Or worse...

This was such a bad idea.

Then he unleashes a devilishly handsome grin. "Well, in that case, welcome."

Relief floods me as the inquisition ends as quickly as it began.

"Would you like a drink...?" He leaves the question hanging, waiting for me to supply a name.

"Tia," I provide. "Just Tia." I suspect throwing around the last name of Guerra might not be the smartest plan right about now. "And yes, a drink sounds wonderful," I add with a smile.

"Well, Tia, let me show you where they are."

The man places a hand on the small of my back, bringing butterflies to life in my stomach as he gestures toward the mirrored wall at the far end of the entry. I follow his lead, and the crowd seems to part around us as we move.

The way they shift raises goosebumps on my arms and a tingling sense of foreboding tickles the back of my mind. This can't be the man himself, right? While still a man, he's too young to be the conqueror everyone fears. Besides, I've been told on many occasions that he never attends his own parties.

Still, this inquisitor of mine must merit enough respect that he doesn't have to say a word.

We turn right around a corner of the mirrored wall and into a ballroom that dwarfs the size of the one in my family home. The entire back wall is made up of windows and French doors, each opening out onto a stunning terrace that runs the expanse of the ballroom.

"Wow," I breathe, astonished by the grandeur that somehow manages to outshine the opulence of my own home.

"You like it?"

"It's incredible," I confess.

We stop in front of the full bar, stocked with every variety of liquor, all in opulent bottles that must have cost a fortune.

"What do you like to drink, Tia?" my inquisitor asks as the bartender turns his attention to us.

I don't. I have no clue what I might like to drink. I quickly scan the bottles, looking for something that might sound remotely familiar. "I'll take a Macallan." I've never tasted it before, but my father offers it to guests as an after-dinner drink.

My guide's eyebrows rise in apparent surprise mingled with a hint of amusement. "We'll take two." He raises two long fingers toward the bartender. "Neat?" His eyes shift back to mine, clearly expecting an answer.

"Neat," I agree, confused by his question. *Is he asking me if that's cool for him to order the same thing?* I have no clue why it would or wouldn't be. But he's been nice enough to speak to me, where most people didn't glance my way.

The bartender takes the beautiful bottle off the shelf and pours us each a small amount of liquid into two cut-crystal glasses. I accept mine and cup it between my palms, too nervous to take a sip right away.

"Tell me, Tia, what brings you here tonight?" my gorgeous guide asks, his hazel gaze probing.

My nerves come to life once again as I sense an undercurrent to his question. Even so, I can't stop the thrill that races through me at the sound of my name on his lips. "Oh, you know, the same reasons everyone goes to parties like these."

"Which is?"

"For fun?" I suggest, my answers coming out as questions as my confidence plummets.

"What kind of fun?" he asks, his eyes mesmerizing in their intensity.

I shrug, attempting to release some of the tension from my shoulders with the nonchalant gesture. "To meet new people and see new things. Am I supposed to be searching for another kind?" My stomach knots as I recall the conversation those three girls were having near the front door. About capturing a certain Moretti's attention and maybe even getting him to take them to bed.

"Forgive me if I might sound suspicious, but it's not every night that a daughter of Don Guerra comes strolling through my door."

My heart slams against my ribcage as I realize just how deep I might have stepped in it. "Y-You know who I am?"

"It's my job to know everyone coming and going from this house, and you, Tia, have piqued my interest. Are you here to spy on me? Did your father send you?"

"No, I—I didn't—I mean, he didn't…" I flounder, once again lost for words as my mind quickly translates the full meaning of his words. Then it hits me. "Spy on you?"

Shit. This must be Leonardo Moretti. I am such an idiot.

But even as the fact stares me in the face, I can hardly believe that the man in front of me is the one who's gotten so far under my father's skin. He doesn't come across as the dangerous and brutal criminal my parents have made him out to be. He can't be…

"You're Leonardo Moretti," I breathe.

He doesn't respond. He doesn't need to.

My eyes drop as I realize there's no way out of this but to tell the truth and pray I haven't made a massive mistake by disobeying my father. Because, as of right now, I'm entirely at the mercy of the Moretti heir. My only chance of survival is honesty and a prayer that he'll believe me.

"I snuck out," I confess, heat radiating from my cheeks as I study the glass clasped in my hands. "My father would kill me if he knew I was here. But I just... I want to *live* my life."

I press my lips closed to stop the rush of words that threaten to spill from me in a flood. And I glance tentatively up through my eyelashes, feeling I've said too much.

But Leo's gaze softens, growing sympathetic even, then a hint of humor glints in his striking eyes. "So, you're not here to kill me, then?" he jokes, his disarming smile returning in full force.

Heat races through my veins as an electric energy crackles between us. "And take that honor from my father? He would never forgive me." The smartass comment is out of my mouth before I have time to think through how wise it might be.

But before I have time to panic, he releases a low, sexy chuckle.

"May I ask you something, Leonardo?"

"Only if you'll call me Leo."

Heat creeps into my cheeks at his request. "Leo." I test it out and find the name suits him better somehow. "How old are you?"

It feels like a juvenile question, but he's not what I would expect of a man capable of tearing apart the town of Piovosa and dismantling generations of family wealth and power in five short years.

The humor in his eyes intensifies, but he doesn't challenge my question. "Twenty-five."

"Nooo." The uncouth word slips from my mouth before I can stop it, and I clap my hand over my lips.

"You don't believe me?" he asks, another chuckle rumbling from his chest.

"I mean... I have no reason *not* to believe you. It's just..." From what I've heard about Leo's conquests, I can hardly believe he's that young. Since he took the reins of the Moretti family, he's expanded their power and territory with alarming efficiency. "I had always imagined you'd be older."

Silence stretches between us, and I take a drink to stop myself from fidgeting. Poor choice. The alcohol burns as it trickles down my throat, bringing tears to my eyes. I choke and cough, fighting hard not to spit out the liquid fire. And when I finally regain a semblance of composure, Leo wordlessly offers me a napkin.

"Thanks," I rasp, wiping my lips and then my watering eyes.

"How old are you, Tia?" he asks, his eyes scrutinizing me perceptively.

It's a fair question after mine, but that doesn't make me any less mortified to tell him. "E-Eighteen," I lie. I mean, I will be soon enough, but I don't want to sound any more childish than I've already managed in this conversation.

Leo's hazel gaze holds mine with a steady silence that seems to slice through my untruth with the ease of a hot knife through butter. Still, he doesn't challenge me. "And you snuck out of your father's house to come to this party looking for an adventure?"

Biting my lip as my nerves get the better of me, I nod. I've made such a fool of myself. I must look like a child to him. I am a child to him, with not just a seven-year age gap but a world of experience that stands between us. But his crooked smile that follows wipes the thought away.

"Well, then, the least I can do is show you around," he offers, leaning close to place a hand on the small of my back once more.

His proximity sends my body into an unexpected frenzy as my breath catches in my throat. I detect the hint of sandalwood, vanilla, and amber cologne in the air around him. The scent quickens my heartbeat, and I can't help but take in the sight of him once more as a heady dose of attraction pounds through my veins. Leo Moretti is nothing like the demon I had envisioned. He's just... hot.

"Where do we start?" I ask breathily, trying to regain my composure.

"How about the library? People come from all over to see it."

"That sounds... wonderful." In truth, that's where I feel most at home. After so many hours immersed in the books that provide my only source of escape, I'm confident a library will put me at ease.

Once again, the party guests move fluidly out of our way, like the Red Sea parting as Leo escorts me down the elegant hallways. He stops before two oversized double doors and slowly swings one open, gesturing that I should enter first.

I stop short as soon as I step inside the two-story library filled with rich cherry-wood shelves that hold leather-bound tomes. The sight of all that knowledge packed into one vast room takes my breath away.

"You like books," Leo observes as we linger in the quiet room that no one else has ventured into.

I nod. "It never ceases to amaze me that something so small can take you all over the world—even to worlds you couldn't find in a million years—with just a few slips of parchment and a well of ink. What's not to love?"

When he doesn't respond right away, I glance up at Leo and find he's standing closer than I had expected. My heart skips a beat as he studies me, his devastatingly handsome face close enough to touch, and I find myself trapped inside his intelligent green-gray eyes.

"What?" I breathe, unsure of why he's looking at me that way. All I know is I like it.

"I wouldn't have figured you for a poet, Signorina Guerra."

Heat pools in my cheeks at the flattering statement, and I glance around to distract myself before I say something embarrassing. "Do you have a favorite book?" I ask, following a row of hardcovers with curling gold print embossed along their spines.

My fingers trace lightly across them as I note their geographical categorization.

"It's been some time since I've read a book for pleasure," Leo admits, following beside me with smooth, long strides. "But *Treasure Island* was always my favorite growing up."

I glance sharply up at him, studying his proud features. "Really?"

The hint of a smile tugs at his lips as Leo stops and turns to me. "Again, you doubt me? It's a wonder you braved my home at all if you're so confident I would lie."

"No, it's not—sorry, I'm just surprised because Robert Louis Stevenson is my favorite author. I've probably read *Treasure Island* fifty times."

"A brilliant book about adventure. 'Hang the treasure! It's the glory of the sea that has turned my head,'" he quotes, his eyes dancing. "Somehow, it doesn't surprise me that you like it."

Is it entirely wrong that I find his ability to quote Stevenson on a whim entirely too appealing?

The energy shifts between us, that electric tension transforming into something more like a magnetic pull as Leo's posture softens. The conversation takes a more personal turn as we stroll around the empty room, talking about the characters that inspire us and the books that hold a special place on our hearts' shelves.

As Leo's tour carries us back out into the hall, our conversation continues. I find myself surprisingly relaxed, my composure reclaimed as our discussion shifts from literature to history, geography, and culture. Things I've cultivated knowledge about through my top-tier education and thirst for information, while he's learned much firsthand.

"I've heard great things about the Guerra daughters. It's an honor to finally meet you and discover for myself that the rumors are true."

My stomach flip-flops dangerously. "What rumors?"

"That you're as intelligent and charming as you are beautiful," Leo says.

The statement is casual, as though he's completely oblivious to what his words might be doing to my body. But hearing a gorgeous, older man like Leo call me beautiful does strange things to my insides. I can't quite tell if my heart is in my throat or if that's the butterflies trying to escape my tummy.

"Leo!" a man calls, walking toward us. He looks just a few years older than I am. "I've been looking all over for you. I... who's your friend?" he asks, his mind seeming to jump tracks as his eyes take me in for the first time.

"Meet Tia. Tia, this is my cousin Vinnie."

"It's a pleasure," he says, extending his hand.

And as I take it, Vinnie leans in to stage-whisper, "Don't let him fool you. He might come across as intimidating and respectable, but he's a sucker for a pretty smile." Then he gives me a conspiratorial wink.

A startled giggle escapes me, and I glance at Leo from the corner of my eye to gauge his reaction. He merely quirks an eyebrow at his cousin, who clears his throat and straightens. Once again, I'm struck by the authority he commands without lifting a finger. Not even my father puts people in line with so little effort.

"You needed something, Vinnie?" he says after a moment's silence.

"Oh, yeah. But it can wait." Leo's cousin gives a slight bow of his head. "Pleasure to meet you, Tia."

"Likewise."

We don't linger long before Leo whisks me toward a door leading off the hall. A moment later, we enter the billiards, where several pool tables have multiple games occurring at once. In here, the scent of cigars lingers in the air, and the throbbing music bleeds through the walls without actually filling the room.

Once again, Leo introduces me like a guest of honor. Though I know several of the partygoers as acquaintances of my family, it becomes increasingly easy to spot the Moretti family members—because I recognize so few.

We travel through several more rooms, Leo showing me the study, the conservatory, the parlor. Each is more finely decorated than the last. As we weave through the crowded house, Leo converses lightly with his guests, introducing me to whomever he thinks I might find interesting along the way.

And the longer I spend with him, the more I start to question all the warnings my parents have given about staying far away from the Moretti family. I sense nothing of the animosity my father has spoken about reflected in Leo's actions.

If anything, his easy charm makes it impossible to avoid what I'm quickly realizing is my first crush.

We finish our tour back in the ballroom, where the party is in full swing, the music filling the space as people move across the dance floor and mingle.

"Would you... be interested in going somewhere a little more private?" he asks after several more guests bombard him, demanding his attention. "Somewhere we can talk without this constant interruption?"

And though I don't quite understand why Leo seems so willing to keep talking to me, I can't deny I like it. My pulse quickens, and I swallow to quell my nerves as I nod.

2

TIA

The separate wing Leo takes me to rings with the silence of leaving the party's music behind, and I'm suddenly intensely aware of each breath passing between my lips. This section of the house is as ornately decorated as the last, with rich marble floors, fine dark-wood wall paneling, and pedestals holding fresh bouquets of flowers that perfume the air.

I can only imagine how many people it must take to maintain the opulent arrangements.

"No one will bother us here," Leo assures me, stopping to open a thick wooden door.

Nervous excitement bubbles up in my chest as I take in the mahogany four-poster bed, the rich furnishings that accompany it, and the deep greens, grays, and browns that fill the space with warmth. A closed-glass gas fireplace with sparkling obsidian at its base occupies one entire wall of the room. And just beyond it is the en suite bathroom.

"Is this...?"

"My room? Yes, I hope you don't mind. It's just the one place I know I can find peace and quiet. No one will disturb us here."

My heart flutters giddily, the excitement warring with a deeply ingrained apprehension. I know my parents would never approve of me being alone with a boy in his room. Especially not Leonardo Moretti. And at the back of my mind, an alarm bell sends off a subtle warning at his words.

And yet, I don't want to say no. For whatever reason, I trust Leo. And it flatters me to think he would invite me into his personal space when he has maintained a polite distance from so many of his other guests tonight. I might be crashing his party, but he's certainly welcoming me into his place of solitude.

"It's beautiful," I admit, taking in the spacious room that feels like an apartment in and of itself.

The door clicks softly shut behind us, and when I glance back at Leo, he gestures to the richly upholstered seating area that fills the space near his large picture window. Outside, the night looms inky and absolute, making the window into a reflective surface.

Fire races through my veins as Leo's eyes find mine in the mirrored glass. His lips curve into a mischievous grin, breaking the sudden tension and freezing me in place; I release a breathy laugh as he seems to read my indecision and takes the lead.

"Have you enjoyed your taste of freedom tonight?" he asks, his smooth baritone low and warm as he settles onto the couch, his arm resting lightly along the back.

Taking the seat next to him, I nod, biting my lip to maintain my silence. I don't dare speak for fear that I might tell him this has been one of the best nights of my life. I snuck out looking for a sense of adventure, and I found not just that but an enchanted castle with a prince charming as well.

But I definitely can't say that.

"Well, I'm glad I got to be a part of it, then." Leo's eyes shift down to my trapped lower lip, a fire igniting in his gaze that makes my stomach tremble. "Tia," he murmurs, forcing his eyes back up to mine as he leans closer. "I would very much like to kiss you."

A potent dose of adrenaline seeps through my core at his words. I've never kissed a boy before, and the prospect of feeling Leo's dangerously sexy lips against mine… it sends heat coursing through my veins, filling me with a foreign exhilaration.

"I think I'd like that too," I breathe, my tongue darting out to moisten my suddenly dry lips.

A slow smile curls one corner of his mouth, and Leo takes my practically untouched glass of scotch, setting it and his own glass on the side table behind him. Then he shifts, drawing closer until our knees meet.

My breath catches in my throat as he cradles my chin with long, masculine fingers, tipping my face closer to his. His eyes drop to my lips once again as he leans in with excruciating care. Heart pounding in my throat, I don't dare move. I don't dare breathe as time stands still.

He closes the distance slowly, as if giving me the opportunity to change my mind. And when our lips finally meet, a jolt of electric heat crackles through my body, leaving my lips tingling. I can't help the gasp that escapes me, and Leo releases a low hum of amusement as I feel his soft smile form against my mouth.

Then he kisses me more ardently, his lips covering mine with a fiery need as his hand brushes slowly across my jaw. His fingers comb into my hair as he cradles the back of my head in a passionate embrace.

A shiver of excitement ripples up my spine as his tongue dances out to trace the seam of my lips. I open them instinctually, and a burning warmth blossoms deep in my core as he strokes between my teeth, tasting me. I've never felt anything quite like it. And I want more.

The smoky flavor of the scotch lingers on his tongue. And my desire to explore this overwhelming attraction makes me bold. Reaching up, I mirror his gesture, combing my fingers into his thick curls. They're silky as they tangle around my fingers, and the low groan that rushes from his lips to mine tells me he likes the way I'm touching him.

A strong arm snakes around my waist, pulling me close, and my heart hammers against my ribs at the feel of his hard chest pressing against mine. The world around us seems to fade as his kiss intensifies, awakening in me an appetite I never knew I possessed.

After a lifetime of reading fairy tales and love stories, I can't help but wonder if this isn't what love is like, that weightlessness that makes a person feel like they can fly. I'm falling for Leo, hard. And though I know that's nothing short of a betrayal when he's my family's sworn enemy, I can't seem to stop myself.

My parents have mistakenly pegged him as a villain, but I don't doubt that they would see the good in him if they took the opportunity to get to know him personally like I have. Leo's charming, funny, intelligent. He gets me in a way no one ever has. And it shouldn't matter that his last name is Moretti. Not when *this* is the kind of love he has to give.

Slowly, Leo lowers me back onto the couch, his weight settling lightly over me as he continues to kiss me with smoldering passion. His body rests against mine, and the prominent bulge that presses like an iron rod into the side of my hip brings sinfully dangerous thoughts to mind. From what I understand of anatomy, that would indicate he's as excited by kissing me as I am by him. At the peak of my thighs, heat builds, making me ravenous for more.

My breath comes fast and shallow as I scarcely recognize myself. I've never done anything so rash. A small voice at the back of my mind questions how smart it is to be alone with a man, an older man whom my parents don't trust. But I only get one life to live, and Leo makes me feel like my wait is over—this is where the adventure begins.

Leo transitions his kisses, finding the corner of my mouth and then the tender flesh behind my ear. Air rushes sharply between my teeth as he sucks the tender flesh between his lips, making my body throb. It's like he knows exactly how to bring me to life, lighting a fire deep inside me.

And as he continues to suck, his hand slowly travels down my body. His fingers whisper across my chest, his touch feather-light as he follows the line of my cleavage that vanishes into my dress.

As he shifts to cup one breast, the warmth of his palm radiates into my flesh, melting my insides. A low, feral groan rumbles from his throat as he kneads my breast through the layers of my bra and dress.

"You're so young and firm," he rasps appreciatively.

My heart skips a beat as I wonder if he might not know I lied about my age. *Could my body possibly give that away?* But he doesn't draw back or accuse me. Instead, his fingers curl around the low neckline of my dress, sliding inside the lacy fabric of my bra until his fingers find my nipple.

Liquid arousal washes through my core as he takes the hard nub between his finger and thumb, lightly rolling it. I gasp as a tingling euphoria follows, leaving me almost numb with pleasure.

"God, I want to see your beautiful body," he breathes, kissing me fervently as he fills me with overwhelming need. "I bet you're the most perfect creature I'll ever see."

"Okay," I murmur, my stomach doing somersaults.

I shouldn't let him. My father would be furious if he found out. *Throwing away the modesty he's ingrained in me since I was a little girl? Exposing myself to a man?* Let alone my father's sworn enemy. But something about Leo makes me want to know, to understand that deep, indescribable connection lovers have.

Leo pauses, drawing back from me just enough to meet my eyes, and in them is a silent question of whether I mean it, a hope that I did. I nod, the motion jerky with the intensity of my nerves. Then Leo reclaims my lips fiercely, rewarding me with his sinfully inspiring enthusiasm.

Strong arms pull me up off the couch and back onto my feet a moment later, and Leo holds my waist until I'm steady. Then he steps back to watch me. Biting the pad of my lower lip, I shrug out of my coat to reveal my flirty blue bodycon dress. Reaching behind me, I unzip it with shaking hands.

His warm fingers curl around the straps of my dress a moment later, and he guides them slowly down my arms. Then he pulls the stretchy fabric past my breasts and hips.

I let him, shivering at the suddenly intense exposure of bare flesh. My hair tickles as it falls down my exposed back in a thick waterfall. My nipples pucker, pressing adamantly against their lace cage.

Leo's smoldering gaze travels appreciatively down my curves. Heat blossoms in my cheeks as I realize I'm wearing a rather childish pair of cotton underwear with blue bows speckling the white fabric. They don't even match my lacy black bra.

But Leo doesn't seem to care. He issues a low whistle of approval as he steps back to admire my body. Then a smile graces his perfect lips. "You're fucking hot, Tia."

With a groan that sends a jolt of nervous anticipation through my core, he closes the distance between us once again.

Goosebumps ripple across my flesh as his strong arms enfold me, pulling me against his solid chest, and he kisses me with a hunger that leaves me trembling. Guiding my arms up around his shoulders, Leo slowly walks me back toward the bed.

My heart pounds a mile a minute now as my thoughts start to race. *Are we about to have sex? Am I ready for that?* My father would kill me if he found out. All those years of careful supervision, never letting me out of sight to ensure not just my protection but my chastity, and the first time I manage to evade my guards, I give away my most valuable asset?

I shouldn't. I know that.

But god, I've never wanted to experience something so badly in my life.

"W-What are you doing?" I stammer as he presses me gently onto the soft sheets.

"I just want to make you feel good, Tia. Will you let me do that?" he asks. "I want to show you what it really means to live. To give you the best night of your life."

Skin tingling with nervous anticipation, I look deep into Leo's eyes. And in them, all I can find is sincerity, a truth that sets my soul on fire.

"Yes," I agree, shifting as he settles onto the bed beside me.

His smile broadens, and his touch is soft as he murmurs a sultry, "Good." He follows me as I lie back across the sheets, and then his fingers trail lightly down my skin until they find the top of my panties. "You can tell me to stop whenever you want," he promises, his hand hesitating for just a moment.

Licking my lips nervously, I nod. But I don't stop him. I want to know the pleasure he's offering. And I trust that he can give it to me. I *want* him to. Because Leo is everything I could ever have dreamed I might want in a man. He's smart, engaging, handsome—not like any of the idiots my father has been parading me in front of for months. And he's offering me a freedom I've been craving for far too long.

As his hand slides beneath the fabric of my panties, it blows my world apart. I gasp as his fingers graze the sensitive nub at the peak of my thighs, releasing a tingling pleasure through my body that wipes my mind blank.

His fingers stroke a part of me that no one has ever touched before, and the forbidden intimacy makes me tremble. Like the softest silk, his touch glides across my skin and slowly delves between my folds.

"Holy shit, you're so wet," he rasps, touching me gently.

I groan as the pleasure builds to an inferno, searing my flesh as it consumes my soul.

"I think someone likes when I kiss her," he whispers playfully, his lips hovering over mine.

I nod. Right now, I would confess to just about anything as long as he kept touching me like this. And he does, his fingers stroking me, then circling my most sensitive spot with heavenly precision. At the same time, his lips slant over mine, his tongue pressing between them to taste me deeply.

Every nerve in my body lights on fire, consumed by sinful pleasure. I shouldn't be doing this. I know. I shouldn't let him touch me. But I can't help myself. I can't stop the overwhelming need that fogs my brain and leaves me panting for more. My arousal intensifies, my excitement climbing to a pinnacle of ecstasy I've never known.

Then he slowly presses one finger deep inside my depths. I cry out at the unexpected euphoria that accompanies the foreign penetration. My core tightens around him, filling me with a powerful new desire.

"Does that feel good?" he purrs, nipping playfully at my ear.

I nod, my lips too numb to form words, my breaths gasping from me in short, hard bursts. And Leo gives a low chuckle. Then his fingers stroke more adamantly between my folds, and he eases a second finger inside me.

"Oh god!" I moan as a trembling desire consumes me. My knees shake as my muscles tighten. In preparation for what, I don't know.

But Leo seems to, and his thumb finds the sensitive point at the peak of my thighs, sending a jolt of pleasure up my spine. As his fingers press inside me once more, I topple into oblivion.

Ecstasy blasts through me like a bomb, sending immense, tingling relief out to the tips of my fingers and toes. My core throbs, spasming around Leo's fingers as my clit pulses against his thumb, and my chest heaves as I ride the unexpected wave of all-consuming euphoria.

Leo hums appreciatively, his lips soft as he brushes a kiss across my throat. "You're sexy when you come," he growls.

"Holy hell," I gasp, absorbing his words and realizing I've just experienced my first orgasm. "Do that again."

A dark chuckle rumbles inside his chest as his eyes search mine. "If you'll let me, I can blow your mind. What do you say, Tia? Are you up for knowing the best kind of pleasure you'll ever find?" he suggests.

If he means sex, I'm ready for it now. I want to discover all that Leo has to offer. I want to know the world of pleasure he lives in. *And would it be so bad to have one amazing night with a guy I actually like, who I genuinely find attractive? I'll soon be facing a lifetime of misery with some old perve or a gross, idiotic slob, so don't I deserve one special memory to call my own?*

I nod.

And the light that brightens his eyes is priceless. He wants this as much as I do.

He rises from the bed, leaving me a puddle of bliss as he strips with casual confidence.

It's impossible not to watch as he grips the collar of his dress shirt and pulls it up over his back and shoulders to reveal an impressively muscled chest. His broad shoulders look powerful. And the hard body I felt beneath his shirt is toned to perfection. His abs form an etched six-pack, and as he unbuckles his belt, letting his slacks fall to the floor, I find hard lines that form a V tapering down his hips to vanish suggestively inside his boxer briefs.

My heart stutters as his hard cock comes into view for the first time. I've never seen one before—beyond what's in the anatomy books—and though I don't quite know what I expected, this isn't it. It looks far larger than any I've seen images of.

That's supposed to fit inside me?

Leo reaches into the drawer of his bedside table and pulls out a small square foil. Ripping into it, he takes out the circular rubber and slowly rolls it onto his impressive length. My mouth goes dry at the thought of what comes next.

Then, as he turns to me, I'm suddenly aware that I'm overdressed.

I sit up, reaching behind myself to unclasp my bra, drawing my feet protectively toward me at the same time. It's surprisingly hard to find the courage to expose myself completely. And yet Leo stands before me, naked in all his godlike glory, without a hint of trepidation. He approaches slowly, his eyes patient as he takes me in like I'm the most beautiful thing he's ever seen.

And that gives me the strength to be vulnerable, to take a chance. Sliding my bra straps down my arms, I set it carefully aside.

Leo prowls onto the bed, his gaze predatory as he stops at my feet.

Desire ignites in my core once again as his hands slide slowly up my thighs, feeling every inch of me. I lie back, watching as he takes silent control. His fingers hook inside the waist of my panties, and I lift my hips to let him strip me, the last shred of my childhood slipping away as he drops my undies to the floor.

His hands are gentle as they rest lightly on my knees, and without breaking eye contact, he slowly guides them open. Heat blossoms in my belly as he eases between my legs, his hips spreading my thighs as my legs quiver with anticipation.

"Are you ready, Tia?" he murmurs, his hazel eyes brilliant as he hovers on top of me.

"Yes," I breathe.

His lips capture mine, stealing my breath away. As he aligns our bodies, I'm sure he must be able to hear my heart; it's beating so loud. He reaches between us, guiding his cockhead to my wet entrance.

I tense as he presses inside of me just a fraction, the sensation both foreign and almost painful. He feels far too large, already stretching me to my limit.

"Easy, Tia. Relax. Breathe," he murmurs, his low voice by my ear sending a shiver down my spine. "It might hurt a little right at first, but I'll take it slow, and I promise you're going to like it. You're in good hands."

Trying to regain control of my erratic heart, I take a shuddering breath in and release it slowly. Then, peering deep into his riveting eyes, I nod. The pad of his thumb finds my clit a moment later. As he starts to circle it, rolling over it in tantalizing ways, I ache desperately to have something inside me once more.

My need is so intense it's hard to think straight.

As nervous as I am, all I want is to feel that euphoria he drew out of me with his fingers. And the thought of experiencing it with him, of knowing what it's like to come *with* someone, that chases away the fear threatening to suffocate me.

Leo eases forward, his movement gradual as he stretches me to an almost painful degree. It's the most intense feeling, and yet, at the same time, the pleasure of his thumb circling my sensitive nub makes me crave more.

"Fuck, you're so tight," he groans, his voice agonized.

And my walls clamp around his hard length at the erotic sound. He presses more adamantly into my depths, and fiery pain mingles with overwhelming relief. I cry out as he sinks inside me to the hilt, filling me up until I feel as though he might rip me in two. At the same time, it's heavenly as tingling electricity dances through my body, numbing my limbs.

Then, he slowly starts to withdraw.

My fingers press into the rippling muscles of his back as I hold on for dear life.

Leo moves carefully inside of me, his motion gradual as he slides in and out, in and out. And each time he fills me up, my excitement mounts, slowly overriding the pain. I can feel the tension building deep in my core, that pleasure that will send me toppling into oblivion once again.

He grunts, the sound low and carnal as his pace begins to quicken. With each thrust growing more passionate than the last, I feel my own release drawing close.

"You feel so *fucking* good," he groans, his lips leaving mine for only a moment.

I'm so consumed by the new and glorious sensation that I can't form the words to respond. Instead, I whimper, my breaths coming hard and fast as my pleasure builds rapidly inside my core, threatening to explode, it's so intense.

Leo's hand slides from between us and scoops beneath my hips, raising them and shifting the angle so his pelvis grinds against me with every penetrating thrust.

"Oh god!" I gasp, my hands shifting to the sheets above my head as I brace myself for the impending oblivion.

"Come with me, Tia," he commands, filling me up until I'm ready to scream.

And I can't do anything but obey. Unraveling around his hard erection, I throb and pulse, gripping him like a vise as I orgasm so powerfully that stars explode behind my eyes.

Leo snarls, slamming inside me. A moment later, I can feel him swelling and twitching as he matches my glorious spasms. For a few brief seconds, we reach euphoria together, our panting breaths in unison as our lips brush in passionate bliss.

Leo lingers on top of me, staying inside of me until my throbbing orgasm finally subsides. Then he presses a last tender kiss to my lips and eases out of my depths.

I feel devastatingly hollow without him now, and I bite back the sudden and unexpected sting of tears. I have no clue why I'm emotional—though the experience was both the most intense and profound I've ever known.

But I refuse to cry over one of the best moments of my life.

I watch Leo stand and strip the condom before tossing it into the trash. Then he bends to scoop up his pants and pull them on. Slipping off the bed, I quickly do the same, snagging my undies and dress.

"Can I drive you home?" he offers as he puts his shirt back on.

His thoughtful concern moves me. That he would be willing to give me a ride rather than staying to enjoy the party means the world to me, and my heart swells with fresh emotion.

"That would be wonderful."

3

LEO

The slight muss to Tia's thick black locks and the fresh flush in her cheeks, combined with the knowing shine in her dark chocolate eyes, could leave no doubt in anyone's mind that tonight was her first time. Not that I couldn't have known that from the hundred other signs.

But no one dares to say a word as I escort her through the house and out the front door to my canary-yellow Ferrari. The shy smile that graces the oldest Guerra daughter's lips contains a secret that makes my cock throb. Because I know what it is.

She lost her virginity tonight. And I have to admit, something about her purity, the raw trust she placed in my hands, made it beyond fucking enjoyable. Not many girls could spend an entire night with me and not bore me to disgust. The Guerra girl might be young, but she's smart.

If not entirely too naive.

Still, I did exactly as I promised. I treated her gently. I gave her the best kind of pleasure a man can provide. Her first time was with someone probably far better than she would have had to endure otherwise. Because I wanted her to feel good, to know just how incredible sex can be.

It's the least I could do, really. Considering what comes next.

I open the door for her and offer my hand to make climbing inside a bit easier. The dazzling smile she unleashes is filled with such innocent trust, such silent gratitude. God, she's young. Sheltered. Naive.

My conscience hits me like a punch to my gut. I quickly crush the moment of weakness, strengthening my resolve because there's no turning back now. What's done is done.

I make my way around the front of the car and slip behind the wheel.

Tia keeps her delicate hands resting lightly in her lap, her long pianist's fingers soft and relaxed. "Thank you for giving me a ride home," she says as the motor purrs to life.

"Don't thank me just yet." I flash her an insincere smile as I focus my attention on the fortune of having one of the Guerra girls waltz through my door this evening.

The puzzling turn of events still has me reeling slightly, but after tonight, I'm sure I'll have the old man beneath my thumb in no time. All thanks to his archaic sense of parenting and a rebellious teen.

The Guerra family has been a challenge to overcome. Their influence in the community has made my family's attempt to take over their territory far less simple. While some of the smaller crime families in the area crumbled under little pressure, I've found it would take far more than that to crush the Guerras.

But their fall is inevitable.

And Tia is going to serve as the perfect message to send to them —I'll fuck Don Guerra as surely as I did his daughter. And there's nothing they can do to stop it.

We drive through town in silence, my Fararri taking the curves with silent ease as I make it to her house in record time. And I vaguely note that it was no short walk to reach my party from her parents' estate.

She's a determined piece of work. I'll give her that.

I glance at her from the corner of my eye to find her observing the dark night outside the window, the street lamps that dimly illuminate the narrow sidewalks. Her hands shift, pulling her appealing blue dress further down her slim thighs and crossing her legs in an attempt to ward off the unseasonal chill. When I notice the goosebumps breaking out across Tia's legs, I turn up the heat in the car, and she gives me another grateful look.

A short time later, I turn down the long driveway of her family's estate, a thrill going through my chest as I dare to enter the enemy territory with blatant disregard.

Even in the dark of night, I can see the Guerra house is a grand one, with creeping ivy climbing up one stone wall and the classical flavor of a New England mansion gracing its corners and edges. Older than the structures on the Moretti estate, but no less grand.

Tia worries her lip nervously, her face paling slightly as she looks up at the darkened window like a child about to get caught with her hand in the cookie jar.

"Something wrong?" I ask, a hint of amusement slipping into my tone.

"I should have thought to ask you to drop me at the end of the drive," she murmurs, casting an embarrassed glance my way.

"First time sneaking out?" I tease. I can't help myself. I shouldn't play with my prey. But after tonight, she's going to hate me regardless of what I say now.

Tia releases a soft, nervous laugh. "Is it that obvious?"

I shrug, pulling up right outside her front steps. "Look, Tia. I want you to know that tonight... well. You're a beautiful girl, and it's nothing personal..."

Her demure flush from my compliment fades as quickly as it came, her mind deciphering my words at a rapid pace. "Nothing personal?"

The blood drains from her face, turning even her lush lips a chalky white as I blast my horn relentlessly, my eyes never leaving hers.

"What are you doing?" she screams, her eyes shifting to my hand on the steering wheel as if she's contemplating whether she can physically remove it and rectify the situation.

But it's too late.

Lights flick on throughout the house, casting a golden glow across the lawn and pillared front porch. Horror consumes Tia's face as she realizes the full gravity of her situation, and her eyes level me with a penetrating hatred.

"You're a monster," she states. Then she scrabbles for the door handle and flings the car door open.

The armed guards that pour out of the front door aim their guns, freezing Tia in place. Then Don Guerra and his wife step out onto the front porch of his home. His face is livid, and it fills my soul with wicked satisfaction.

Daring to tempt fate, I open my door to speak to him over the roof of my car. In the absence of my horn, the night is deathly quiet.

All that I can hear are Tia's sobs as she stumbles toward the porch —where her mother waits with open arms, a look of torment on her face. I grind my teeth to drown out the sound, doing my best to ignore the painful scene.

Instead, I turn my eyes on my mortal enemy.

"What have you done?" Don Guerra growls, his eyes shifting between me and Tia until I'm unsure of who he's posing the question to.

"Your time is over, old man," I state, my voice carrying across the space between us with the confidence of my success to back me. "The Guerra family's reign is over. You need to face the music and accept your fate."

"You can go straight to hell if that's what you think," the don snarls.

I scoff. "Thanks for the fuck. I hope you didn't have any grand plans for your little girl. Though I heard you've been trying to barter her off for an alliance that might be strong enough to stop me. Good luck with that now. I doubt any of her prospective husbands will want her now that I've been inside her."

Tia's mom gasps as her daughter buries her face in her mother's shoulder, her entire body trembling with her sobs.

"Shoot him, god damn it!" Don Guerra bellows at his stunned guards.

Looks like that's my cue.

Dipping back into my car before they can get a clear headshot, I throw my car in gear and punch the gas, peeling out so quickly that it closes Tia's still-open door. Bullets ping off the sides of my yellow sports car, and on any other day, I would be furious about someone punching holes in something that's mine.

But tonight was worth it.

Fuck Don Guerra.

Seeing the look of apoplectic rage on his face is worth more than a Ferrari.

That was priceless.

A hint of guilt burrows inside my chest as the sound of Tia's sob echoes in my ears. But it's not like I hurt the girl. Honestly, I probably did her a favor. Because I know the list of men she might have been obligated to marry if I hadn't taken her virginity. And not one of them is even close to worthy of her—regardless of who her father is.

I chuckle darkly as the thought instantly relieves my misgivings. Because I meant it with all sincerity that Don Guerra's going to have a hell of a time finding someone who wants to form an alliance with him now. Not when the very man they're supposed to be uniting against managed to fuck the virgin Don Guerra was supposed to be offering up for marriage.

That leaves Tia to forge her own path in life, maybe find someone without such a fancy name who's willing to look past her very brief history of rebellion.

If her father doesn't kill her, that is.

4

TIA

"Tia, come outside with us and play in the garden," Anna says from my doorway, making me nearly leap out of my skin.

I quickly minimize the screen on my computer before turning to her.

Vienna and little Sofia stand hopefully behind her. My trio of younger sisters watches me with wide, innocent, dark eyes, looking the picture of hope as they wait for my answer.

"Maybe later," I suggest from my seat at my desk, trying to keep the impatience from my voice. Somedays, I wish I could find just ten minutes alone without having to worry someone might walk in on me.

Three pairs of shoulders droop because they know what that means. I'll be hiding away in my room for the day—and I intend to stay here until I can leave this town and never look back.

"Okay," they agree in chorus before trooping off with apparent disappointment.

Sighing heavily, I lean back in my chair and scrub my face.

Being relegated to the house for the foreseeable future hasn't nearly been the punishment my father might have hoped. Mortified by what happened with Leo and fully aware of the ripples it's caused, I have no desire to show my face in society anymore.

I find it hard to even venture into the garden.

It's been a month now, and still, I can hear the whispers. I know that I'm the reason our great family is going to collapse. Because no man will have me now that Leonardo Moretti has. I've doomed our chance of alliance, and Father won't even speak to me now. He can barely look at me.

My stomach knots as I think about how horribly I screwed up—and how much worse it could still get. Not that I've dared tell anybody yet. Glancing nervously at my computer screen as my sisters shuffle outside, I try not to imagine what my father would say as I pull up the web page once again...

He's still furious. With me definitely, but more importantly with the Moretti heir who so crudely sullied my honor. Which means he's been holding business dinners with the few families still standing.

Therefore, I've grown accustomed to taking meals in my room.

"Knock, knock," Maria says, stepping into the room and plopping onto my bed a moment later.

"Damn it, Maria. You're supposed to wait until someone invites you in!" I scold, quickly minimizing the icon once again.

"I said 'Knock, knock,'" she says defensively.

And normally, that's more than an adequate boundary between me and my sisters. I know my stress is just wearing my nerves thin. I just really don't want anyone to see what I'm googling. "Sorry. I know. It's fine," I say, closing my eyes and rubbing my temples.

"Sooo... are you ready to get going?" she asks playfully, her smile telling me she's already forgotten my sharp tone.

"I already told the other three I might join you outside later," I state, turning in my desk chair to face the oldest of my younger sisters.

"Tia, you're starting to transform into a vampire. You need sunlight. Fresh air. A bit of laughter... and we miss you." Maria pulls one of my decorative pillows onto her lap and hugs it protectively. "I miss you. Won't you at least talk to me?"

What is there to say? I had the best night of my life only to discover the man I thought I liked was using me, lying straight to my face. I can't thank Leo Moretti for much, but I can thank him for the very effective education he gave me.

Men are not to be trusted, especially men with the last name Moretti.

And what weighs on my mind this morning is not something I'm ready to talk about—definitely not with my younger sister. Changing my focus to direct the attention to Maria, I prop my chin on the back of my chair as I fiddle with a lock of my hair. "What do you want to talk about?"

"Your birthday?" Maria suggests.

"What about it?"

I turned eighteen three days ago, but the usually lavish parties our parents throw to celebrate the occasion didn't happen. Not that I need a party. I'm an adult now. But it does sting a little that Father forbid my mom and sisters from anything more than telling me a happy birthday. Somehow, that made their birthday wishes seem all the more ironic.

"I got you something." Maria glances toward the door, checking to make sure the coast is clear before she pulls out a small box.

"Maria," I scold. "Father told you not to."

My younger sister levels me with a look that says, *Really?*

Yeah, I have no room to speak.

Then she passes me the box.

"Thank you," I say more gently this time, accepting it.

"You're welcome." Maria watches me with an intent gaze as I untie the ribbon and lift the lid.

Inside is a beautiful glass millefiori necklace, the tiny floral discs forming a ring of colorful circles that spread across the beautiful pendant. It's roughly the size of a quarter and hangs on a delicate silver chain.

"Maria, it's beautiful," I gasp, stroking the smooth glass with my fingertip.

She must have had it shipped all the way from Murano, the only place in the world that makes this traditional Venetian glass. No wonder she wanted to give it to me despite Father's orders.

Fighting back the tears, I look up once more to meet my little sister's eyes. "Thank you."

Maria smiles, hopping up off the bed. "Now you can go back to moping alone on your computer if you want. But really, you should come join us."

"I'll be down in a bit," I promise.

My sister plants a quick kiss on my cheek before skipping from the room. Heart thawing after over a month locked in ice, I take a moment to smile after her. Then, only after I'm sure I'm alone do I don the sweet piece of jewelry.

Its cool, smooth surface resting just above my heart gives me the strength to turn my attention back to my computer screen. Clicking the icon to retrieve the webpage I minimized, I take a fortifying breath and resume my research. Nerves tremble in my stomach, pushing me to the brink of nausea, and a fresh wave of panic fills me.

Is that an early sign of morning sickness?

I don't even know when that might begin.

Chewing the inside of my cheek, I scan the results for what I'm looking for—anything to discredit my suspicion, really. But so far, it doesn't look so good. It's too early for morning sickness, so the fact that I'm not throwing up, unfortunately, tells me nothing.

I have been pretty stressed lately—for good reason—but I haven't really lost weight, and pregnancy seems to be the primary cause of a delayed menstrual cycle. My fingers shake as they hover over my keyboard, and I scan my frantically racing mind for another question I could ask that might ease my anxiety.

I try again, this time typing *How late can a period be?*

There, I find results that would indicate two weeks overdue isn't unheard of. The website suggests that a hormone imbalance is most likely if my cycles are irregular. But they aren't really. This is the first time I've been late since I started menstruating.

God, please, please, let this be a hormone imbalance. I'd even take a stress-induced mental breakdown over pregnancy.

That website suggests that tender breasts could be an indication of imbalance. And when I cup mine, they feel fairly tender. *But didn't the previous website say that sensitive breasts were a sign of pregnancy?*

Trying to contain the wave of panic that washes through me, I hover my fingers over the keyboard, thinking of what words to put in next. *How can you be certain you're pregnant?*

I really don't want to bring this up to my parents until I'm sure. Even then, I would rather not, but what else can I do?

"You're late?"

The sound of my mother's voice behind me feels like a bucket of ice being dumped over my head. My heart skips a beat, and I whirl in my seat to find her staring at my computer screen over my shoulder. I didn't even hear her come in. *Did she knock?*

"Mom, what are you doing in here?" I ask breathlessly.

"I think you're the one who should be answering that question. You told us he used protection." Her eyes flash with fresh betrayal, her refined features twisting into a look of anger and despair.

"He did!" I insist, my cheeks flaming as the worst night of my life comes roaring back to my mind.

The pure bliss of my freedom, the wild adventure I never wanted to end, followed by the worst kind of humiliation and rejection. *How has my punishment not been enough?*

My mother grabs my wrist, pulling me from my chair as tears shimmer in her eyes. "We're going to your father. You'll take a test so we can know once and for all just how thoroughly you've ruined all of us."

My stomach drops into my feet at her words, and I follow numbly as she drags me down the hall to the stairs. Heart hammering in my chest, I fight the fresh waves of mortification I must endure over one stupid night.

That night changed everything for me. *That* was the night I stopped being a child. The night all my juvenile fantasies were shattered. It destroyed my relationship with my family. Left me ruined, unlovable, a worthless burden my parents would rather be rid of than have to support. That night destroyed my naivete. It destroyed me. I only wish I hadn't needed Leonardo Moretti to educate me.

"Giuseppe," my mother says, knocking on my father's office door.

"Come in."

His booming voice makes my heart stutter, and I ball my fingers into fists to hide the way they shake. His demeanor shifts as soon as he sees our faces.

Utter disappointment darkens his eyes when he looks at me now, and he can only seem to spare me glances before he has to look away. As if the very sight of me offends him. Every time he does, it reopens the wounds of that night, reminding me of just how terribly I ruined things.

"Get out," he commands the men he'd been meeting with.

Both send startled glances in my direction, then they rise from their chairs and leave without a word, closing the door behind them.

"Your daughter has been researching signs of pregnancy." My mother's tone could turn water to ice, and it doesn't escape my notice that I've officially become *your daughter*, as if she no longer wishes to be associated with me.

At first, she'd been gentle, concerned when I came home that night. She thought I might have been kidnapped, violated. It was much harder for her to wrap her mind around how I could willingly walk myself into the Moretti house of my own free will. How I could give myself to him of my own volition.

The truth makes me less of a victim in her eyes because I was too ignorant and childish to see the foolishness of my behavior. Maybe she's right. But that didn't make me any less hurt, any less scared, any less angry. I hate Leonardo as much as the rest of them now, and I hate myself because I ruined our best chance of destroying him that night.

Father levels me with a silently furious gaze, the disappointment radiating from him in waves. But still, he doesn't speak to me. Instead, he gives curt orders to my mother. "Send for the doctor. I want confirmation. And make sure it's discrete. The last thing we need is rumors of a pregnancy scare getting out to further tarnish our good name."

As much as I want to scream at my father, tell him to say something—anything—to me, even if it's to yell, I bite my tongue. I've never felt so isolated, so utterly alone. My hand instinctively reaches for the millefiori necklace tucked beneath my shirt, but I stop myself so as not to arouse my father's suspicion.

I turn without a word and exit his office with my mother, leaving her behind as I head straight up to my room. I suppose one good thing came out of my parents finding out. At least now I'll know. That has to be better than all the worrying and then wondering if my worrying is causing the problem but being unable to control it.

Closing the door behind me, I fall back on my bed to stare up at my ceiling. *He did use protection, right?* I had assumed so that night. It looked like a condom. But the one thing I know about Leonardo Moretti after that night is I can't trust him. About anything. I don't know what his motivations were that night—aside from using me as a crass statement.

But I wouldn't put anything past him now.

The bastard needs to be put down.

I just wish I'd understood that before I destroyed our family's chances of uniting to take him out.

5

LEO

Don Valencia stares me down with thinly veiled hatred as I scan the docket of his most recent profits. I can't help the smirk that tugs at the corner of my lips as his face slowly turns a deep shade of red, then purple. It's taking all his willpower not to say something, and I take my time scanning the numbers to give him every opportunity to lose his temper.

And if he does, I'll crush him.

"This looks sufficient," I agree, handing back the papers after I've had my fun.

"And you'll let my sons continue to run production?" Don Valencia asks, his tone clipped as he hands me the deed to his company.

I step close to him, lowering my voice as I give him a warning look. "They'll do whatever the *fuck* I want them to. And right now, they have the opportunity to prove they can be good little minions who answer to me. If they get that right, then maybe I'll let them keep their positions."

Taking the deed from his hands, I fold it and slip it inside the breast pocket of my coat. Don Valencia swallows visibly, his body trembling with fury.

"You should be happy, Aldo," I say more amicably, straightening my suit and drawing up to my full height as I bring our meeting to a close. "I'm letting you keep twenty-five percent of the profits in your company. That makes me pretty magnanimous, don't you think?"

Not many of the dons in Piovosa have received as generous of offers. But the Valencia family is too prominent to exterminate completely, so I have to make concessions if I'm going to maintain my hold. The smaller families have been easy to trap under my thumb. But I'll have to be more clever if I want to overthrow the last few in my sights.

"Magnanimous. Just the word I was looking for," Don Valencia growls.

I give a curt nod. "I'll be in touch."

Then I turn, striding from his warehouse as my men fall into step around me.

The workers busy themselves as we pass, keeping their eyes focused intently on the tasks at hand. When I step out into the brilliant late afternoon sun, I take a deep breath and look out across the trucking yard I now own. This is a big move toward running this town.

With a few choice law enforcers in my pocket and the Guerra family out of my way, I'll be unstoppable.

Time to head home and deliver the good news.

∿

THE HOUSE IS quiet as I enter, our butler Luigi holding the door open as I step inside.

"Where is he?" I ask, scanning the open space.

I don't need to clarify who "he" is. Luigi knows.

"In his study."

With a curt nod of thanks, I turn in that direction.

"Signor Leo," Luigi says, making me pause.

I turn to face the loyal servant, one eyebrow rising in silent question.

"Prepare yourself."

It's a subtle warning, one that tells me my good news about the Valencia warehouse is not going to be met with a good mood.

"Thank you, Luigi," is all I say before turning toward the study once more.

The door is open, and my father is staring out the picture window to the wooded mountains that serve as a backdrop to our estate.

"Valencia Transport is ours," I state, opening with the good news.

My father turns, his expression one of poised disdain. "Come in and shut the door."

Fighting the irritation that rises in me at his commanding tone, I do as he says, closing the door behind me before coming to a stand in the center of the richly furnished room.

"I just finished a meeting with Don Guerra." His steely tone highlights his fury as my father levels me with a cold gaze. "It would appear you got their oldest daughter pregnant."

I'd all but forgotten about Tia and our night together over a month ago. I've been so busy crushing the families they had once hoped to become allies with that I haven't had time to reflect on my abuse of the girl beyond how it nearly hamstrung her family.

I snort. "They can't possibly know that already."

"You idiot. You think he would come to me if it weren't verifiable? He wants the truth about her reputation swept under the rug. Now you've gone and knocked up a girl from the very family we're trying to take down!"

Bristling at the insult, I grind my teeth and force my temper back under control. "You weren't so upset about me sending the Guerras a message in the first place," I point out.

He'd laughed when I told him the story. A very different tune than he's singing now.

"Fucking her weakened their position and took away their best tool to form an alliance against us. But getting her pregnant just gave them power over us. How could you be so careless?"

"I used a fucking condom. What more do you want from me?" I snap defensively.

"You need to take responsibility."

"Hardly," I scoff. "Besides, she's probably just pretending to be pregnant because her feelings are hurt, and she wants to get back at me." But the niggling guilt in my gut sours my words.

"Obviously, condoms don't always work, Leo. And if you're the big shot you think you are, I would expect you to know that!" His voice rises with each word in an uncharacteristic display of uncontrolled fury. My father's lips pale as they form a thin line of frustration, and when he speaks again, his tone is cool and collected once more. "The Guerra girls have a reputation for their virtue because their father guards them so obsessively; so that Don Guerra came to me willing to discuss his daughter's loss of virginity would definitely mean the girl's pregnant. You think he wouldn't be absolutely certain before exposing that information to anyone? Least of all our family."

"And how is he so certain it's me? A hundred guys could have knocked her up by now. She was far too easy to get into bed to be the virgin they claimed her to be," I sneer. I know I was her first—no matter what I say. But that doesn't mean she isn't trying to entrap me in some way.

"I assure you, there will be a paternity test before we announce the engagement. But if you are, in fact, the father, to make things right, you *will* marry the girl."

"The hell I will." I'm not a pawn in this game. I'm the one controlling the board. Our family was nothing before my ambitions earned us the territory we now own. And my father will not be dictating the terms of my personal life over some girl's pregnancy.

"If this child is yours, we will form an alliance with the family rather than absolve them of their power," he commands, his gaze imperious as he looks down his nose at me.

"I won't marry just to satisfy your whim," I state flatly. "I'm a conqueror. We don't need an alliance with the Guerra family. And now that we have the Valencia family under our command, they won't be able to stand against us for long. So, it doesn't matter if the girl's pregnant. I will finish what I started. *My* way."

Sighing heavily, my father rounds his desk to stand before me.

We're roughly the same size now, though I have a few inches on him while he's several pounds heavier around the middle. But he has the same Roman nose and angular jaw. He's a picture of what I will likely be in twenty-odd years, though I have no intention of growing soft with age.

Placing a hand on my shoulder, he holds my eyes, his gaze intense. "Blood is thicker than water, Leo, and allowing your bastard son—if the child proves to be a boy—to be raised by our enemies could end up destroying everything we've built if the child comes to claim his inheritance. The only way to ensure our family's hold on Piovosa is to bring that child into the fold."

My stomach knots at the grave truth in his words.

If I had legitimate children, then a bastard might not be such a threat, but regardless of the child's legitimacy, he would be my eldest and, therefore, have a solid claim to inheriting my empire according to Piovosa's traditions.

If the baby proved to be a girl, I would have far less to worry about. Women rarely came into an inheritance in families like ours, and an illegitimate girl would have even less of a claim. *But can I really take that chance?* My odds are fifty-fifty at best.

And if the child did prove to be a boy, the Guerras would be raising that child with every intent of vindicating themselves one day.

"Fuck," I snarl, jerking away from my father's grip as I scan the room for something to smash. Things really couldn't look worse.

Just when I'm on the cusp of taking it all, I fall victim to my own schemes.

"An alliance may not be the victory we hoped for, but it's better than the alternative," my father states, his words rational now, seeming to have lost their heat now that my own fury is consuming me.

"If she isn't pregnant—if I'm not the father—I'm going to crush that family so brutally their name will vanish from history," I state coldly.

My father observes me silently, his eyes following my path as I pace the study.

"When are we doing the test?"

"Today. The Guerras have already called the doctor with the understanding that we both wish to keep this... discrete."

I nod, my mind racing to think of the implications that might go into this unwanted pregnancy. I need to blow off some steam. "Tell me when he gets here. I'll be in the gym."

Striding from the room, I signal for my guards to follow, ready for a proper sparring session. I need to knock somebody senseless—or have my bell properly wrung. Right now, I'm not sure I care which one.

6

TIA

"Signorina Tia, the don would like to speak with you downstairs," my maid says with a nervous smile.

"Thank you, Linda," I say wearily, rising from my bed. I've come to dread these summons over the last few weeks, knowing that if my father wishes to see me, it can't be for anything good.

Finger-combing my hair into place, I check my image in the mirror to make sure I don't look too terrible. Then, I follow Linda downstairs to the drawing room. Both my parents wait for me there; my mother has become something of a translator for my father, seeing as he still refuses to speak to me.

"That will be all, Linda," she says as the maid ushers me into the room.

Linda gives a slight curtsy before departing, closing me in the room alone with my parents. I stand silently, waiting for whatever it is they have to say now. I know better than to speak—let alone argue anymore. I've ruined everything, and all I can do is hope that they know how to fix my childish mistake.

"Sit down, Tia," my father says, and hearing my name leave his lips after all this time makes my chest tighten. Whatever he needs to tell me must be bad if he's talking to me again.

I do as he says, settling onto the couch across from my parents and lacing my fingers on my lap, my back ramrod straight.

"I've spoken with Don Moretti, and we've come to an arrangement," he states, his tone measured, his sharp eyes intent on mine.

"An arrangement?" That can't possibly mean what I think it does. Not after years of hatred between the two families, a growing animosity that has only exploded after my indiscretion.

My gaze flicks naturally to my mother for an explanation, and her expression puts me slightly at ease. But she doesn't speak; instead, her eyes implore me to understand.

"To avoid the humiliation of having the world know that our enemy got our daughter pregnant, you and Leonardo Moretti will get married—quickly, before the baby is born."

My heart stops at my father's declaration, the reality of his words striking me like a physical blow. I can feel the blood draining from my face as the room swims dangerously before me. And I force air into my lungs to try and regain my composure.

"You must be joking," I demand, shifting to clench my hands into fists. He can't possibly expect me to marry that asshole.

"I'm not."

"Do you really hate me that much now? Do I disgust you to the point that you'll get rid of me at all costs?" I know my parents aren't thrilled about helping raise the child of their unwed daughter, but I can't believe my father would sell me off to the Morettis when I know just how much he hates them.

"Believe it or not, this isn't about you, Tia. This might be our last chance to save the Guerra name. Because the Morettis won't want a bastard child to be raised outside their control. That means they've actually agreed to an alliance they never would have before."

My objections die on my lips as he throws my mistake back in my face. Because as much as I want to deny it, I know that my actions that night are what put our family in such dire straits. Snapping my mouth shut, I force my hands to relax, lacing my fingers once more as I wait for him to go on.

"But..."

I scarcely dare to breathe as I wait for the other shoe to drop. Because marrying Leonardo Moretti couldn't possibly be bad enough. Focusing on my father's onyx gaze, I wait for the noose to tighten.

"Tia, could this baby possibly be anyone else's?"

I can't tell if the hint of emotion behind his question is pain or hope, but it brings a knot to my throat. My father, a man who once had pride in me as his daughter, can barely look me in the eye anymore. And as much as I hate that my virginity could matter so much when it comes to deserving my father's love, I hate more that the consequences of my actions have impacted everyone I care about so completely.

But most of all, I hate the man who took so much from me.

"I wish it could be anyone else's," I breathe, my gaze dropping as I pick at my cuticles. "Leonardo Moretti is a monster, just like you said, and I would rather die than marry him. But I know that you can't marry me to anyone else—especially now." *Now that I have a child growing in my belly.* Not that I wanted to marry any of my potential suitors, but the reality of my situation feels far worse than it did just a month ago.

A sharp silence lingers between us, and I wonder if my father might be considering the benefits of my death over the alternative of having to accept the Morettis as allies.

But he presses onward, his tone resolved. "They're asking for a paternity test before announcing the engagement."

I scoff. "They have the gall to accuse me of sleeping around after what he did?" I snap, my temper overcoming my composure. *The bastard. He takes my virginity, and then he wants to question my chastity?*

I've never wanted to murder someone so violently. I can't imagine spending my life with him. Not after how he treated me. He must be a psychopath to be capable of such callous disregard for another person's wellbeing.

And I would have to be insane to accept his proposal. Or a complete masochist.

"Well, if those are his conditions, he can go right to hell." I cross my arms over my chest defiantly, slouching against the back of the couch as I turn my face away from my parents.

"Would you let your sisters die to spite him?" Father asks, drawing me from my caustic thoughts.

The question cuts like a knife. *Is that what it's come down to? My sanity or my sisters' survival?*

"We're running out of options, Tia," he states as if he could hear my thoughts. His eyes are grave as they hold mine. "Either we use our leverage from your pregnancy to enforce this alliance, or we prepare to be annihilated because we are out of allies."

"What do you mean?" I breathe, my stomach knotting uncomfortably.

I've been entirely out of the loop since the night Leonardo dumped me on the front steps of my parents' home. My father has kept me from sight both as punishment and in the hope that gossip about my poor choices would dissipate before it caused too many problems.

But it would seem his efforts have been in vain.

"The Valencia family, our last hope of legitimate support in this bloody battle, just buckled under the Morettis' pressure."

My hand covers my mouth in horror as I realize what that means. I don't know where the Fiores, the Amici, or the Russos must have fallen, but if this is what it's come to, their fates can't have been good.

It will take far less effort to crush us now. Because no one hated the Morettis as adamantly as Don Valencia. And as much as I would have loathed being married to Tony, it couldn't possibly have been worse than a lifetime subjected to Leonardo's mind games.

"I don't see how this is even a choice," my mother says, her tone cold and condemning. "But as your father insists, I can only hope you'll do the right thing for your family—your sisters—this time. So, what'll it be, Tia?" Her expression is stern with unspoken tension.

"I'll do it," I murmur, the words like acid on my tongue. "I'll marry him."

"Good." My father's expression softens slightly. He seems to have found a hint of forgiveness now that I'm willing to do what it takes to correct my mistakes—as best I can.

But nothing I do can turn back time. And all I want is to go back and smack my young, naive self upside the head. Because I'm in so far over my head, I don't know what to do. The fate of my family rests on my shoulders.

And now I have another innocent life in my hands.

Only my child will be going with me into the lion's den.

"The doctor will be here shortly to perform the paternity test." Father rises from his chair, ready to depart now that the conversation is done.

A lone tear trickles down my cheek as I consider just what this means for me and my unborn child. We will be trapped with a man who used me, made me fall for him, and then tossed me to the curb when it would be most cruel.

Brushing the moisture quickly from my skin, I steel myself, standing as well. And to my surprise, my father stops in front of me to rest a hand on my shoulder.

"Our survival depends on your ability to make this marriage work, Tia," he says gently. "So you can't disappoint me this time."

Swallowing hard, I nod. *No pressure or anything.*

My mother follows my father, pausing to cup my face in her hands. It's the first ounce of affection she's shown me in a month. "I'm proud of you for doing the right thing for your family," she murmurs. "That's the girl I raised."

The words bring tears to my eyes, and I close them, trapping the salty moisture inside. Pressing her lips to my forehead, my mother gives me a soft kiss. Then she departs with my father, leaving me alone in the drawing room.

For a moment, I stand alone in my despair, utterly lost.

But then, I'm not alone anymore.

Resting my palm on my stomach, I do something I've never done before. *We'll make it through this. I promise,* I think to the tiny life growing inside me. And though I know it's far too early to feel the baby move, I can't help imagining a warmth radiating from my core—an unconditional love that fills me with astonishing new strength.

It still feels so strange, so surreal. I'm too young to have a baby. Hardly old enough to be a mom. And yet, in all the crazy chaos around me, having this child is the one thing I'm confident of.

No matter what it takes, I want to make my baby's world safe, loving, and good.

I never want my child to be forced into a marriage they disagree with, to be used like a pawn in a sick game of power.

I *will* give my child a world that is fair and just, and free. I don't care if I have to tear down the entire town of Piovosa, brick by brick.

7
LEO

"I can't believe we're going along with this farce," I state, straightening the knot of my double Windsor and tightening it around my throat as we wait in the entry for our first guests to arrive.

My father levels me with a look that warns me not to say what he knows I'm thinking. That, though Don Guerra sent us the labs confirming I'm the father of Tia's child, I still wonder if they might not have found a way to manipulate the results. To make her look pregnant when she's not. Maybe they paid off the doctor. I don't know.

I don't see how the odds could be stacked so high against me. It was one time, for Christ's sake, and I used protection. Besides, it would suit the Guerra family to force us into an alliance rather than admit defeat.

But my father is past hearing my objections.

And I know if I say them now, minutes before the start of my engagement party, he might just clock me.

"You will behave tonight, Leo," my father commands, his gaze layered with ice.

"I know how to work a fucking dog-and-pony show," I snap, turning my eyes back to the entryway to collect myself.

Just in time, too, as Luigi announces the arrival of the Guerra family and opens the front door. Don Guerra leads the way with his rather stunning younger wife, Francesca, on his arm. I can see where Tia got her looks, and as my betrothed walks across the threshold, I'm struck by her beauty once more.

I haven't seen her since the party, and she would catch my eye just as easily tonight, her long raven locks drawn into an intricate knot of curls on top of her head. Several ringlets cascade down one shoulder, luxurious and shiny, reminding me of just how soft they felt.

Her makeup has been done to make her look older, more sophisticated, the dark points of her eyeliner drawing attention to her near-mercury-colored eyes. And her lips have been painted a deep rose color, both enticing and elegant.

She looks like a princess in her gold silk evening dress. The lines are simple, yet cut perfectly to flatter her curves before tapering into a flowing train. And I would say without a shadow of a doubt that by the looks of her, she can't possibly be pregnant.

She's fucking perfect, her pert breasts filling out the sweetheart neckline before her waist tapers down to her full hips. If I didn't have more important things on my mind—like a town to conquer and unite under my family's name—I might be tempted by such an enticing figure.

But when her eyes flick up to meet mine, I see none of that innocent child who snuck into my party. Instead, a cold composure settles over her, making her look years older as she studies me with an inscrutable gaze.

"Don Guerra, it's a pleasure to welcome you and your family to our humble home," my father says, striding forward with a grand sweep of his arms.

Biting back my snort of derision at his unnecessary theatrical performance, I follow as we close the distance between our two families.

"You chose to keep your other daughters home for such a special occasion?" he continues, glancing behind Don Guerra and his wife for any of the other four Guerra daughters.

I can hardly say I blame them, considering what happened the last time one of their daughters stepped foot inside this house. But once again, I bite my tongue. Instead, I step forward, donning my charm as I extend my hand to Don Guerra.

"It's an honor to know I'll soon call you father-in-law." I smile as he clasps my hand with a considerable amount of force—not quite enough to be a statement, but enough to make me think it's taking a good amount of self-control.

"And I look forward to welcoming you into the family, Signorina Tia," my father states, turning his attention from Signora Guerra's hand to face my betrothed.

"I'm sure the pleasure will be mine," she says, her words formal but her delivery as sweet as honey. Not at all the breathlessly awestruck teen I encountered a month ago.

Tia is transformed.

A woman in full.

"And, of course, you remember my son, Leo," my father says, inviting me to step forward.

"Wonderful to see you again, Tia," I say, holding her eyes with my own.

Because tonight is about mending fences as well as showing to the town of Piovosa that our union–and our families' alliance—is both real and possible.

"You look well," she observes, her smile warm. But the charm doesn't reach her eyes. They remain guarded despite her best efforts to hide the pain behind them. "Have you been sucking the souls out of other young ladies lately?"

The barb is sharp and delivered with impeccable finesse, making it sound as casual as if she were asking about the weather. I'm rather impressed. I might just like this new, more catty side to her.

Smirking, I watch as my wordless response lights a fire of hatred behind her eyes. It seems everyone is going to let her impertinence slide, and knowing that it will piss her off more to ignore the slight, I pretend it didn't happen. Let her get through any slights before the party begins.

Of course, she hasn't forgiven me. I've done nothing to earn it. And frankly, I don't intend to. I might have to marry her and make this alliance work, but I don't have time for her hurt feelings, nor do I have the inclination to make amends when I still suspect her family is using this to avoid relinquishing their territory.

"You look more than well," I observe, my smirk stretching into a wolfish grin as I dare to let my eyes take in her striking figure, and I gesture to her gown. "I don't think I've ever seen a dress worn so well."

"Charming," her mother observes flatly, speaking for the first time. When I glance her way, she gives the slightest of eyebrow raises to confirm the subtle sarcasm.

The tension is palpable as Tia's cheeks color, her arms wrapping protectively around her stomach, as if to cover herself, and her father's eyes narrow in my direction at the same time as my father's do.

But before either have the chance to confront or chastise me, the first of our guests start to arrive. We all turn toward the door, posing a united front to welcome them. It turns into something more of a parade of people, with over three hundred guests on the invitation list and most seeming to make an appearance despite the very last-minute nature of the party.

The whole grand affair was put together in less than a week. Invitations were sent out the same day the Guerras provided the proof of paternity. Since then, the estate has been a madhouse of preparations. Of which I've given no input at all aside from a few guests I most definitely want to attend.

Mayor Romney being first and foremost on that list. And as he and his wife walk through the front door, for the first time tonight, I'm actually grateful for this monstrosity of a party.

When all the guests have finally arrived, we enter the ballroom to mingle. It's a beautiful June night, and the French doors are flung wide to let in the fresh summer air, allowing the dance floor to expand onto the terrace.

People have already started to eat, grazing from the rather impressive buffet tables full of finger foods and bite-sized treats. Tia takes it all in quietly, her delicate fingers resting lightly in the crook of my elbow as we follow our parents into the room.

"Don Guerra, Signora, would you care to join me? I was hoping to introduce you to my nephew from New York," my father suggests, already taking advantage of the alliance my marriage will form. "I think you might find him a rather interesting acquaintance."

"Of course," Tia's father agrees, his eyes shifting to her momentarily.

She gives him a measured smile, then her eyes shift to me.

"Would you like something to drink?" I suggest, gesturing to the bar as flashes from the night I met her unexpectedly fill my mind.

"I'll take a water, thank you," Tia says, her voice sickly sweet as she rests her hand subtly across her abdomen.

It's slight, but the message is there. Just a hint of undercurrent that suggests my insensitivity to her condition—one that is supposed to be kept secret until after the wedding. I clench my teeth, the tendon in my jaw popping as I note the hidden threat—that she could reveal her secret at any moment, should she be so inclined. But I can't call it out for what it is.

"Of course," I agree with a forced smile.

We head to the bar and collect our drinks—ice water for Tia and a stiff whiskey for me. I suspect I'm going to need it before this night is over.

Then, we start to make our way around the room. Fulfilling my obligation to spend the event at her side, I introduce Tia to my family's acquaintances, several she met at the party she crashed. On rare occasion, she introduces me to someone from her side of the aisle. But everyone we engage with, she charms with demure smiles and witty conversation.

She's in her element now.

I wonder if, at the party that night, she was too nervous to maintain her composure. Or perhaps she was so nervous her parents would find out that she came across as shy and unprepared. But tonight, she's captivating, her charisma winning over everyone she sees.

"Would you like to take a break and have a bite to eat?" I suggest after over an hour of entertaining our guests.

"I'm starving," Tia confesses, her eyes lighting at the suggestion. "After all, I'm eating for two now."

Despite the fact that she lowered her voice, her words have their desired effect as my stomach drops and I cast a sidelong glance to make sure no one is near enough to have heard.

"You'll hold your tongue if you know what's good for you," I warn, my voice even lower as I barely move my lips.

"Of course," she says, her voice breathy with dismay. "How careless of me." But the slight curve to her lips is enough to tell me she's enjoying her small victory.

Still, I'm determined not to let her get under my skin. Even if she's good at it. In truth, I was starting to get a bit baffled by her lack of spiteful comments—like the one she opened with at the start of the night.

I expected her to be more challenging. But seeing that smile now, the subtlest of celebrations after getting a rise out of me, sparks my suspicion. I can almost see the wheels turning in her head, and though I have no idea what she's thinking, I suspect she's not walking into this arrangement as willing and accepting as she pretends to be.

We gather our plates, Tia collecting an impressive mountain of food on hers, before heading toward the tables set up off to the side of the dance floor. And to my delight, I spot Mayor Romney and his wife occupying one.

Lightly gripping Tia's elbow, I steer her in their direction. She follows willingly, her eyes cast up to study my face for the briefest of moments before landing on the table where we're heading.

"Are these seats taken?" I ask, adopting my most charming tone as

I set my food on the table to pull out the chair next to Mayor Romney so Tia can sit.

"No, by all means," he says, his gesture welcoming, though his tone is somewhat stiff.

The sharp-witted mayor I've been trying to put in my back pocket for over a year now has proven particularly challenging to win over. And after more failed attempts than I would like to admit, I'm starting to wonder if my time might not be better spent on other high-ranking officials.

But Romney has the position—and the reputation—to open many more doors for me. So, though I can tell his guard is up, I'm not ready to throw in the towel just yet.

"Thank you." Tia settles gratefully into her chair, her smile sincere as she turns it on the couple next to her, who both look to be in their forties.

Mayor Romney has a considerable belly, the effects of a lifetime spent in meetings and sitting behind desks. His wife, on the other hand, is petite with just a hint of gray at her temples, her hair pulled up into a simple French roll.

"Tia, I believe I had the honor of introducing you to Mayor Romney and his wife at the beginning of the night," I say in an effort to hold their attention.

"Oh, yes. Thank you so much for coming," Tia says, her eyes lighting as if their presence means the world to her.

"I believe congratulations are in order," Signora Romney says, smiling at Tia as I sink into the chair next to my betrothed. Her gaze shifts to me next, her blue eyes soft but somehow less open.

No doubt, her husband has had plenty to say about me and my family. It's not like our prowess comes without a certain... reputation around town.

"Thank you." Tia beams, her cheeks warming to a beautiful shade of rose. "I must admit, it astounds me how many people can come and show their support for two young people getting married."

Her words are impressive without a bitter edge, like a light switch she seems to turn off and on.

"It's a beautiful thing, marriage. When you find the person you're meant to be with for the rest of your life," Mayor Romney says, his eyes affectionate as he takes his wife's hand to give her fingers a squeeze.

She returns his loving gaze, her smile doting.

"And from the looks of it, you two are a perfect example of that kind of commitment." Tia's voice floods with admiration.

"We're going on our thirtieth wedding anniversary," Signora Romney admits.

Tia pauses, a bite halfway to her lips as her eyes grow wide. "That's amazing. Just beautiful."

"I wish you the same happiness, my dear," Mayor Romney says, patting Tia's hand that rests upon the table. Then, his eyes cast doubtfully in my direction.

Hardly a winning review.

"You know," Tia cuts in, setting her food back on her plate as she looks at me. And in her gaze is an open devotion that would have knocked me off my feet if I'd been standing. "I never dreamed that kind of love was real before now."

Her delicate pianist's fingers rest lightly on top of mine, and I take her hand, my heart drumming an unsteady beat. Then she levels me with a smile. Just as quickly, it's gone as she turns to face Mayor Romney once more.

And his expression reveals as much astonishment over her open devotion as I feel.

"My Leo took me completely by surprise. And though I know he has a reputation to uphold, I don't think he'll mind if I tell you a little secret."

Fuck. This can't be good.

Tia leans closer to the couple, casting a wicked glance my way before she stage-whispers conspiratorially. "He's actually quite a sweetheart."

Before I can come up with a single thing to say, Mayor Romney bursts out laughing, the sound hearty and loud as his head tips back in uproarious mirth. Signora Romney laughs as well, her eyes dancing as she looks at me with newfound appreciation.

And suddenly, I feel as though the rug has been pulled out from under me.

"I assure you, my girl, your secret's safe with me," Mayor Romney says when he's finally regained his composure. "And Signor Moretti, if you can win this charming girl's heart, I assure you, it's worth whatever price you might have to pay to keep it. Even if that makes you… sweet."

My gaze shifts to Tia with newfound respect. She managed to soften the couple I've been working on for so long in just a matter of minutes. As she slides the bite-size portion of mozzarella, tomato, and basil off a cocktail stick with deliberate sass, I can't help but appreciate her in a new light.

"I assure you, Mayor Romney, I have no intention of letting this girl go."

"Well then, I wish you both the very best of happiness," he says, raising his glass along with his wife as they toast us.

Perhaps it's a fluke, but Tia seemed to wrap her mind around my reason for choosing this particular table, and she knew exactly how to help me without instruction.

The night carries on until well past midnight, and when the final guests depart, I'm astounded by the Guerra girl's ability to hold her own in a crowd. She's just eighteen and could charm even the hardest of men without a second thought.

Perhaps it's her inherent innocence. Or maybe her sharp intelligence and quick wit. Whatever it is, she keeps it for the guests.

At the end of the night, I walk her to the door as our parents exchange pleasant parting words.

"Good night, Tia," I murmur, brushing my lips over her knuckles as the high of our celebration makes it easy to play nice.

"Good night, Leo." Her tone is cordial, her hand willingly accepting my touch.

But the devotion she unveiled earlier, the soft affection and demure charm, is now gone, replaced by an iron wall of protection I can just make out in her deep brown eyes. As much as I would like to think that things could be so easy, there's clearly a chasm of distance between us.

Not that I can blame her after what I've done.

8

TIA

"Ready?" Father asks, his presence suddenly looming beside me as Leo and I stand near the front door of the Moretti home.

"Yes." Slipping my fingers from Leo's grasp, I give him one last measured smile, then I follow my parents outside onto the front steps of the grandiose home.

Soon to be my home, I suppose.

That thought hits me for the first time, and as we step into the black Escalade that will carry us home, I glance back at the imposing structure. The first night I saw it, I'd been in awe of its beauty. But tonight, it looks like a haunted mansion that might star in some horror novel. The sharp spires pierce the night sky, and the grotesque gargoyle faces sneer down at me, daring me to try and run.

I won't.

I refuse to be intimidated.

And after tonight, I actually think I might have a chance of doing something more than just endure a life of misery to protect my family.

Because tonight, I discovered Leo's aspiration.

A smile threatens to lift the corner of my lips as I settle onto the seat of the SUV and buckle in. Then I turn to look out the window into the inky sky beyond. I can't wait to get home and think over exactly how I want to go about what I found.

I stumbled upon it while in the midst of trying to follow my parents' instructions and win over my betrothed—for the sake of my family and my unborn child. But I wasn't about to let Leo forget about *why* tonight was necessary.

I know I shouldn't have, and for the most part, I actually managed to behave, but I couldn't help the few slights I sent his way. I just… reminded him about the baby he put inside me. Subtly. While in a roomful of people who aren't supposed to know. I was careful, of course, to make sure no one actually overhead me.

But once I saw it got under his skin—far better than my more juvenile and caustic remark at the start of the evening—I just couldn't help myself. I fight to keep the smile off my face as I recall Leo's growled warning that I should hold my tongue.

He really has no idea what he's in for.

I did come into tonight intending to put aside my personal disdain for the Moretti heir. To find a way to bridge the gap between us. I would have done my best to achieve that goal to protect the people I love. But what I got out of our engagement party was worth so much more than Leo's approval.

Because if there's one thing I've learned about him, it's that he's a man of ambition.

And more than anyone else in that room tonight, Leo wants to win the approval of Mayor Romney. So, to prove I can be useful to him, I stepped up. I helped garner some good will between him and the mayor—something Leo appeared in desperate need of.

I succeeded, of course.

But it also gave me an idea.

Perhaps this marriage won't be the end for me. If I can truly win Leo over, if I can gain his trust, then I might just learn how to destroy his family from within. Because any vulnerability can be exploited if I understand the motivation underneath.

But why would Leo care so much if the mayor liked him? Why does he need the man's approval? And why is he struggling so hard to get it?

All questions I need to answer before I can start tugging at that loose thread. But at least I have a lead, something to help motivate me down that aisle. And thankfully, I'm more than willing to spend some time charming the mayor and his wife while I figure out the answers to my questions. Because they seem positively lovely.

And right about now, I could use all the friends I can get.

"Well, that went better than expected," Mother says, a slight smile gracing her lips as my father rests his head back and closes his eyes.

"I think Leo and his father are almost as eager to make this situation work as we are," I confess.

"Don Moretti, yes, though I'm less confident about your betrothed." My mother's sharp eyes match mine, waiting for my assessment.

"He's a psychopath. Of course, it would be harder to read him. But I made myself indispensable tonight, so you have nothing to worry about. He'll marry me. Besides, like you said before, this baby all but guarantees the alliance."

Lifting his head from its reclined position, my father looks at me for the first time. "You did well tonight," he says. "You've grown a lot this past month."

"I grew up fast when I realized the world has no patience or sympathy for children—or childish mistakes," I state flatly.

Then, as my hand rests gently on my belly, I turn my attention back to the black night outside my window. I've been doing that a lot more lately, touching my tummy as if seeking comfort. Somehow, it helps me feel less alone, though I can't yet feel a baby bump.

The vehicle falls silent after my rather chilly statement. My mind soon returns to thoughts of what I've learned tonight and how it might help my newly forming plans.

Because I'm not about to settle into a lifetime of misery if I can find a way to bring the Moretti empire crashing down.

The best part is, no one would suspect my family of retribution because the Morettis are just as keen to hush up my extramarital pregnancy as my family is. So, no one will know my motive except for the family I intend to take down.

And by the time they find out I've betrayed them, they'll hopefully be unable to stop their fate.

Then, out of their ashes, the Guerra family can rise again.

9

LEO

"Put them on their knees," I command, glancing at my watch to check the time.

I'm going to be late to my own wedding at this rate. Still, I have a message to send, and what better way to get the point across to the Valencia family than to show them I mean business. Even on my wedding day.

My men do as I say, shoving the three simpering thieves to their knees in the back alley beyond the Valencia trucking warehouse. Each in their early forties, and I can guess they're loyal workers who have been with the Valencia family for a long time. But they're not high enough in the ranks to have come up with their plan on their own.

"I've made your boss a very generous deal," I state, standing before the kneeling men who sweat visibly through their business shirts, "allowing him and his men to keep a share of the profits. Not everyone gets so lucky."

They're nervous—as they should be. They stole from me, and today, they get to learn what happens when they take what's mine. Regardless of who put them up to it.

"But you men weren't satisfied, were you?" I ask, stepping close to straighten the middle man's collar.

His lips twitch with fear, but no words come out, and after a moment's silence, Johnny slugs the man nearest him with brutal force, sending several teeth flying across the cement ground.

"You answer the boss when he's talking to you," Johnny states.

"N-N-Noooo," the man stutters a reply, blood burbling between his lips.

"So, tell me, did Aldo Valencia put you up to this?" I turn my gaze on the man whose teeth Johnny just knocked out, hoping the punch might have loosened his jaw.

The three men share a glance, utter terror in their eyes.

"If you tell me the truth, I'll let you live," I promise, placing my hand over my heart in a gesture of good faith.

"H-He said you wouldn't notice... if we just took a little," the middle man says, his eyes round with fear. "I swear we didn't take much!" The man starts to snivel, curling in on himself as he prepares to take a blow.

I nod and look at the men on either side of him, who nod vigorously in confirmation.

"Thank you for your honesty," I state. Then I glance at my men standing behind the three thieves, a silent command that they understand without question.

Sharp cracks echo in the narrow space, followed by a scream of pure terror as the middle man covers his head as best he can with his bound hands. The two men beside him fall heavily to the ground, their eyes staring lifelessly before them.

"What the fuck!" the last man screams upon seeing his dead buddies' brains on the sidewalk. "You said you'd let us live!" His voice climbs several octaves in his hysteria.

"I did." Eyeing either of his compatriots with cold disdain, I crouch in front of the lone survivor. "You told me the truth. They didn't."

Intense relief floods the man's face at my cold-blooded reasoning.

As long as I intend to keep him alive, it seems he won't question my blatant manipulation. Once again, I glance at my men standing behind him, and the last thief is hauled to his feet before they guide him into a paint-spackled metal chair. They push him into it with more force than necessary, considering his knees give out before he even tries to resist.

Beside him is a plain wooden table that looks worse for wear. Like it's been used as a cutting board one too many times. I'm idly curious as to how the trucking warehouse men must use it. Not likely what I intend to use it for, I would assume. But I'm not curious enough to ask.

Accepting the handle of a large knife from Johnny, I step toward my prisoner. Fresh panic washes over his face as I reach for his hands. Then, once again, relief takes over as I cut him free of his bonds. Before he can get too comfortable, Rasco grabs his arm, slamming it down on the table beside him.

"Wait," he pleads, his eyes growing round as I raise the knife. "Wait, wait, wait!" he cries, nearing hysteria as he sees what's coming a moment before I bring the knife down.

And as cold steel meets wood, I cleave his hand from his body.

He releases a bloodcurdling scream.

At the same time, an impressive amount of blood spurts from his severed arm, catching me across the neck and cheek and nearly sullying my wedding attire.

I turn my head just in time, avoiding the worst of it. And as Rasco wraps a quick tourniquet around the man's elbow, Johnny passes me a clean towel. I wipe my face and neck clean, trying to make myself presentable because I won't have time for a shower after I'm done here.

Then I turn my attention to the thief once more as the man's agonized screams taper into whimpering moans.

"This is what happens to men who steal from me. Next time, I might not be so merciful," I state coldly.

He cradles his ruined arm against his chest, his face chalk-white as he looks up at me with bloodshot eyes.

"Go tell the rest of your family that under the Moretti rule, they don't try skimming off the top. Understood?"

"Y-Y-Yes, sir," he stutters, stumbling to his feet in his desperate effort to run away.

I watch him go, ensuring that he makes it back inside the warehouse building before I turn my attention to the mess we've made of the alleyway. "I'll leave you boys to clean this up," I state, nodding for Johnny to take charge.

"Sure thing, boss," he agrees.

I glance at my watch once more, then I flash Rasco a grin. "I'm overdue at church."

He chuckles darkly. "We'll be praying for you that you won't light on fire as soon as you walk through the door."

Snorting a laugh, I throw my blood-stained towel at him. "Fuck off." Then I turn toward my waiting car.

∽

I'VE ONLY SEEN my intended bride a handful of times during our very brief engagement. And that suits me just fine. I'm busy making a name for myself, elevating my family to a level of power and prestige that no single mafia family has achieved in this town's history.

Still, I hadn't intended to be quite so late to the ceremony when I left my house this morning. Running down the Valencia culprits took longer than I had anticipated.

Well, I suppose it won't hurt Tia to learn the lesson now. I'm often late to dinner. So she can expect it of me.

"You're very late," my father growls as I climb the church steps to meet him, adding the cufflinks to my tux as I go.

"I ran into a few complications."

"Is it taken care of?"

"I wouldn't be here if it weren't." I accept my suit jacket from him, shrugging into it and closing the buttons before finger-combing my hair into place. I only pause a moment to check that my bowtie is straight before I push the inner doors to the chapel wide open with a resounding thud. The congregation is already gathered, and the music is done.

And my bride stands at the altar, waiting for me.

She looks stunning in a strapless white dress with intricate beading that covers the bodice and cascades down the back of the train. Her veil sits like a crown atop her head, her face left uncovered so I can see her elegantly natural makeup and the carefully blank expression she turns my way.

She can't be pleased with me. I've kept her waiting for almost half an hour.

And yet she looks the picture of calm as she holds a beautiful bouquet of white roses, purple-centered calla lilies, and sunflowers between her palms.

"Sorry to keep you all waiting," I project to the room. I stride down the aisle toward my bride, giving a nod to one side of the congregation and then the other, acknowledging their patience and showing my appreciation.

I lope up the steps to meet Tia at the altar, stopping with a huff before her.

"Are we ready, then?" the priest asks, his tone censored with the appropriate amount of inexhaustible patience.

After what we paid him to officiate our wedding today, he better be willing to stand up here and wait all night if that's what I want.

Tia turns to pass her bouquet to the younger teenage girl behind her—Tia's sister, by the looks of it, as the resemblance is uncanny. Then my bride turns back to face me, her composure unshakable as she prepares to marry me.

"I swear I didn't forget," I tease, trying to break the tense moment.

"My mother was starting to worry you got cold feet," Tia jokes.

"But you weren't?" I challenge, quirking an eyebrow as I unleash a cocky smile.

Rather than answer, Tia shifts her gaze from my face down to the collar of my shirt. Wordlessly, she reaches inside the breast of her white dress and pulls out a tissue. The material still feels warm as it brushes against my throat, her fingers working swiftly to clean up what I can only imagine is some gory remnant of my morning.

My lungs freeze at the lightness of her touch, the unexpected poise with which she handles me. I'm being an ass. I know it. And still, she's the one unsettling me.

I catch a glimpse of the crimson-stained tissue before she tucks it away inside her dress once more. And my jaw nearly hits the floor. *How is she this nonchalant?* It doesn't make sense to me.

Then she turns to look at the priest, offering me a perfect view of her elegant profile. "We're ready," she confirms with a gentle smile.

A moment later, Tia turns to face me. And for an instant, I'm lost in the dark depths of her rich brown eyes, unable to see my way free of their inexplicable power.

Then, the ceremony begins.

10

TIA

"**D**early beloved, we are gathered here today to celebrate the union of two great families, the Guerras and the Morettis, as we sanctify the marriage of Tia and Leonardo before God. Thank you all for witnessing such a joyous occasion. Please be seated."

Joyous occasion, my ass. As the congregation settles into their seats with a chorus of rustling and wooden creaks, I'm an utter wreck inside. Ripples of hot and cold anxiety flash through my body like a faucet in the hands of a four-year-old—scalding one second and ice-cold the next.

I can scarcely breathe, my vision slightly hazy before me, and I couldn't say whether the corset of my wedding dress has anything to do with that or just the fact that I'm about to become the bride of Leonardo Moretti.

My heart is pounding so desperately against my ribcage, I'm certain Leo and the priest can hear it at the very least. The humiliation of being made to wait, paired with the blatant violence Leo must have been a part of before coming to our wedding, doesn't even begin to describe the reasons for my tumultuous feelings.

My entire life feels like a cruel joke to be standing here like this, willingly handing over my freedom to a monster.

On the inside, I feel as though I'm screaming bloody murder. But on the outside, I keep my face a mask of serenity. Because I refuse to let Leo see how he affects me.

It gave me great pleasure to see the stunned and slightly baffled expression on his face when I managed to keep my cool through his grand entrance. In truth, I barely held it together, forced to stand at the altar and wait like *I'm* the one who wants this. Then to realize that he was probably late due to losing track of the time while he enjoyed inflicting horrible pain—or death—upon some poor, unfortunate soul. God only knows why.

I know it would have pleased him to see me lose it.

So I won't.

The priest delivers a long, verbose speech about the sanctity of marriage, the oaths we give as man and wife, and the importance of keeping those promises—the promise of honesty, fidelity, and loyalty.

It takes every ounce of my self-discipline not to snort derisively. Because I have no intention of keeping any of them—and Leo broke every one of those vows the night we met.

We can't possibly uphold the "sanctity of marriage." Not to each other.

This wedding is a farce. But there's no turning back now.

I study Leo's features as the priest continues on to talk about how marriage is a gift from God—that as Leo's wife, I will have the duty to honor and serve him, to bear his children. A slow smile curves one side of Leo's lips as his hazel eyes search mine.

And I wonder, does he smile because he thinks that's what I'm signing up for? To be subservient? Submissive? Meak? I'll do what's necessary to lull him into a false sense of security. But he'll come to rue the day he ever mistook me for weak.

My caustic thoughts are all that get me through the agonizingly long Catholic ceremony without collapsing. And thankfully, I don't have much part to play. And I wonder how many women have had to endure this same torture for the Church to realize it's best if we don't have to speak.

Finally, we come to the moment I've truly been dreading.

The priest steps forward to take our hands, and he brings them together, joining them in a formal display of union before the gathered witnesses. A jolt blasts through my body like an electric shock as my fingers meet Leo's, and my heart breaks into a nervous sprint.

I don't want to be anywhere near him. I don't want to touch him. And at the same time, that slight connection brings my body to life, stealing my breath away.

The priest turns his head regally to look at me and asks, "Do you, Tia, take Leonardo as your lawful husband, to have and to hold, from this day forward, for better or for worse, for richer or for poorer, in sickness and in health, to love and cherish until death do you part?"

Hell no. "I do."

My chin lifts defiantly at the smirk that spreads across Leo's cruelly beautiful face.

"And do you, Leonardo, take Tia as your lawful wife, to have and to hold, from this day forward, for better or for worse, for richer or for poorer, in sickness and in health, to love and cherish until death do you part?"

"I do." His voice is low, calm. It rings with the authority of a man capable of ordering the deaths of hundreds on a whim. A man who likely ordered someone's death on our wedding day.

And I'll soon call him husband.

My stomach gives a dangerous quake.

As the priest passes me Leo's ring, I quickly dart my tongue out to wet my suddenly dry lips. Leo's eyes miss nothing, and something flickers just behind them, an emotion that makes me wonder if he sees how nervous I am.

It's bad enough, I could almost vomit.

"Now, Tia, place the ringer on his finger," the priest says.

My hand shakes as I follow his instructions, my heart in my throat as my body urges me to flee before it's too late. It's the first outward sign of the battle waging within me, and Leo's eyes flick down to my hand with quick understanding.

Rather than waiting for me to thread his finger into the ring, he does it for me, shifting his palm and straightening his ring finger so it slides seamlessly into the gold circle. And when our eyes meet, an inscrutable emotion bubbles beneath the surface of his hazel gaze.

"Now, Tia, repeat after me," the priest says. "Take this ring as a sign of my love and faithfulness in the name of the Father, the Son, and the Holy Spirit."

I do, my lips numb as I stumble over my tongue and somehow manage to complete the sentence.

Then Leo takes my ring from the priest. He repeats the same phrase, his words ringing clearly through the church as he holds my gaze, and a shiver runs down my spine.

I look down, catching a glimpse of my wedding ring for the first time, and I'm stunned by the size of the oval-cut solitaire that rests at the center of the delicate, twining platinum band. It's simple, beautiful, and looks far too extravagant beside my dainty hand.

When his warm fingers slide softly up mine, guiding the ring into place, he uses the same gentle care with which he touched me the night he took my virginity. It turns my mouth dry in an instant, and I can't help but look up to meet his eyes once again.

The heat in his gaze is unmistakable.

He likes touching me. He wants to.

And now, he owns me.

So he can have me whenever he wants.

The priest's next words slice through me like a knife. "In the sight of God and these witnesses, I now pronounce you husband and wife! Leo, you may kiss your bride."

My stomach drops somewhere between my feet as Leo closes the distance between us, one arm snaking around my waist as his other hand cradles the back of my neck. I lean away instinctually, wanting to put as much distance between us as I can.

But his strong arms pull me firmly against his body, arching my back as he molds me against his hard chest. I gasp as our lips meet in a pointedly romantic kiss that makes the crowd go wild.

And though I know it's just for show, I can't deny my attraction to Leo. Even after how horribly he treated me, after how little respect he's shown me, my body still awakens at his touch.

A fire lights across my skin, bringing me to a feverish temperature in a matter of seconds.

And though I'm terribly torn between wanting to give in to my attraction or flee, I know that I have a groom to convince and a crowd to please. Though it goes against every instinct, I force my muscles to relax, allowing me to melt in Leo's arms.

He dips me just far enough to make my heart flip-flop, and when I release the tiniest of squeaks, he responds with a wickedly low chuckle. Then, only after he's convinced everyone and their grandmother that we are very much in love, Leo brings me back up to set me gently on my feet.

"Please welcome, for the first time, Mr. and Mrs. Leonardo Moretti!" the priest announces.

And Leo twines our hands together, raising them above our heads as the audience cheers. Forcing a smile, I scan the sea of faces, my eyes falling first on my father, who gives me the subtlest of nods, a sign that he's forgiven my transgression now that I've given everything to make it right. Then to my mother, who smiles with tears in her eyes. Her hands cover her mouth as if she's so happy for her baby girl on the best day of my life.

Beside her are my three youngest sisters, their eyes wide as they take in the lavish scene of the day, oblivious to the true meaning behind it and how this will come for them, too, someday. I dare a glance over my shoulder as Leo pulls me toward the stairs. And Maria's face is the only one that reflects the horror inside me. Our eyes meet for the briefest of moments.

Then I turn, the world seeming almost to move in slow motion as I follow my husband down the aisle.

Like a lamb to slaughter.

I can't stop the horrible, icy feeling in my chest as I realize just what I've done.

I did it for my family. To protect my sisters. And still, I don't know that I'm strong enough to survive the lion's den.

Steeling myself, I square my shoulders and pick up my pace.

I *will* be strong enough. I have to be. Because I refuse to simply roll over and play dead.

I won't give up until I have Leonardo Moretti dead at my feet.

11

LEO

I glance at Tia from the corner of my eye as the plates are delivered to our guests as one. We hired as many servers as we have wedding guests filling the grand ballroom of the Moretti estate. And the opulence of the moment as the servers lower the plates before them in perfect synchronicity is like a dance. Because my family is nothing if not the image of sophistication and class.

But to Tia, it might as well be a typical Tuesday night.

She leans back subtly, allowing the server to deliver her own plate, then she offers him a soft thank-you before taking up her napkin to spread it across her lap.

"You look lovely today, Tia," I say, curious what kind of mood she'll be in now that we have a few relatively private moments at our sweetheart table.

Her gaze snaps in my direction, her mercury-colored eyes scrutinizing. Then she glances down at the intricate embroidery of her dress as if only just noticing what it is she's wearing.

"Oh, this old thing?" she jokes, delivering a coy smile that hits me right in the solar plexus. "You're too kind."

I snort, unable to filter my response, as she catches me by surprise. I'll need to keep that in mind in the future. She's quick.

Clearing my throat, I collect myself. Then I take my glass of red wine from the table and sip it.

Her eyes flash, then shift back to the sea of people that sit around the tables spread before us, letting my silent taunt roll off her shoulders. I think I might learn to like this game. Like chess—or battle strategy—but perhaps a lot less deadly.

"You're upset with me for being late to the ceremony," I state rather than asking because regardless of how well she handled herself, it's a given that she would expect me to arrive on time for our wedding. But I'm curious what she'll be willing to say to me.

"I'm sure whatever the delay, it must have been important," she says, her attention turning to the perfectly golden-browned baked chicken on her plate. She lifts her fork and knife with the grace of someone born to privilege, who's spent her life eating as if it were a performance.

"It was a matter of life and death," I confess gravely, taking up my own utensils and cutting into the beef wellington before me.

Tia coughs, her composure vanishing momentarily as she practically chokes on the piece of chicken she is chewing.

"Are you alright, my dear?" I ask with feigned shock, resting my palm on the soft, cool flesh of her exposed back.

Tia guzzles water, her eyes watering as she chokes down her food. "Fine," she rasps.

Then our table falls notably silent.

We exchange a few more pleasantries between dinner and dessert, performing the traditional cake cutting in between as a moment of reprieve.

Then it's time for the first dance. And though I'm loath to do it, my father made sure I knew how. So, as the first notes of "A Ti Korita Vu" filter from the band's instruments, I guide Tia onto the dance floor and bring her into a proper ballroom frame.

Her arms rest lightly on mine, her fingers delicately gripping my shoulders, and her head tips away from me in a picture of elegance that stuns me. Her dress fits her perfectly, revealing just a hint of her pert breasts over the sweetheart neckline before the start of the beaded corset that tapers down her thin waist. A perfect bustle cascades from the top of her skirt, giving her pronounced hips beneath the layers of fabric.

For a moment, I'm captivated by her, unable to move as I feel the soft warmth of her body pressed against mine, the confidence with which she waits for me to make the first move, to lead her to our wedding song.

I don't know why, but I hadn't anticipated she would be a dancer.

My hesitation is fleeting, and I regain my composure as the music starts to build, ethereal in its haunting notes. Sweeping her around the dance floor in a traditional Viennese waltz, I try to focus on my steps, not the way she glides before me as if carried on angel wings.

Though we haven't practiced this dance before, she responds to the lightest of signals, spinning and twirling in my arms as I guide her across the ballroom. A hush falls over the guests, who watch with rapt attention.

And when the music finally fades, I lower Tia into a dip. She stretches her arm elegantly over her head, extending the line with a beautiful flourish as if we'd been practicing this very move for months.

Applause follows her back onto her feet as I right her, and for a moment, I hold her, spellbound by the energy vibrating between us. Then I lift her fingers to my lips, brushing a soft kiss across her knuckles.

As the rest of our guests move onto the dance floor, I leave her standing there, making my way to the bar for a stiff drink.

"Whiskey. Neat," I tell the bartender, leaning an elbow on the counter as I turn back to look at the dance floor.

I half expected Tia to be standing alone, but before she has a chance to look lonely, her sister—the one who stood as her maid of honor during the ceremony—joins her amidst the crowd.

Tia releases what must be the first genuine smile I've seen since the night I met her. The ones she's been delivering all day have been quite convincing, but I can see the difference as soon as she smiles at her sister.

Clever girl. Too clever.

My suspicions rise as, once again, I'm privy to the intelligence that lurks beneath Tia's innocent demeanor. She might have everyone else fooled—even my father. But not me.

She's stunning, yes. But I'm still not convinced that she's being honest with me.

"A beautiful first dance," Don Guerra says as he comes to stand beside me, holding an empty wine glass as his eyes look out on the transformed dance floor.

What had been a sophisticated performance just minutes before has devolved into a lively scene as people dance to the high-energy music delivered by the band.

"You taught her well," I acknowledge, raising my glass in solute before taking a drink.

Don Guerra turns to the bartender to request another glass of wine. Then he joins me in leaning against the marble counter so we can both watch the revelry.

"I find it is my duty to thank you, Leonardo, for doing the honorable thing," he says after several moments of pregnant silence.

I glance sharply in his direction, surprised by his statement. "How so?" I ask, my guard up as I scrutinize him. "And please, call me Leo."

"You didn't have to go through with the marriage. But you did. You saved my family—my daughter—a humiliation that could have broken her. So, despite our differences, and the rather rocky history between us, I want to thank you. Sincerely."

Stunned, I study his weathered face for several moments. "You're welcome," I say, when I can find no malice behind his words.

In truth, I'm astounded by the fact that he could hold himself with such dignity, even after the blatant insult I gave him by dumping Tia on his doorstep that night. Grudging respect rises inside me as I stand beside him, at a loss for words. Giuseppe Guerra knows what is best for his family and can set aside his pride to protect his daughters. That takes a lot of strength and nerve.

"You played your cards well, given the hand you were dealt," I confess after another long pause.

Don Guerra turns his eyes on me now, the same dark, penetrating gaze as his daughter. And behind them is an intelligence that makes me think twice about my cocky determination to crush him before this unlikely alliance.

"Soon enough, you'll learn that when it comes to your children, you'll risk anything to ensure their happiness."

The statement lies heavily between us, the meaning behind it far deeper than the words themselves. Of course, he's talking about the child that drove this entire alliance into being. But beyond that, I sense that he's telling me just why he insisted on this marriage in the first place.

But which of his daughters' happiness is he referring to?

He can't possibly mean Tia's.

I'm not stupid enough to believe that she could possibly be happy about marrying me. Not after what I did to her.

My eyes find her on the dance floor as one song transitions into the next. She looks young and carefree as she twirls her younger sisters, all five dancing together in a giggling group of giddy camaraderie.

The corners of my lips twitch involuntarily, threatening to smile. Beside me, Don Guerra watches them as well, his emotions less guarded as his eyes light with fatherly affection.

"It must be hard raising five daughters with a last name like yours," I observe, the statement made more out of curiosity than anything.

What a stark contrast to my father, who could pour all his ambitions into his one and only son.

"You have no idea," he says, his voice low and rich with meaning. Then he turns to level me with a solemn gaze. "Hear me well, Leo. You now possess one of Earth's greatest gifts. You can either cherish it as it should be cherished, or you can squander it and learn too late about the consequences."

I bristle at the don's bold words, and a scoff bursts from me as I stand to my full height. "Is that a threat?" From where I stand, it sure sounded like it.

Guiseppe assesses me with a calm gaze, his eyes searching my face as the silence stretches between us. "No, it's just a fact," he says, his tone measured. Then he tips his chin in the direction of the dance floor. "Perhaps you ought to spend more time dancing with your new bride."

In a flash, the exchange between us feels like a different game entirely. This is a power play meant to destabilize me. My temper flashes white-hot, and I bite down on the words that threaten to spring from my mouth without proper consideration.

"Thanks for the advice," I state, downing the rest of my whiskey in one go. Then I set my tumbler on the bartop and stalk away, heading for the exit.

12

TIA

My feet ache from dancing in my heels, and my carefully styled hair falls loosely around my face by the time the night is over, and Leo and I depart. We aren't going far—just to Leo's suite, where he took me the first night I met him.

Though I haven't had a drink, I stumble as I walk, my soles aching and blistered as I danced to my heart's content, determined to enjoy one last night of fun with my sisters. The wedding went off without a hitch. It was a grand affair, and despite the circumstances, I ended up enjoying the reception immensely. In part because I hardly saw Leo after our first dance.

But now, as he leads me down the hallway to our new shared living accommodations, I'm faced with the fact that it's what comes after the party that I fear.

I haven't been with anyone except Leo. After the way he made me feel so good before utterly destroying me, I'm terrified of what he might have in store for me tonight. Still, I hope I might have the opportunity to enjoy myself, even if it's only a little.

Because the one saving grace going into this marriage is that I know I'm attracted to Leo—and that he's very good in bed. It doesn't matter that he also makes my heart ache, and my skin burn with fiery rage.

Today proved as much. Despite how much I hate him, my body still craves his touch.

Not to mention, the survival of my family rests on my shoulders. This alliance is only as real as the marriage we've entered into. So I need to make this work—at least until I find a way to crush Leo and bring down the Moretti family once and for all.

"This is us," Leo says, leaning his back against the heavy wood door to his room. His hand twists the doorknob, and he steps back to welcome me inside.

I can smell the lingering scent of whiskey on the air behind him, and I suspect he's had a decent amount to drink. But he's as dexterous as ever, his strides confident and measured as he stalks into the room and starts to undress.

Closing the door behind us, I watch him for several moments, unsure of what to expect.

My heart slowly calms from its frantic beat as I realize he doesn't intend to pounce on me now that we're alone. In truth, I had no idea what to expect walking into tonight.

Now that I'm his, he could do anything.

And after the electric feel of his touch during the wedding ceremony, I thought he just might demand I fulfill his conjugal rights. But right now, he seems more inclined to get ready for bed as he undoes his bowtie with deft fingers before he shrugs out of his black tux.

I'm tempted to follow his lead and pretend like he's not there while I take off the confining white casing that's made it challenging to breathe for more hours than I can account for at this point. But if I'm going to win over my new husband and get close enough to learn his secrets, I can't fall prey to the temptation of keeping my distance.

"Do you mind?" I breathe, turning my back to him to expose the satin buttons running down my spine. They're low enough, I'm sure I could undo them myself without too much trouble. But this gives him an excuse to touch me.

Leo pauses, his green-gray eyes flashing to my face momentarily.

Then he turns his attention to the buttons of my dress as he makes swift work of them.

"Thank you," I murmur, peering at him over my shoulder as I look up through my lashes.

He simply grunts, returning his attention to undressing himself.

Positioning myself so I'm well within Leo's line of sight, I reach behind my back to drag the zipper of my dress down in what I can only hope is a seductive motion. Once again, his gaze flashes in my direction, and a slight scowl buckles his brows.

With a sigh of relief, I let my wedding dress fall to the ground, pooling around my feet as I shed twenty pounds in an instant. Mother insisted it was the perfect dress for the occasion, but I've never felt such immense relief as I do to be rid of the confining fashion.

This merits a more distinct pause from Leo as his fingers hover over the buttons of his shirt. His eyes drop from my face to my suddenly bare breasts, and a shiver runs down my spine at his heated gaze. My nipples pucker, growing hard in the sudden cold of his room.

No fire burns in the fireplace tonight. Not at the end of June.

Before my nerves fail me, I step out of my dress, wearing nothing but my high heels and a lacy white thong, as I slowly approach him. Trying my best at a seductive gaze, I peer up at Leo as I rest my palms on the firm muscle of his shirt-clad chest.

I can feel the powerful beat of his heart against my palm, fast enough to make me think I'm doing something that appeals to him. Then I lean in, tilting my chin up and tipping my head as I kiss him, slow and sweet.

Heat radiates through my body as he stands motionless for several seconds, our lips locked in a passionate kiss. But he doesn't deepen it or take control like he did the first night he was with me.

Strong hands grip my upper arms, and a second later, Leo guides me firmly back a step, breaking the kiss as he removes me from his personal space. Then he turns to finish removing his shirt, his demeanor cold and distant.

"What, you don't want to?" I ask, halfway between baffled and antagonizing. *How am I supposed to make any headway with him if he doesn't even want me? Was I wrong in thinking the attraction between us is mutual?* "It's our wedding night, Leo. People will expect us to make the most of it—especially since we're delaying our honeymoon."

I throw the last part in to try to drive the point home. I don't actually believe Leo intends to take me on the honeymoon he casually promised once his responsibilities calm down. But it's something I can use as leverage to make my argument more convincing.

Dropping his dress shirt casually onto the floor, Leo eyes me for a long moment, his handsome features working to find an expression they can settle into comfortably. Then they soften.

"You're right. I'm sorry. It's been a long day, but we should enjoy tonight. Right?"

A fire lights in his eyes, awakening unexpected excitement in my belly, and my breath catches as he closes the space between us once more. His arms wrap around me, pulling me close as the heat from his bare skin radiates into my exposed flesh.

Despite myself, I moan as his lips capture mine in a passionate kiss, his tongue stroking the seam between them, encouraging me to let him in. I do, my heart pounding a mile a minute as I try to make sense of how I managed to convince him so easily.

It shocks me—how readily I can forget how much I hate Leo when he holds me like this, kissing the sanity from my brain in an instant. His tongue strokes tantalizingly across my own, tangling with it in a seductive dance as his hands travel slowly down my back.

Tingling anticipation races up my spine as he reaches my butt, his fingers splaying as he grips the exposed flesh greedily. Then he bends to scoop me up, his hand gripping my thighs as he lifts me off the ground like I weigh little more than a feather.

I gasp, my arms shifting to wrap around his neck as he guides my leg around his hips, and my core tightens at the sudden and intense closeness of feeling his bare skin pressed against every inch of me.

His belt buckle digs adamantly into the tender flesh of my inner thigh, and I arch my back as the slight discomfort triggers my excitement.

"Fuck, you're sexy," he breathes, kissing my neck as my head tips back, my breasts pressing firmly against his hard pecs.

Then he turns, carrying me toward the bed.

But he doesn't lay me down like he did last time. Instead, he carries me to the glass door of his balcony just to the side of his bedside table.

"What are you doing?" I gasp as the fresh summer night breeze whispers across my back, raising goosebumps in its wake. Fear tightens around my throat as I think of the house full of guests sleeping in the rooms all around us.

Anyone on the floor above us could easily look out their window and know exactly what we're doing.

"Leo," I whisper, desperation tinging my tone, "someone might see us."

"Isn't that what you wanted?" he taunts, his arms like iron around my waist as he carries me to the balcony railing.

Cold sandstone bites into the tender flesh as he sets me down on the coarse railing.

"I think we ought to make a show of it so no one will doubt that the baby I put in your belly is legitimate. Don't you agree?" His tone is arctic, as cold as ice.

"Leo, please," I beg, panic rising in my chest as I realize what his intentions are. "Someone will see."

"Isn't that the point?" he breathes, leaning close to press his lips to mine.

And despite myself, my stomach flutters, my desire awakening at his sensual kiss.

A moment later, his fingers hook around the skimpy lace of my panties, and with a forceful yank, he shreds the fabric as he tears it off me. I squeal at the sudden, intense sting, then press my lips fiercely to his to try and muffle the sound.

He chuckles, low and wicked, his bare chest vibrating against my breasts as he holds me close with one arm. I can feel him unbuckle his belt with the other, then undo the button and zipper of his slacks, and cold anxiety mingles with a molten heat deep in my belly.

I know I shouldn't want it, but despite my mortification, despite how much I hate Leo, I can't help the aching need that consumes me at the thought of having him inside me once again. It felt so good the first time, I nearly lost my mind. Maybe, if I stay quiet, no one will notice our complete lack of decorum.

Clinging to his muscular shoulders as Leo brings my hips closer to the railing's edge, I gasp as his silken cockhead finds my entrance. It feels different than before, when he was wearing a condom. Somehow intensely more intimate, daring even. My stomach knots with anticipation, my skin tingling. Then he presses inside me with one powerful thrust.

I break our kiss, burying my face against his chest to stop any sound from escaping me. Because somewhere over the past few months, I forgot just how big he is. And this time, he's not taking it slow.

He drives forward relentlessly with his hips as he fills me up, stretching me to my limit, and I want to cry out as he fucks me hard and fast. But I refuse to make a sound and give him the satisfaction of embarrassing me when, so far, I don't think we've woken anybody.

This is nothing like the first passionate night we had together. It's rough and carnal, and to my utter mortification—despite the pain of being taken so indecently—it turns me on.

"Come on, wife. Don't you want everyone to know how much fun we're having? It's our wedding night. They expect us to seek each other's pleasure," Leo taunts, not bothering to keep his tone low.

I don't respond, biting my lips to stay silent just to spite him—and because if I try to say anything, it might come out as a lascivious goan. He's trying to goad me, his message loud and clear. I don't get to control him with sex. That's his domain. And here, he owns my pleasure.

When I don't answer, he grips my hips firmly, lifting me from the balcony, then he turns me abruptly to face away from him and bends me over the railing. A moment later, he guides his cock between my thighs to find my entrance from behind.

Our skin slaps together audibly with each driving thrust, and tears sting my eyes as I try not to cry. Not because it hurts. In truth, the pain subsided after the first few deep, penetrating thrusts.

But I don't think he's going to stop until I give in to him and wake the whole house, and I hate him for manipulating me once again.

Worst of all, though, I find myself dangerously close to enjoying the abuse as Leo reaches around my hips, his fingers finding my clit with expert precision.

"You think you're going to stay quiet, pet?" he murmurs, leaning close to my ear as his strong chest grazes against my back.

And the low, silky sound of his voice makes my core tighten involuntarily.

"I assure you, I won't stop until I make you sing. So unless you want people to see me fucking you in the broad light of day, you better give me what I want."

Horror grips me as I realize just how terribly I've miscalculated the depravity of my new husband. I'm so far in over my head that I don't know if I could find my way back to the surface. Still, I can't stop the shudder of arousal that ripples through me at his threat.

His fingers circle my clit with merciless greed, awakening the ravenous hunger deep inside my belly despite the mortification that sets my cheeks ablaze. And I'm torn, desperately, between the desire to succumb to my baser instincts and the need to defy Leo.

I want to show him that he doesn't own me. As much as he would like to think he does, I'm the master of my own body. And I hate him so much right now that he can't possibly make me want him.

But the stimulation is overwhelming, the tingling euphoria so all-consuming that I'm not entirely sure I have the control over my body that I so desperately want.

I open my lips, ready to tell him *fuck you*, the most caustic comeback I can come up with at this moment. But the only sound that escapes me is a deep, guttural moan.

Leo releases a dark, sadistic laugh as he pounds inside me harder, his fingers torturing me with pleasure. "My little slut," he breathes, his lips feather-light as they graze the hollow of my neck. "I think you might just like being fucked where everyone can see, don't you?"

And when his finger and thumb lightly pinch the sensitive bundle of nerves at the peak of my thighs, I can't help myself.

I scream.

Then, I explode into oblivion.

13

LEO

Fucking Christ, it feels good to be inside Tia—no condom, wrapped in her warm, wet depths, taking her as hard as she can handle. *And when she comes around my cock because I called her a little slut?* I'm about two seconds from losing my mind.

Her tight little pussy throbs around me with impressive force, gripping my cock like a vise as her body silently begs me to come inside her. She's still just as fresh as the first time I fucked her, all tight and firm and waiting for me to break her in. And the desire to fill her up is almost unbearable.

But that's not what this is about.

As much as I like fucking Tia—and I can't deny that I do—this is about teaching her a lesson. Her and the rest of the Guerra family who think they can manipulate me with underhanded threats and throwing their daughter at me with the responsibility of an illegitimate child.

Even now, after a wedding and a day of celebration, they're my enemy, trying to find my weak points through subversive means. Because they know they can no longer defeat me in a proper fight. So now they want to outmaneuver me using the pretense of a baby.

And I intend to show them that they have no chance against me —regardless of their deceit.

Above us, I can hear the slide of a window opening, and a smirk spreads across my lips as I know we have our first witness. Tia must hear it too, as her head turns, her eyes glancing up toward the facade, and a single tear trails down her cheek.

Her expression is an explosion of emotions. Hurt, anger, embarrassment. But beneath it, I can see the heat of arousal, the lingering flush of lusty satisfaction from her first orgasm. Despite her apparent determination to defy me, she likes the way I fuck her.

"Looks like we have our first witness, my pet," I taunt low and soft.

"Fuck you," she hisses, turning her face forward once more, perhaps in an attempt to hide it.

"You already are," I sneer, then I thrust forcefully to make my point.

Tia whimpers, her fingers curling to dig into the stone veranda.

I pant as I keep up my grueling pace, abusing her pussy as I take her hard and fast. And Tia takes all of me, her tight hole stretching like a glove around my cock. She fits me perfectly, like she was made for me.

Claiming her fills me with an overwhelming satisfaction—not just because having her means I own one of Don Moretti's most valued possessions, but because she's gorgeous. Even more so now with her newfound maturity. I could tell the night I met Tia that she's smart. But now, Tia seems to be applying that intelligence toward survival. And that makes her even more sexy.

"God, you feel so fucking good," I groan.

Tia breathes heavily, her lips pressed together as if to make as little noise as possible. But that's not why we're out here. Our witness has closed their window once again, and I'm not going inside until I'm sure I've driven my point home.

"You ready to give them a show?" I ask. "Let them hear just how hard your new husband makes you come?"

Leaning over her, I change the angle of my thrusts to penetrate her more deeply. Tia whimpers, the sound not quite a confirmation but still provocative enough to guarantee she doesn't want me to stop what I'm doing. And I don't want to either.

As little as I want to admit it, I could easily get addicted to the heavenly feel of her pussy wrapped around me. She moves beneath me with just the right amount of passion, needing me inside her but still trapped beneath my palm.

And all the while, I tease her clit, demanding another orgasm before she's even recovered from the first.

Biting down on her lip, Tia turns it white in the pale glow of the moon as she tries not to make another sound. And that makes me want to break her all the more. *She thinks she can tempt me, tease me, make me into her plaything?* She should know better by now.

And after tonight, she's never going to forget it.

She might be beautiful—intoxicating even. But in this relationship, I own her pleasure, not the other way around. And apparently, she needs to be reminded of that now.

"You think you're done, Tia? You think you get to decide when you've had enough?"

She doesn't answer me. Her only response is to cast an agonized look of pleasure over her shoulder as her pert breasts bounce against the railing.

"That's right. You belong to me now. You're *my* plaything. And if I tell you to scream, you sure as *fuck* are going to." I flick her clit, demanding her release, and she squeals, bucking against me involuntarily as the change in pressure shocks her.

Tia's cry of pleasure dies into a muffled sob, and her shoulders dip precariously forward, her body leaning over the edge of the railing as the strength leaves her arms. My heart dives with her as I fear she might literally topple over the ledge.

Releasing the nape of her neck, I wrap my arm around her chest and shoulder, palming one glorious breast. My other hand grips her hip so she's securely in my arms. But I don't stop my punishing pace.

And as Tia trembles against me, I know she's too overcome with pleasure to fully grasp how close she came to falling.

"That's it, my pet. Let them hear you," I purr in her ear, nipping her earlobe as I let my fingers slide slowly around her hip to find her slick folds once more.

"Please, Leo," Tia sobs, her voice agonized.

And it makes my balls tighten, my cock throb.

"Please let you come again?" I tease, collecting her slick juices on my fingers before I resume circling her clit.

Tia cries harder, her body shuddering against my chest as I pound inside her. Playing with her nipple, I tease the peak of her slit at the same time. Her walls tighten around me as I feel her edging closer to climax once more.

"Sing, little bird," I encourage, trapping her earlobe between my teeth as I drive her wild.

She mewls, the sound just long and loud enough that I'm confident the lights that flick on behind us are in response. But she seems too close to release to notice this time.

Hips rolling, Tia jerks in my arms, her body spasming as she comes a second time, this time with overwhelming force. I groan as her walls milk me, egging me to come inside her.

And as Tia softens in my arms, turning to putty as I manipulate her body with ease, I know I want to do just that. After years of discipline and wearing protection to ensure I wouldn't have any bastard children running around, I finally don't have to think about it anymore.

Because what's done is done.

For better or worse, I have a wife, and I fucking love being inside her without a condom.

Grunting as the intensity of my arousal reaches the breaking point, I thrust deep inside Tia and release my seed in several throbbing bursts. Her pussy flutters around me, eagerly accepting all I have to offer.

And for a moment, as we come down from our orgasms together, I'm filled with a deep and instinctual satisfaction. It felt so good to claim Tia, to use her so completely. There's nothing more carnal than taking a woman roughly, passionately, and filling her with my cum—no surer way to mark my territory.

We breathe heavily together, my heart hammering a rhythm against her back as I hold her close, unsure of whether she'll be able to stand on her own two feet if I let her go. The patio dims as the lights from our witnesses darken once more, leaving us alone in our marital bliss.

Finally, after several minutes, Tia stops trembling, and her breathing grows more steady. I ease out of her, slowly loosening my hold on her body as I stand to my full height. And as soon as I release her, Tia flees inside, her heels tapping at a rapid pace across the stone balcony as her sobs fade into the night.

It was mean and manipulative, treating Tia the way I did. I could see the embarrassment and discomfort on her face, mingled with her pleasure. I could almost feel bad once again for using Tia to make my point. But I also know that the Guerra family is anything but innocent in trapping me in this marriage, and now, my guard is up.

I've questioned whether Tia was even pregnant from the start or if it was a lie strategically told to save the Guerras' necks from my noose. It frustrates me, knowing that they outsmarted me by trapping me in this marriage. And I won't let it happen again. The subtle threats from her father and Tia's attempt to seduce me. She must have an ulterior motive.

But watching her run inside after—despite the pleasure I drew from her—awakens a pang of guilt inside me. Perhaps I took it too far. I don't think I actually hurt the girl, but I wouldn't want to either. It's her family I want to destroy, and as my wife, Tia is under my protection.

Sighing heavily, I look up at the now-dark windows above.

In our world of backstabbing and manipulation, I wouldn't be surprised if her goal tonight was to try and demonstrate that she's willing to move past the horrible way I treated her the night I took her virginity.

And in my burst of temper, I've only made things worse.

Combing my fingers through my hair, I scrub the back of my neck as fresh guilt tightens my chest. Perhaps I overreacted. I shouldn't have taken my anger out on her.

I won't make the same mistake again.

Turning, I follow my bride back inside. *What a terrible farce of a wedding night.*

14

TIA

I'm tired of wandering the labyrinth of hallways that make up the Moretti estate. After three days of exploring the house and grounds, it no longer feels like a maze of endless corridors and vaulted rooms. I know the entire layout by heart—even the twenty-five guest bedrooms the manor houses.

Undoubtedly, the estate is nearly twice as large as my family's, with the main, three-story mansion containing two separate wings that extend on either side. The terrace outside the ballroom that I fell in love with the first night Leo showed me around sits in the center of it all, a beautiful outdoor space paved with flagstone. It's large enough to house three fountains spread evenly across. Their ornately carved centers each depict a different Greek myth.

But that's not where I'm headed this morning. Rather than wasting another day wandering, I want to dig deeper into the library. The grand collection has more books than I could read in a lifetime. And seeing as I have nothing productive to do with my time, it seems like a good challenge to finish them before I die.

My steps echo across the granite floors of the entryway in my new home, resonating loudly and reminding me of just how alone I am. From the corner of my eye, I catch my reflection to my right, a ghost floating past the mirrored wall I found so spectacular the night I crashed the Moretti house party.

Now, it mocks me and the circumstances of my new life.

At a glance, anyone would think I'm perfectly content, my appearance well maintained, dressed in the finest designer clothes. I keep my expression passively open and friendly. But slowly, I'm drowning, overcome by the circumstances of my new life and the ugly world I find myself in.

I've finally recovered from my wedding night, though it took several days of a deep ache between my legs and sore muscles that aren't used to being used before I could finally walk comfortably once more.

And every time my core throbbed, or my muscles groaned in protest, they made me think of Leo. The way he kissed me so passionately, lifted me into his arms with ease. Then carried me out onto the patio to fuck me for everyone to see.

My stomach knots as I think of the humiliation. And the pleasure in Leo's arrogant face. He liked teaching me a lesson, and the statement was glaringly clear. I don't get to dictate terms in this marriage. I don't get to have a say—not unless I want to be punished.

The worst part about it is I still came. It turned me on when he touched me. Even when he took me roughly. I don't know what that could possibly mean about me. I still hate him, passionately. I want to destroy him. But feeling him inside me… the way he ignites my senses… it sends me to a place of sweet oblivion. A place where, for a moment, I could care less who sees.

Bile rises in my throat, and I turn abruptly, suddenly repulsed by my reflection. And slam into the Moretti butler as he rounds the corner into the entryway.

"Ah, Signora Moretti." His tone is formal as he steadies me for the briefest of moments before releasing my arms to step back.

"Sorry, Luigi," I gasp, warmth radiating in my cheeks.

"That's quite alright. The master requested that I inform you there will be a meeting in the library today. You're to occupy yourself somewhere else." He gives a stiff bow before striding away to carry on with his duties.

Well, there goes the only escape I've found from this dreadful place. I guess I'll need to find another way to fill my time. Looks like another day of wandering around the grounds. Sighing, I change direction, heading toward the terrace doors at the back of the ballroom.

On my way, I pass several suited men, their scowls a clear indicator I should mind my own business. I give them a silent nod, but their eyes simply slide over me as they walk by.

Leo's house is filled with self-important men who scarcely notice my presence. Except to tell me where I'm expected and when. The guards keep their eyes carefully focused on the middle distance. The maids whisper from the room every time I enter one, as if they've been told to remain invisible. Only Luigi seems willing to speak to me. And even then, it's just to relay messages Leo wishes me to receive.

But even Leo pays me little mind. He goes out early in the morning and comes back in the evening, often arriving late for dinner. I doubt the tension between us is helping. During our engagement party, I thought I might have been making a little bit of headway with him. After our wedding night, I don't think we could be farther from it.

And with so many hours left alone, I can do little more than dwell upon it.

Breathing in the fresh summer air, I make my way down the terrace steps into the garden below. It's a beautiful day, the sky blue, the birds whistling happily from the potted fruit trees that line the windows.

Strolling idly through the colorful garden, I slide my Millefiori necklace back and forth along its chain, thinking about my new life. Overall, it hasn't been too challenging to get used to. This gilded cage isn't much different than my own family home. I'm expected to stay within the confines, make an appearance at all meals and functions, and stay out of people's way otherwise.

The grounds here are somehow more impressive than the acres of space that surround the Guerra estate. A backdrop of the dramatic Allegheny mountains lies just beyond the Morettis' backyard, and a dark, mysterious forest covers the distance between the sprawling house and the sharp peaks. The view is breathtaking, certainly my second-favorite amenity to my new home—after the library.

But I miss my sisters, even my parents. My sisters would love it here—all the stunning gardens and colorful flowers growing with wild abandon, the countless rooms to explore and play hide and go seek through.

Even though my relationship with my parents has been somewhat strained over the past few months, I miss them, too. After I agreed to marry Leo, I managed to recover a shadow of the closeness my parents and I once had.

But then I had to leave them all, to move miles away and into an entirely new world—it might as well be light-years. And it feels like I'll never have the opportunity to fully repair the rift that my actions caused.

Instead, I can only move forward, and learn the expectations that come with being Signora Moretti. I can't say it's very fulfilling. Even my revenge plot is dead in the water as of now. Because I can't do much of anything to learn Leo's weaknesses if I never even see him.

Plucking a dianthus, I hold the fragrant bloom to my nose and take a deep breath, trying to calm my frustration when I think about my husband.

My initial plan to get close to Leo is failing miserably because he's hardly ever around. Whether he's intentionally trying to avoid me, or if he simply lives to work, I don't know. Even in our bedroom, he hasn't attempted to touch me, since our wedding night.

I can't decide if I'm happy or sad about that. He humiliated me, fucked me for all our wedding guests to see, and did it with a brutality I wasn't ready for. But at the same time, I can't deny I liked it. He made me orgasm multiple times—despite the mortification and the shame. Something about his unapologetic way of touching me, his confidence as he manipulated my body, set my soul alive.

I've had sex with him two times now. Both very different. And yet, each time, I feel such an intense connection, a rapture that's almost like a spell falling over me. I want his touch. I crave it. And yet, I fear what unexpected consequence might come from it.

Sex clearly isn't how I'm going to manipulate Leo, so I need to find another way. Because I refuse to fade into the background and watch my family's once-great name get raked through the mud by associating with the Morettis.

It's my fault we had to form this alliance. And I intend to fix it.

But how, I have no clue when I'm so entirely isolated.

Usually, I might go to Maria about this kind of thing.

Now, it seems the only person I can speak to is the child growing in my belly.

"You're pretty good company," I assure my abdomen solemnly. I've caught myself doing that a lot more lately to fill the silence of my new home. "Though you're not very talkative," I add. "So I don't really know that you're going to be much help planning my scheme."

My lips curl slightly at my bad humor, and it feels pretty sad that I'm now the only person who laughs at my jokes. Hopefully, my child will find me funny, seeing as they just might be the only person I'll have around.

Continuing my stroll, I round the corner of the well-trimmed hedges, and my heart skips a beat. A gardener kneels on the gravel walkway, his blue overalls coated with fresh soil as he digs in the ground with a spade.

"Oh," I gasp, my hand going to my heart as my body reacts to the surprise of finding somebody when I thought I was alone out here. I hope against hope he didn't hear anything I said to my baby. Because I'm not confident it wouldn't incriminate me.

"So sorry, Signora. Did I startle you?" he asks, turning to face me though he keeps one knee resting on the hard ground. By the gray of his mustache, I would assume he's in his late sixties, and his leathery skin has a permanent tan from years spent in the sun. But his eyes have laugh lines around them, making his face soft and kind.

"No, no, it's fine. I just didn't realize anyone was in the garden." I smile, nervously combing my hair behind one ear.

"I can come back later," he assures me, gripping his knee as he comes to a stand with arthritic effort.

"No, please, there's no need," I assure him, instinctively reaching out to help. Then I pause, as I realize he's already on his feet.

"It's no trouble," he says. "I wouldn't want to disturb your walk."

"Actually…" I give a breathy laugh. "If it's not too odd a request, could I join you? I love gardening."

Stunned into silence, the older gentleman considers my request. And by his hesitation, I wonder if I might not have put him in a bad spot.

"Of course you can join us, Signora," a woman cuts in, her breath heavy as she pushes a wheelbarrow of fresh flowers up the path. "We're replanting this portion of the garden since one of our furry neighbors thought they'd turn it into their bed."

The woman is a stark contrast to her male counterpart, her words verbose as she welcomes me. Rather than his more wiry frame, the woman is on the heavier side with her frizzy gray hair pulled up into a messy bun on top of her head.

Her words send a wave of relief through me as I finally find something useful to do with my time.

"You can use my gloves," the man offers, getting ready to remove them.

"Actually, I love getting my hands dirty," I assure him. Then, I clap my hands together with a broad grin. "How can I help?"

Ignoring the way my pants get dirty as soon as I sit down, I take up the spade the man hands me and get to work. The woman's chatter is friendly and constant as we work, and for the first time since I moved into the Moretti estate, I dare to hope that I've found a few friends.

15

LEO

"Mayor Romney, this is a pleasant surprise," I say as I enter the bank just as he's about to leave.

"Ah, Signor Moretti, it is indeed," he agrees with an amicable smile. "I must congratulate you on such a spectacular wedding. I'm rather impressed by the splendor, considering the limited time you had to prepare."

I chuckle. "I assure you, my family is well-versed in how to plan extravagant affairs. We've had plenty of practice."

Mayor Romney releases a low, throaty chuckle as well, nodding in silent acknowledgment.

"I hope you and your wife enjoyed the party," I add. "My wife and I were honored by your presence." I press a palm to my chest in a sign of heartfelt sincerity.

"Very much so. Your Tia was a vision. And your first dance brought tears to my eyes. It's a rare thing to see two young people so well matched."

My heart twists at the mention of her name, but I maintain my smile. "I'm a lucky man."

"I'll say. I'll tell you, my wife and I have taken quite a shine to her.

In fact, we were just talking yesterday about how we ought to have you over for dinner soon. What do you say? Are you free tonight?"

"To—Yes, absolutely. Tia will be overjoyed to see you both again."

"Wonderful. I'll let Alicia know. Shall we plan on seven?"

"We'll be there," I agree, astounded by the sudden shift in my relationship with the mayor I've been trying to get into my back pocket—the man who would solve a lot of red tape issues for my vision of expanding my family's reach.

I take his offered hand, giving it a firm shake. He departs a moment later, leaving me rooted to the spot as my mind races. It's a perfect opportunity to further garner his trust. But I know I've dug myself into a rut.

Because I haven't done anything to make amends with Tia. In truth, I've done nothing but expand the gaping chasm between us. I can't stand the steady guilt that's been gnawing at me since our wedding night. To avoid it, I've spent as little time with Tia as possible, giving her space rather than showing her that I do, in fact, know how to be a decent husband. Or human being.

Swallowing my pride, I know that I'm going to have to make a convincing argument for why she should help me. To win the mayor's approval, I might even be willing to do some groveling.

Rather than attending to the business I came for, I turn and exit the bank, climbing back into my car to head home early.

It only takes me fifteen minutes to drive across town. I park on the far side of the courtyard fountain outside my home, then take the steps two at a time, stepping inside the entry as Luigi opens the door.

"Tia?" I ask by way of greeting.

"Out in the garden, I believe, sir."

Something in his tone catches my interest, but I set that aside to think about later. Right now, I'm on a mission. With a nod, I straighten my suit coat and head toward the balcony beyond the ballroom.

Her soft, melodic laugh catches my ear as soon as I step out onto the terrace, and I turn in the direction of the sound. It's gentle and feminine, and it reminds me of the smart, innocent girl I met a few months ago.

A sliver of jealousy needles its way into my chest as I wonder who might be making her laugh. But as I reach the stairs to look out over the gravel walkway, I'm stunned by what I see.

Tia's on her hands and knees, dirt covering her fine clothes as she digs in the garden alongside two of the groundskeepers. The woman beside her chatters happily, scarcely coming up for air as she tells some outlandish story. The smile on Tia's face is warm and soft, her happiness sincere as she sets a flower into the hole she's dug and scoops the earth back around it, tamping it down gently.

I rush down the steps, making a beeline toward my wife, who seems completely oblivious to her inappropriate behavior. Or perhaps she doesn't care. Whatever the case, I fully intend to correct her on it.

"Tia!" Reaching her, I grasp her arm and pull her up off the ground, bringing her to her feet.

She stumbles into me, her palms finding my chest in an attempt to balance herself because I handled her too roughly. Clenching my teeth in frustration, I soften my grip, trying to steady her without doing more harm.

"What do you think you're doing, rolling around in the dirt with the help?" I ask once she's firmly on her own two feet. "It's completely inappropriate."

The gardeners shrink away from us, silent as they stare up at me in shock, and when I glance their way, they quickly drop their eyes, busying themselves with their work once more.

"I was *gardening*," she says, her voice immediately defensive as she yanks her arm from my grasp. She peers up at me with guarded eyes, her laughter of a moment before, gone.

"Why?" I demand, looking her up and down.

Dirt darkens her fingernails and mars her creamy skin. She even has a smudge on her chin, and my fingers itch to wipe it away. But I restrain myself, confident she doesn't want me touching her right now.

"Because I would prefer to do something useful with my time than wander around the grounds any longer, and since I'm not allowed to leave, you can hardly judge me for doing what I can with the limited options available." Her onyx eyes flash passionately as her hands land on her hips, her body language telling me she's gearing up for war.

I straighten as I study her delicate features in her sudden fury. I like this side of Tia, the outspoken young woman who's not afraid to say it like it is.

"What do you care if I get dirty?" she continues, her voice scathing. "It washes off easy enough—far better than blood, I'd wager. And at least I'm doing some good, trying to add beauty back into the world. I'm not hurting anybody. So, what's so terrible about planting a few flowers, even if it's *beneath me*? That's far better than the butchering you've most likely performed this morning."

Taken aback by her sharp tongue and willingness to speak her mind, for a moment, I'm left speechless. But I'm also unable to argue with her reasoning. And as she glares up at me, I let my shoulders relax.

"You're right. I'm sorry. I should have thought about how you might have to fill your time."

Tia falters, seeming surprised that I would have it in me to apologize. "Well... perhaps you could at least give me a car or allow my sisters to visit."

Her tone is grudgingly accepting of my apology as her arms cross defensively over her chest.

Such a simple request. I would have granted her far more to keep her out of the dirt and behaving more appropriately as my wife. "Done," I agree readily.

Again, Tia seems startled, and her arms drop as her perfectly shaped brows press into a frown. "Really?"

The simple question brings me back to the night I first met her, and I can't help but smile. "You doubt me?"

Her expression tells me she recognizes the line immediately, and she does not look happy. Instead, hurt flashes across her face, quickly followed by resentment. "Can you blame me?"

Touche.

Sighing, I hang my head as I nod, giving a moment to acknowledge the injury I caused. Then I raise my eyes to give her a grave look. "I mean it, Tia. I'll hire you a car and driver, and your sisters are welcome to come here whenever you want them to visit—and stay as long as you like."

"Thank you," she murmurs.

I give a single nod. Then I glance down the pathway. "Will you walk with me?"

Confusion washes across her features before she quickly dons her mask of passive complacency. "Okay. Sure," she agrees.

And when I offer her my elbow, she takes it, resting her delicate fingers in the crook of my arm. Somehow, it doesn't bother me that she's dusted in earth, dirt packed beneath her fingernails. Her hands are still elegant even after their menial labor.

"Thanks for letting me join you," she says sweetly to the two gardeners.

After casting a furtive glance my way, they both give her wide, toothy smiles.

Tia follows me down the path, her steps light, and I can't help but notice the fresh, earthy scent combined with a slight tang of salty sweat that surrounds her. It's not the oversweet perfume girls often wear. With just a hint of citrus spice, it's a pleasantly appealing and natural scent, and I swallow as I find myself drawn to her.

16

TIA

Unsettled by Leo's sudden amiability when it comes to my happiness and what I do with my days, I walk beside him, stealing glances out of the corner of my eye. The gravel crunches in the silence that stretches between us, slow and steady as we stroll along the garden pathway.

He looks as sharp as ever in a full, navy blue suit and crisp white shirt. A silver tie draws attention to his hazel eyes. I almost feel bad for the slight smudge my palm left on his chest when I fell into him. Almost. Though he is the one who chose to yank me out of the dirt.

"Are you settling in well—aside from the lack of entertainment in your day?" he asks lightly, seeming to take an interest in my well-being for the first time.

"Well enough," I say cautiously, wary of where this conversation is going or why he's taken a sudden interest in me.

"Can I do anything else to make you more comfortable here?"

Aside from dropping dead? "I don't think so. More freedom of mobility and my sisters for company will do me some good."

"You miss them," he observes. "You must be very close."

"We are." I smile, thinking of my four sisters dancing at the wedding, little Sofia giggling every time I twirled her.

Affection swells in my chest as I think of my four sisters, and my hand automatically reaches for the Millefiori pendant around my neck once again. Leo's eyes miss nothing, and they land on my necklace with open curiosity.

Pausing, he turns to face me. "May I?" He gestures as if to take the pendant from my fingers.

I drop it, letting my hand come to rest at my side, and Leo leans in, his body suddenly dangerously close as his fingers lightly pluck the glass from my skin to palm it carefully by my throat.

"A gift from one of them?" His hazel eyes flick up to meet mine momentarily, and my breath catches in my lungs.

"Maria, the oldest after me. She gave it to me for my birthday." For a heartbeat, I think about how silly I was to have lied to him about my age. I wonder, if I'd told him I was seventeen the night I met him, would anything have changed?

"It's beautiful," he murmurs, placing it lightly back against my skin.

The glass is warmer now, and I shiver as that warmth settles into my chest.

"Will you tell me about her?" he asks as we resume our ambling pace, making our way toward the estate's arboretum.

The sun pours down on us with impressive force, and the well-placed trees along our path offer a wonderful respite from its heat. Glancing sidelong at Leo, I wonder once again what could possibly be the purpose of him seeking me out in the middle of the day. *Why talk to me now, when he's all but avoided me since the wedding?* He must have something up his sleeve, some underlying motive, and I refuse to let down my guard.

But I refuse to let my suspicion enter my tone as I humor him. "Maria's sixteen and very outspoken. She and my father butt heads often because she's confident she can bend the world to her wishes if she stands her ground long enough."

"She must take after you then," he teases, his eyes dancing as they meet mine. "Two women not afraid to speak their minds. It's a wonder your father's survived this long."

Despite myself, a giggle bubbles up in my chest, and I smile. "He's said those exact words more than once over the past few years. Though I hardly think a woman who says what she's thinking is anything to be discouraged. You miss out on half of the world's intellect when you expect them to hold their tongues and simply obey what the men around them say."

"At *least* half the world's intelligence," he inserts, his tone playful.

I cast him a sharp glance, unsure of whether he's making fun of me or laughing with me. But the grin that spreads across his beautiful lips is conspiratorial rather than condescending.

"Then you prefer opinionated women?" I challenge. Somehow, I doubt it, though I can't think of a single instance with Leo that would directly counter my statement. But I hardly see how he could have respect for women when he's treated me so cruelly.

"I think it would be a disservice to society to assume all men have a more valid and worthwhile opinion than women. Take Tony Valencia, for example." He gives a theatrical shudder of horror. "I would much rather listen to your opinions over his on almost any matter. Because yours at least stem from intelligence and a rather expansive education. I can't say the same for him."

The flattery, while bringing a shy warmth to my cheeks, reminds me of the night I met Leo. I can't deny he's a great conversationalist when he wants to be. And he has a dry sense of humor that makes me laugh before I can stop it.

He chuckles with me, the sound low and enticing, and the moment feels incredibly natural as we have a laugh at Tony Valencia's expense. I suppose the one thing I can be grateful about in my marriage is that it saved me from spending a lifetime with the degenerate gambler.

It would be too easy to fall into the fluid and engaging conversation and forget about why I can't trust Leo. Even for a second. He must be after something. And he simply masks it with such finesse, that I could almost believe he's spending time with me simply because he enjoys my company.

But I'm unwilling to fall for his tricks again. It infuriates me to watch how masterful he is at manipulation. With a few well-placed words, he's disarmed me, boosting my confidence and making me feel like he sees value in me. My thoughts and opinions even.

I would love nothing better than to destroy him for it, but I know I can't do that without playing the long game. So, I keep my temper under tight control, waiting to see what he wants in case I might be able to use it against him.

"How have you been feeling with the pregnancy?" he asks casually, and it's the first time he's addressed the topic directly.

My shoulders tense slightly, and I work to lower them, calming myself as I rest my palm instinctively over the still near-invisible bump. "Well enough," I say shortly. The hurt that lies beneath the consequences of losing my virginity is more potent as I discuss it with the person responsible.

"You seem to be sleeping well. Still no morning sickness?"

He delivers the question with impressively innocent curiosity, but after having to take a paternity test before he would even agree to marry me, I'm not blind to the undercurrent between us.

"Just because you're not home enough to witness it doesn't mean I haven't been experiencing morning sickness," I state flatly, stopping as I remove my hand from his elbow.

Caught off guard by my sudden vitriol, Leo pauses, his expression surprised as he turns to me. "Forgive me. I didn't mean to imply…"

Of course, he did. I'm not so naive as to not recognize he had doubts about the truth of my pregnancy. But that he would still be entertaining them is like a slap to the face. *How can he possibly pretend that anyone but me was taken advantage of in this situation?* If I had the strength, I might throttle him right here in the garden.

His expression softens into an unspoken apology. "Let me know if I can do anything to make you more comfortable, my love." The endearment rolls right off his tongue, so sweet and affectionate. But directly following his underhanded question, it might as well be a punch to the gut.

"Don't call me that," I warn, my temper starting to get the better of me.

"Why not?" he asks, one eyebrow rising.

"Because you don't love me."

A pregnant pause lingers between us as Leo studies my face carefully, his hazel eyes calculating. Then he gives a single nod. "As you wish."

He offers me his elbow once again, and as I take it, we resume walking, the break in eye contact a relief. I'm doing a far worse job of masking my anger toward Leo than I had hoped. I need to do better if I'm going to play a convincing role.

After several minutes of silence, Leo releases a sigh. "I realize we haven't gotten off on the best foot, Tia, but I hope that eventually, you might learn to find me a tolerable companion."

"I'm sure I will," I say, trying my best to get myself back on track.

"I know I have no right to ask it of you now, but I need your help," he says, turning to face me once again. "A favor, really."

It's my turn to raise my eyebrows as I wait silently for him to reveal what possible use he could have for me after pretending I don't exist for the past three days.

"You recall Mayor Romney and his wife, who I introduced you to at the engagement party?"

"Yes, they came to the wedding as well," I acknowledge, thinking back on the sweet older couple who had wished us happiness in our marriage. That was the exchange that gave me the brilliant idea of getting close to Leo, so I could learn how to hurt him.

"They've invited us to dinner tonight, and I need you to make a good impression. They seem to have taken quite a shine to you, and I would like to build on that."

It's like some merciful god heard my pleas and chose to take pity on me. This is the window into how I can ingratiate myself with Leo, make myself indispensable—and once I've gotten close enough to discover his weak point, I'll be able to exploit it.

"Of course," I agree readily. "If that's what you need."

Perhaps I was too heavy-handed in my performance of the obedient wife because Leo seems taken aback once again.

"Why are you so willing to help me?" he asks, his brows pressing into a frown that's unreasonably sexy.

"Because we're married. We're in this together now, whether we like it or not, and I don't see the point of shooting myself in the foot by refusing to help you with your goals."

Leo assesses me carefully, his expression inscrutable. Then he seems to shift, his demeanor softening as he takes my hands in his, completely disregarding the dirt that still clings to my nails, darkening their beds.

"Tia, I'm sorry for having treated you so poorly," he says, his eyes deep wells of sincerity that steal the breath from my lungs. "I let my ambition—my bloodlust—run away with me. I was so focused on the conquest that I didn't stop to think of you as a person."

Stunned by the apology I never dreamed he would stoop to give me, I stand speechless, unsure of what I could possibly say.

"I think you are an exceptional woman, and you didn't deserve any of it. I want to make it up to you," he continues passionately. "And I believe this could actually prove to be a decent partnership if we work at it. I intend to. From now on. I will show you the care and consideration—the respect—you deserve. Will you give me that chance?"

His thumb brushes lightly over my knuckles, releasing tinglings up my arms to my heart, and my chest tightens at the persuasive apology. If I were any more naive than I am, I might just have believed him.

But there's no doubt in my mind that he's only apologizing now—being so kind to me—to butter me up so I'll follow through and help make a good impression on the mayor. It doesn't mean anything. This is just his new attempt to manipulate me.

I can't trust him. I know I never will.

But this does present a golden opportunity.

"Yes," I breathe, letting the strength of my emotions fill my voice to be all the more convincing. And inside, I smile. Because this is one step closer to bringing his family to its demise.

The relief that washes across Leo's face is surprisingly moving. And as his eyes dip to my lips, my heart skips a beat. Cautiously, he leans in to kiss me, and this time, it's soft and warm, full of promise.

17

LEO

Tia's soft lips taste of honey, and they move with such supple willingness, molding to mine as if made specially for me. I'm tempted to keep kissing her here, in the middle of the garden. But it's getting late, and we both need to get ready.

Drawing back slowly, I keep her cheek cupped against my palm as I look deep into her rich brown eyes. She looks up at me with gentle wonder, as though unsure of why I would kiss her.

And I know that's on me.

I've given her no reason to trust me. But moving forward, I intend to be better. Because Tia's full of surprises. Her strength of mind is particularly appealing. I'm also coming to terms with the possibility that a treasure might accidentally have fallen into my lap.

Yes, our marriage formed an alliance with a family that would have been one of my most challenging adversaries. But Tia herself is proving rather exceptional. Her father's words from the night of our wedding spring to my mind. At the time, I'd taken them with a grain of salt, considering them a subtle threat rather than a sincere observation. But now I'm starting to see the potential in our alliance.

Smiling as my eyes land on the smudge of dirt coloring her chin, I wipe it gently with the pad of my thumb, ridding her flawless skin of the blemish.

"What?" she asks, her lips stretching into a smile as well.

"I think you're wearing about as much of the garden as you planted."

Tia scoffs a laugh, swatting me playfully. "You're not supposed to stay clean while you're gardening. Don't you know?"

"No, actually. I've never educated myself on the rules of horticulture, seeing as I have people to maintain the garden for me."

"You're a terror," she accuses, narrowing her eyes at me. But her smile remains, assuring me that she knows I'm teasing.

"Come on, then. Let's go clean up for dinner." This time, as I lead her down the pathway, I take Tia's hand, and the simple gesture feels intensely intimate, the energy rippling up my arm in waves.

The conversation between us is somehow lighter now, reminding me of the carefree way we talked the night I met Tia. She's less defensive, more willing to laugh, and I find that I enjoy this side of her.

We enter the confines of our room, and I shut the door behind us as Tia makes her way into the bathroom to turn on the shower. I shrug out of my jacket, taking my time, as I intend to shower after she's done.

Not that I wouldn't love to shower with her, but our conversation in the garden ate up most of the afternoon, and I don't want to be late for this dinner. As I fold my jacket, my eyes land on the smudge of soil Tia must have put there when I hauled her out of the dirt.

It brings a smile to my lips, recalling her sharp tongue as she came to the defense of her gardening. Perhaps I ought to give her more freedom to enjoy it if she likes it so much. I shake my head at myself. *When did I get so concerned about ensuring Tia's idle hours?*

Unbuttoning my shirt, I toss it on top of my jacket over the back of a chair, then strip my shoes and slacks so I can go into the bathroom and shave. Tia's back is to me, her face under the stream of water as she rinses her face and long black hair.

When they're wet, the dark locks reach nearly to the dimples at the base of her spine, a waterfall of mahogany that draws my eyes to her full hips. She's a thin girl with modest breasts and a trim waist, but damn, she has a round, gorgeous ass.

My cock twitches at the salacious thought, and I turn my eyes purposefully to the mirror above my sink. Lathering my neck, I shave a precise line, leaving the shadow of a beard on my jaw and chin but shaving my throat clean.

As I rinse my razor, the shower water stops, drawing my eyes to the scene behind me. I watch the reflection as Tia rings out her long hair, then steps around the glass barrier of the shower to collect her towel from its rack.

She tips her head to the side, letting her hair fall over her shoulder so she can towel it dry, leaving her creamy skin wet and glistening. Straightening, she then wraps the towel around her waist, tucking the corner between her breasts in a makeshift dress.

Then, as if sensing my gaze, her eyes shift to meet mine in the mirror. A soft rose colors her cheeks, and she smiles at me. I return the gesture, caught in the act of admiring her body. Returning my focus to the task at hand, I only see her padding from the bathroom out of the corner of my eye.

I take a quick shower, during which time Tia comes back in to dry and style her hair. Still wearing her towel, she offers up the perfect view of her long legs beneath the hem. Her makeup seems to take hardly any time at all as I towel off and finger-comb some styling gel into my hair.

Returning to the bedroom, I pull out a fresh suit and shirt. Tia follows a moment later, stepping into our expansive shared closet to search through the dresses. "How fancy should I be?" she asks. "Is this a formal dinner party? Or just... dinner?"

"Just dinner, I believe." Mayor Romney didn't say anything about how many guests would be coming tonight, but the invitation seemed rather impromptu.

Tia comes into the bedroom a moment later carrying a black dress still on its hanger. Laying it out on the bed and setting a pair of heels beneath it, she then goes to her drawers. I'm shrugging into my shirt when her towel comes off.

And I can't help myself.

I look.

With her hair done up in a loose braid and her makeup soft and natural, Tia's at her most stunning, her perfect figure making me ache to be close to her. And as she bends to step into her black lace panties, I almost groan with appreciation.

Tearing my eyes from her as she straightens, I focus intently on buttoning my shirt. Then I grab the crimson paisley tie I laid out and turn to the mirror to tie it. Tia's temporary dressing station at the bed happens to be right in line with the floor-length mirror I'm using. Once again, my attention strays as she unhooks the dress from its hanger and steps into the soft, stretchy fabric.

She pulls it slowly up her body, slipping one arm into its capped sleeve, then the other. Her eyes flick up to meet mine in the mirror, once more catching my wandering gaze. And this time, a coy smile stretches across her lips.

"Like anything you see?" she teases.

I turn to face her with a smile, and she allows me a full view of the black tea-length dress's modest front. Then she turns to reveal its low-scooping back with several strings of gems hanging in soft arcs from one side of the open back to the other.

I release a low, appreciative whistle. "I do," I confess, my smile broadening. "And I might just want to take you home with me later."

"We're home now," she points out playfully, slowly lifting the skirt of her dress to give me another peek of her sexy black lingerie.

Christ, woman. Suddenly, my collar feels too tight—as do my slacks—and I close the distance between us in three long strides, unable to resist any longer. Wrapping one arm around the small of her back, I cradle her head as I bring our lips together in a passionate kiss.

Tia gasps, her lips parting from my unexpected assault, and my tongue strokes between her teeth, tasting her warm honey lips. After a momentary pause, Tia returns the kiss with equal verve, her fingers wrapping around the collar of my shirt as he keeps our lips firmly joined.

Holding her against my body, I relish the feel of her soft breasts pressed against my chest. She's not wearing a bra because of the dress's low back, and I can feel it. The way her nipples tighten, pressing adamantly into my shirt and skin.

Consumed by her beauty, I spin Tia, turning her to face away from me and pulling her against my chest as I shift until we're both facing the floor-length mirror. Her eyes shine with lust, their dark depths captivating me.

I brush her thick braid over one shoulder, and Tia tips her head as I brush the lobe of her ear with my lips.

"Watch," I command softly, holding her gaze as I work my way down the curve of her neck and across her shoulder.

And with one arm encircling her waist, I let my other hand travel down her body and along her thigh. Tia's breaths quicken as my fingers find the hem of her dress, and I slowly start to make my way back up the inside of her thigh.

One delicate hand reaches up to tangle into my curls. The other rests on top of my hand at her waist, and when I reach the peak of her thighs, her fingers tighten instinctually. She gasps, her body melting against mine as I run my fingers over the soft lace of her panties.

Heat radiates from her, and as I push the fabric aside, my cock throbs to find her already wet and needy. Never breaking eye contact, I stroke my fingers between her folds. Excitement colors her cheeks as Tia starts to pant, her lips parting slightly in the sexiest look of lusty pleasure.

And as I press two fingers inside her slick entrance, she starts to tremble.

"You like that, *bella mia*?" I breathe against her skin, raising goosebumps beneath my lips.

"Yes," she gasps, her gaze smoldering.

She moans, her eyelids sinking and her head falling back against my shoulder as I finger her more adamantly, brushing her clit with my palm at the same time.

"Look at me, Tia," I murmur, my body aching with the need to see the pleasure in her eyes.

She does as I say, her head tipping lazily as she opens her eyes to reveal the intense lust, turning them dark and distant. Her pussy tightens around my fingers, telling me she's getting close to orgasm. So I lean in to capture the lobe of her ear between my teeth.

Tia cries out in pleasure, her clit twitching beneath my palm, and her knees buckle. I hold her close, supporting her weight as I finger her more adamantly now, stroking inside her and curling my fingers to find that special spot that drives her wild.

"Oh, god!" she whimpers.

"Say my name, and I'll let you come," I breathe in her ear.

"Please, Leo," she moans.

And though it's the same plea she gave me on the balcony during our wedding night, I can hear that they're worlds apart in meaning. And this time, her gentle request nearly undoes me.

"Come for me, Tia," I command, compressing her clit with the pad of my thumb as I drive her toward oblivion.

Tia sobs as she topples over the edge, her walls clamping around my fingers as her clit pulses beneath my thumb. She breathes heavily, her fingers softening in my hair as her euphoria leaves her weak and trembling in my arms.

"Beautiful," I murmur, pressing a kiss behind her ear as I relish the feel of her pussy begging me to stay deep inside her.

A fist pounds unceremoniously on my door, making Tia yelp, and she jerks upright, the motion removing my fingers from her.

"Get a move on, Leo. You're going to be late," my father growls through the door.

Groaning, I know I'm in for a painful night. Because he's right. It's time to go. Fresh color blossoms in Tia's cheeks, and we both laugh breathily at the abrupt interruption.

"We better get going," I say, and she nods her understanding.

I release Tia only after I'm certain she's steady on her feet once more. And as she straightens her dress and panties, stepping into her black heels a moment later, I turn to collect my suit coat.

Before we walk out the door, I adjust myself to mask the intense arousal still thrumming through me. This is going to be a very long and painful dinner.

18
TIA

I'm not sure I'll ever get used to Leo taking my hand. Which is exactly what he does as he walks me down the ornately decorated hallway toward the front door, where our car awaits. He did it walking in from the garden earlier as well, and each time, it sends my heart into a frenzy.

I might hate him, but I can't deny that Leo is sexy as sin. And I don't see the harm in enjoying the way he touches me while I still can. Not to mention the pleasure I get out of knowing it's torturing him. Because despite his best attempt to hide it, I can still see the bulge in his pants from our unfinished business. And it can't be comfortable.

I still fully intend to destroy Leo, so the mind-blowing attraction between us most definitely has an expiration date. But in the meantime, I plan to utilize sex as best I can.

He glances at me from the corner of his eye, and I smile, sharing in our secret as he gives my hand a slight squeeze.

I love the fact that he's going to have our unfinished business on his mind during this dinner that's so important to him. It's a minor victory, and one I imagine will tell me a lot about his ambition and self-restraint—or lack thereof.

We arrive at the mayor's house with three minutes to spare, and Leo offers me a hand as I slide from the back seat of the black escalade. It seems tonight he's forgone the canary-yellow Ferrari for something a little more understated. A wise choice if he's trying to make an impression on Mayor Romney, I think.

As I look up at the charming colonial-style house of our host, it most definitely would appear that he's not the extravagant, showy type because, while the house is by no means small, it's certainly modest for a man of his position.

"Ah, here are the newlyweds we've been waiting for," Mayor Romney says, throwing the front door wide before we've even reached the top steps. "Welcome to our humble home."

I can't help but smile at the portly man's friendly demeanor, and behind him, his petite wife beams at me.

"You look lovely, Tia," she says, pulling me in for a hug as soon as I step inside.

"What a beautiful home you have," I say, scanning the space and immediately feeling a sense of home and happiness wash over me.

"Oh, you're too sweet," she says.

"And may I introduce you to the lights of my life, my daughters Leah and Hannah?" Mayor Romney says, gesturing to the two giggling girls who stand in the doorway to the living room, their hands cupped secretively over their mouths as they lean close to whisper.

"It's a pleasure to meet you, Leah and Hannah," I say, holding back a soft laugh. I've only just met the girls, but already they remind me of my sisters Anna and Vienna when they were younger, they way they used to constantly whisper in each other's ears. They've grown past that stage now, but these girls appear to be right around six or seven years old.

"I like your shoes," Leah says shyly, pointing at my black satin peep-toes with a bejeweled bow at the center of the front.

"Why, thank you." I twist and turn to show the girls every glittering angle, and they giggle once more.

"Are you a princess?" Hannah asks, and this time, I do laugh as she says it with such sincerity.

"No, I'm not a princess. Do I look like one?" I pat my head as if in search of a crown.

"Yeah, Princess Jasmine," she says confidently, and it melts my heart.

Mayor Romney chuckles as he places his hands on his hips. "They're going through a Disney phase," he explains.

"Don't we all?" I joke, matching his grin.

"Shall we eat?" Signora Romney asks, gesturing to the dining room. "I believe dinner is ready."

The girls lead the way, Hannah grasping my fingers to pull me along behind her, and Leo's palm leaves the small of my back as he follows last, alongside the mayor. It's a shuffle of chairs as we all settle in, the girls arguing over who gets to sit on the one side of me after I settle in beside Leo.

"I think I might quickly get booted to the curb for failing to show my wife the appropriate amount of attention and awe now that I've seen how it's done properly," Leo jokes after Signora Romney scolds her daughters lightly to pick a seat and calm down.

Mayor Romney chuckles. "I feel ousted. Normally, I'm the one who gets fought over."

"Thank you for having us over," I say. "It was a wonderful surprise."

"We just wanted to congratulate you two properly. After getting to speak with you at the engagement party, Alicia and I have been talking about how little we know you and your families, though you have such deep roots in Piovosa. And you seem like such a charming couple. We hoped we might get to know you better," Mayor Romney says.

Then, he reaches for a bottle of red wine. "Can I interest anyone in a drink?" he offers, gesturing to my wine glass.

Heat radiates through my body as I find myself caught between a rock and a hard place. I don't want to drink and potentially endanger the baby, but I can't come right out and say that after Leo and I have only been married for three days.

"Actually, Mayor Romney—"

"Please, call me Luke and my wife Alicia," he insists, cutting me off as if he's shocked he hasn't already told me to do so.

I smile, taking a moment to recenter myself as that brief interruption bought me the time I need. "Thank you, Luke. But believe it or not, I'm not quite of drinking age, so I'll have to pass. I couldn't possibly accept a drink underage from the mayor himself!"

He chuckles, placing a hand apologetically over his heart. "Forgive me, my dear. You're so mature; I didn't give it a second thought. I appreciate your consideration—and honesty."

My stomach knots at the slight I know he didn't mean in the least because he couldn't possibly know my real motivation for turning down the drink.

"And you, Leo?"

"I'm definitely of age," he jokes, extending his wine glass.

But as he retrieves it with a healthy pour of crimson liquid, his eyes turn to me with a look of respect for having covered my predicament smoothly. The conversation is light and lively as I put on my best performance to prove my worth to Leo.

And though I haven't quite figured out what Leo's particular interest in Mayor Romney could be, conversing with the mayor and his family comes surprisingly easy. Because they're positively charming.

After a light salad starter, the main course arrives shortly, and I lean back in my chair to allow the serving staff to set the beautifully prepared plate of veal parmesan before me.

In an instant, the warm and wonderful atmosphere of the evening turns, as the smell of the meat hits my nose. Nausea hits me with overwhelming force, and though most of my bouts of morning sickness have come earlier in the day, there's no doubt in my mind that I'm facing a heavy dose of it, triggered by a smell I once would have savored.

Bolting up out of my chair, I nearly slam into the server behind me in my desperation to escape the smell, and I cover my mouth and nose to try and help.

"Tia?" Leo's voice is tinged with concern, but I don't even have time to look at him.

"I'm so sorry. Your restroom?" I ask, panic filling me as the bile creeps up my throat.

"Down the hall, first door on your left," Signora Romney says, her eyes widening. "Are you alright?"

I can't even answer her. It's taking all my willpower to keep the vomit in my stomach until I find the bathroom. Striding toward the dining room doorway, I break into a run as soon as I'm out of sight.

I barely make it in time, slamming the door behind me and throwing myself onto my knees as I shove my face toward the porcelain bowl and throw up violently. The contents of my lunch come up far too eagerly, and I pant as I catch a momentary reprieve, but I know I'm not done.

Groaning with frustration over my body getting in the way of my plans, I slump onto the cold tile floor, preparing to wait out my nausea. My hands are shaky as I wipe my suddenly clammy brow, and I breathe deeply in through my nose to try and steady my nerves.

The doctor assured me I would start feeling better in my second trimester, and I suddenly can't wait for that day to come because it's exhausting to be throwing up so constantly. Rubbing my sternum to try and calm the burning sensation, I lean my head back against the edge of the tub behind me.

A light tap comes at the door, and my stomach knots as I imagine Signora Romney on the other side, coming to check on me. *What can I possibly say now?* I wasn't prepared to have to come up with a litany of excuses for all the signs of my pregnancy. And, of course, Leo and I haven't discussed it at all. My parents' solution had simply been to keep me hidden away from everybody but family.

"Someone's in here," I say shakily, praying that's enough of a hint for the person on the other side of the door to go away.

"Tia? It's Leo... Can I come in?"

I groan, closing my eyes as my situation keeps getting worse. I don't want Leo to see me like this, the air around me reeking of vomit and making my stomach queasy once again.

But before I can work up the nerve to tell him to go away, the door handle turns, and a moment later, Leo comes into view. He fills the doorway in all his gorgeous glory, his curls falling casually across his forehead as his striking gray-green eyes take me in.

Tears sting my eyes at the mortifying contrast between us—Leo, a god among men, and me, a childish girl fallen from grace and at her worst moment.

"What do you want?" I ask miserably.

19

LEO

I hadn't fully believed the Guerra family's story about Tia's pregnancy until she bolted from the dining room like her tail was on fire. And now, as I stand in the bathroom doorway, observing her face, flushed with embarrassment, and her beautiful hair all mussed from her sorry state, I suddenly know it's true.

"Oh, Tia," I breathe, quickly stepping inside the modest bathroom to shut the door behind me. "Are you okay?"

I know she's not by the hint of acidity in the air. I've smelled vomit enough times from the untried men who witnessed an execution for the first time to recognize it.

But Tia says, "I'm fine," as she sits up.

She only gets halfway there before her face turns a dangerous shade of green, and she pivots, gripping the toilet bowl as she gets sick once again. Crossing the distance between us in one long stride, I kneel beside her, scooping her braid back over her shoulder and out of danger. Then I rest a hand on her cold, clammy back, hoping it will comfort her as I guide the loose strands of her dark hair away from her face with my fingers.

It's my best attempt at being supportive, though I'm entirely out of my element here. Gore and violence, I'm used to. But seeing Tia be sick and knowing I'm the cause of it makes me feel both helpless and like a complete ass. *How could she possibly forgive my abhorrent behavior these past few months when this is the result of what I've done?*

"Don't look at me," she moans miserably over the toilet, then spits to try and clean her mouth.

I chuckle softly, brushing my knuckles across her temple. "What, are you worried I won't take you home with me now?"

Tia snorts a laugh and reaches shakily for the toilet handle to flush the sick away. Then, she leans back against the side of the shower once more.

"Feel better?" I ask, grateful to see her coloring has returned to normal, if not slightly more flushed.

"I think so," she says shakily, wiping the sweat from her brow with the back of her hand.

Turning to the cabinet, I dig in the drawers beneath the sink to find a washcloth and soak it with cool water, then ring it out.

"Thanks," Tia says gratefully as she accepts it from me. Pressing it gently to her face, neck, and chest, she dabs away her perspiration without disrupting her makeup.

"Can I help you up?" I offer.

She nods, taking my hand, and I pull her to her feet, steadying her when I find her uncharacteristically wobbly.

"I'm fine," she assures me again when I keep a hold of her hips longer than strictly necessary, worried she might fall.

Releasing her reluctantly, I watch closely for any sign that her legs might give out, but she seems more stable on her high heels now. She walks to the sink and leans over it, giving me a wonderful view as she turns on the faucet, slurps a mouthful of the water, and swishes it around to wash the taste from her mouth.

Then she focuses her attention on the mirror, running her fingers beneath her eyelashes to remove the excess liner that started to smudge. Next, she tidies her hair, making the routine look easy as she puts herself back together with impressive precision and speed.

I watch her, at a loss for what to do but wanting to somehow help.

Finally, she takes a deep, steadying breath and releases it.

"Ready?" I ask, slightly amazed at the transformation she managed in a matter of minutes.

"Ready," she agrees, and I open the door to let her out.

In the hallway, I offer her my elbow, unsure of just how stable she could be after feeling so shaky and weak. She takes it, her touch light as she walks with me back to the dining room.

"Everything okay?" Mayor Romney asks, rising from his seat as we enter.

While the children have continued their meal, I can tell that both the mayor and his wife have sat waiting, likely worried for Tia and not wanting to eat until they could be sure she's alright.

It hits me that Tia and I haven't discussed what kind of excuse to make in this situation. I'd been so confident she was faking the pregnancy that I hadn't concerned myself with it.

But Tia doesn't hesitate a beat. "Yes, fine. Thank you. So sorry to keep you waiting. It's rather embarrassing, really, but I have a history of spontaneous bloody noses. Poor Leo hasn't witnessed one before. But I'm perfectly fine now."

We settle in at the table once again, and I glance subtly in Tia's direction as I wonder if it might not have been the food that set her off. *Will she be able to eat it if so?*

"My brother used to get terrible nose bleeds as a child," Signora Romney says kindly. "Thankfully, he grew out of them in his twenties. Hopefully, you will, too."

"Wouldn't that be a blessing?" Tia says with a breathy laugh, and she cuts into her breaded meat.

"So, tell me, Tia, were those younger girls dancing with you at the wedding your sisters?" Singora Romney asks.

Tia hums affectionately, moving to twirl her spaghetti without taking a bite of the veal parmesan she cut. She's mimicking the process of eating, moving the food around her plate more than actually consuming it. A masterful way of covering her lack of appetite. But it makes my stomach knot.

"Yes, I have four sisters." She smiles warmly at Leah and Hannah. "You two actually remind me very much of them."

The girls grin back at her with red-sauced smiles.

"And what about you, Leo? I believe someone told me you're an only child?" Mayor Romney says.

I clear my throat, wiping my mouth with my napkin to give myself a moment. "Yes, an only child. My mother struggled to carry her other pregnancies to term. She died during the birth of what would have been my younger brother. But he didn't make it either."

Signora Romney covers her mouth, her eyes sympathetic. "How terrible. She must have desperately wanted a second child to keep going through the pain of losing a baby."

I nod, turning my eyes to my plate to avoid the truth of the matter—that my father wanted more children. As she was his wife, he believed it her duty to secure him with a second son, in case something should happen to me.

"I didn't know that," Tia says beside me, her voice gentle.

And when I meet her eyes, I find equal parts sadness and fear in their depths.

"How old were you when she died?"

"Seven." I keep the emotion out of my voice.

"That must have been very hard for you and your father," Signora Romney says, drawing my attention back to her.

I give a brief nod and attempt a smile. Then, I deliberately change the subject before the atmosphere grows too stifling. "This veal is wonderful," I praise. "Incredibly tender."

"Oh, thank you. It's a family secret, actually," she says, accepting my shift in topic with all the grace of a politician's wife. "Though we've hired an in-house chef, my father was actually a butcher, so we have a few tricks up our sleeves when it comes to meals like these."

"What does a girl have to do to be let in on these secrets?" Tia jokes.

Our hosts both laugh, and Signora Romney beams.

"I supposed you'll just have to keep joining us for dinner and find out," she says.

"We'd love that," Tia agrees.

The rest of the evening goes smoothly, Tia winning over the

mayor and his family with an ease I never thought possible. For years, I've had my sights set on forming a relationship with the Romney family, and my wife has managed to get us an extended dinner invitation after three short visits with them. I'm blown away.

At the end of the night, after the girls have gone to bed and we've shared a nightcap in the Romneys' sitting room, Signora Romney wraps an arm affectionately around Tia's shoulders, and they walk us to the front door.

This is my chance—the opportunity to move things forward with the mayor without sounding too aggressive or presumptuous. "Thank you, Luke, for welcoming us so warmly into your home. I think it did Tia a lot of good to spend some time in your family's company."

"It was our pleasure, my boy," he says paternally, clapping me on the shoulder.

I suspect part of his unrestrained show of affection has to do with the number of drinks he's had tonight—not enough to make him drunk, but just enough to make him more agreeable than usual. Perfect.

"You know, I would love to sit down with you sometime and discuss some ideas I've had that would help Piovosa grow as a town," I say. "I have a vision for just how great we can become as a community—and an infrastructure—and you seem like the best man to include in that vision."

And though the mayor has turned me down countless times before, when I've asked for a private meeting, this time, he seems more than willing. "That sounds wonderful. Why don't you come by my office later this week? Perhaps we can grab some lunch. I'd love to hear about this grand vision of yours."

"Wonderful, I'll do that." I grin as I extend my hand, and Mayor Romney grasps it, giving me a firm handshake.

"Such a lovely night. We'll have to have you over again soon," Signora Romney insists, giving Tia's hands an affectionate squeeze.

"That sounds lovely. Or we could have you over as well, right, Leo?" she says, her megawatt smile dazzling as she turns it on me.

"Absolutely," I agree, resting my palm on the small of her back.

And I can't help but note the silky smooth warmth just moments before goosebumps rise across her skin at my touch. Once again, it awakens a hunger in me, that hunger I found at the start of the evening, when we were getting ready for this very important meeting.

"Good night," Tia says, stepping through the doorway with a last smile.

And as I follow her, I can't help but hope our night is only beginning.

20

TIA

Leo's arm is steady, his hand gentle as he helps me from the car, and despite my best effort to remain unaffected by him, my heart skips a beat at the heat in his gaze.

"Luigi, send some broth and crackers to our room," he says evenly as we walk through the front door, the butler holding it open wide for us.

"Signor," Luigi agrees, with a slight inclination of his head.

I glance at Leo, taken aback by his request, but keep walking, my hand resting lightly inside the crook of his elbow.

He glances at me from the corner of his eye, and our gazes meet. "You hardly ate," he says by way of explanation.

Butterflies erupt in my stomach at his observation. In truth, I'm starving because I couldn't manage to swallow more than a few bites of my veal parmesan—delicious as it was. But I never imagined Leo would care enough to notice.

I managed to recover from my morning sickness without tipping off anyone in the mayor's house to my pregnancy. I even made good headway with the mayor and his family. I could see Leo going so far as to notice and appreciate that. *But to realize I wasn't eating?* He must have been watching me more closely than I realized.

My skin warms.

We step inside our room, and Leo closes the door behind us as I kick off my heel, sighing gratefully the moment my feet find the cool wood.

"I got a meeting, thanks to your charms," he says behind me, his voice rich and warm.

Bending to scoop up my shoes, I carry them to the closet, glancing coyly over my shoulder as I go. "You really think I was the determining factor?"

"You were," he states confidently, and from the corner of my eye, I catch him shrugging out of his coat.

I turn my attention to removing my jewelry, setting it gently into the beautiful mahogany box my parents gave me as a sixteenth-birthday present.

"I've been trying to crack the mayor's defenses for going on a year now, but you're the one who softened the stickler's heart."

I smile, letting my affection for the Romney family show on my face to mask the satisfaction of knowing Leo can see my worth. And he's opening up to me about his desire to get close to the mayor. Definitely a step forward.

A light knock interrupts our conversation, and Leo strides across the room, his shirt halfway unbuttoned to reveal the light smattering of soft dark hair that graces his muscular chest.

"Thank you, Trudy," he says to the maid, who bustles into the room, a tray of food in hand.

She flushes, keeping her eyes averted as if she can hardly believe he spoke directly to her. For the first time, I notice that he actually calls the staff by their name. Not something I would expect of someone so arrogant. Someone who didn't want me working in the garden "with the help."

But she seems affected by it all the same. Our eyes meet as she sets the soup and crackers on the vanity table before me, and I give her a soft smile.

"Thank you."

"Signora." Trudy gives the quickest of curtsies before rushing from the room once more.

"So, what kind of meeting did you get with the mayor?" I ask and nibble on a cracker. To my immense relief, it goes down easy, and the churning discomfort subsides a little.

"A meeting about some thoughts I have on the direction of Piovosa's future," he says, his hazel eyes gleaming with mischievous enthusiasm. "I think the mayor will find our vision and motivations might align more than he would like to think."

"And what motivation might that be?" I ask, turning my attention to the broth after finishing off several saltines.

"Progress. We're in the perfect location for an infrastructure far greater than what we're utilizing. But we squander the opportunities Piovosa provides, though we're in the most ideal valley on this side of the Allegheny range. Mayor Romney wants what's best for the people here, and I want to bring us out of the dark ages."

It's the most passionate I've seen Leo about anything, and for a moment, I get a glimpse into the fire that drives him, the ambition that leaves him blind to the destruction left in his wake. I could almost admire him for his vision—if it didn't crush families just like mine along its path.

"And you think you can achieve that by meeting with him?" I ask, keeping my tone light and my thoughts to myself.

"It's a start." Leo heads into the bathroom, and I can hear the faucet turn on, him brushing his teeth a moment later.

After the night I've had, that sounds wonderful. Quickly drinking the rest of my broth, I head into the bathroom to brush my teeth as well.

Leo and I move around each other in the spacious room as we complete our bedtime routine. And despite the innocuous crossing of paths on occasion, my awareness feels heightened. I'm not used to feeling Leo's presence.

Since our wedding night, it's as if Leo's intentionally *not* occupied the same space as me. But tonight, he does, sharing it with a strange amiability that makes my nerves tingle. Like I'm waiting for the other shoe to drop.

He leaves me to finish my bedtime routine, and I wash my face clean of makeup, then undo the braid in my hair. Taking a deep breath, I look myself in the eye with the mirror. *I got a meeting, thanks to your charms.* Leo's words run through my head, and I dare to hope that my efforts might actually be paying off. That I haven't given up everything in vain.

Heading out into our luxurious suite, I almost come up short at the sight of Leo in nothing but boxer briefs. His broad back is to me, showing off the black-and-white mural tattoo that I've only caught glimpses of until now.

It's moving, emotional. Spreading across the entirety of one shoulder blade and down his spine, it looks like the inner workings of a clock, with multiple cogs of various sizes connecting. Only each one is different, some basic and utilitarian, while others look so delicate, they might as well be made of lace. But what strikes at my heart are the two largest cogs, one a compass, only the arrow that should be indicating north is slightly off center, pointing directly at his heart. The other is the image of a clock face, shattered glass obscuring several of the roman numerals. Scrawling cursive follows the line of his shoulders, and I'm intrigued to find it's written in Latin. "*Tempus non est hostis, sed directionis defectus.*" *Time is not the enemy, but rather lack of direction.*

I can't quite say why those words make my heart pound. But before I can thoroughly analyze my feelings, Leo turns, revealing his sculpted body and chiseled abs. I blush as he catches me staring, and a slow smile spreads across his lips.

In my mind, I can hear him throwing my words back at me from before dinner, *Like anything you see?* But he doesn't say it. He doesn't have to. Instead, he prowls slowly toward me, his grin cocky and filled with fire.

"Signora Moretti, you look rather overdressed for bed," he teases, his voice low and soft as he closes the distance between us.

My mind goes blank, though my lips part as if to say something.

And before a sound comes out, Leo's arms wrap around me, pulling me firmly against his strong chest. My heart hammers as he leans in to kiss me.

And as our lips meet, molten excitement floods my belly. Scarcely able to breathe, I lean into him, my heart pounding at the sudden and intense passion in his touch. His tongue strokes into my mouth, and he tastes minty and fresh. He smells even better, the scent of sandalwood, vanilla, and amber swirling around me in a dangerously seductive concoction of masculinity.

His hands trail down the curves of my body, exploring my waist, my hips, gently cupping my ass in his palms. Taking two handfuls of my skirt, he guides it slowly up my legs, undressing me with tantalizing patience.

My stomach quivers with nerves as it crosses my mind that this might be a trick. Some fresh way to torture me. But I don't think so. Something about Leo's energy is different. It has been since dinner tonight.

He's softer, more... attentive.

As he takes my black dress up over my breasts, I raise my arms to let him, willing myself to have the strength and courage to see what happens next.

He drops the stretchy fabric onto the floor, and his eyes travel down the length of my body, igniting as they land on the swell of my breasts and the lacy thong that's the only piece of clothing still covering me.

"Christ, Tia," he breathes, sweeping me into his arms once again.

And this time, when he kisses me, it's with a desperate hunger. He lifts me off my feet, wrapping my legs around his hips the same way he did on our wedding night, and I tremble at the way he holds me so effortlessly. Controls me without a thought.

He carries me to the bed tonight, and the tight ball of anxiety in my chest loosens as he lays me gently across the sheets. And he settles lightly on top of me, aligning our bodies.

"I want you," he breathes, releasing my lips to kiss the tender flesh behind my ear.

The words affect me more than I would like to admit, and excitement roars to life deep in my belly. "I want you too," I breathe, and I mean it—even if I hate how much I do.

Leo slants his lips over mine once more, kissing me deeply. His hips press forward, rolling against me and showing me just what he wants. I gasp, a jolt of anticipation lancing through my body as he brushes against my clit, awakening my desire despite the flimsy fabric separating us.

As if hearing my thoughts, Leo shifts to slowly trail kisses down my body, starting at my neck and chest, then traveling between my breasts. He palms the supple mounds of flesh, his fingers and thumbs closing around my nipples, and I moan at their tenderness. They're so sensitive and growing more so by the day.

But Leo seems to already know that as he kneads them gently, somehow easing the swollen ache. His hands remain as his lips travel lower, pressing soft kisses down to my navel. Then lower still.

His green-gray eyes scan up my body when his lips reach the waist of my black lace panties. A playful mischief dances in their depths, and his teeth close around the fabric as he holds my gaze.

A shiver races up my spine at the dangerously sexy sight of Leo undressing me with his teeth. Which is exactly what he does as he guides my panties down using only his mouth. I lift my hips slightly, mesmerized by the seductive sight.

His hands leave my breasts, trailing down my body as he strips me, taking my panties from his mouth only after my feet slip free. He tosses them casually aside, then his hands find my ankles, and they work their way slowly back up my legs.

"What are you doing?" I breathe as he hooks my knees over his shoulders, his gaze smoldering as he lowers his face between my thighs.

"I want to taste you," he says darkly, making my insides turn to mush.

I don't know why that sounds so sexy, but it makes my core ache with desperate need. Leo leans in, his hands grasping my hips, supporting them as his broad shoulders spread my legs. And then his tongue strokes lightly along my seam.

I gasp, my body tensing at the overwhelming pleasure it releases through my body. And though I want to watch him, my head falls back onto my pillow as my arms press my shoulders off the soft sheets.

Leo hums, the sound low and sultry, and when I look down again, he licks his lips. "You taste as heavenly as you feel," he purrs, making a gush of warmth flood my core.

And when his tongue returns, stroking between my folds this time, I can feel just how wet I am. It's sinful—the level of ecstasy that consumes me. My breaths come hard and fast as my body transforms into an inferno of desire.

With all of the hardship of missing my family and worrying for their welfare, after being stuck in a house surrounded by people who I consider my enemies, it feels so good to just feel good. And Leo makes me feel very good as he wipes my mind blank of any thoughts but here and now. The bliss of his tongue pleasuring me.

His lips close around my clit a moment later, and as he lightly sucks the sensitive bundle of nerves, his tongue circles me relentlessly.

"Oh god!" I cry out, my legs trembling violently as the intensity of my pleasure becomes overwhelming. I pant, my fingers curling around the sheets as I try to hold on to something—anything—that will stop me from flying apart.

Leo hums approval, the vibration blasting through me, and I can't stop myself. I buck against his lips as I come hard and fast, my clit twitching between his lips. With one hand, he releases my hip to ease a finger inside me, and I shudder. My walls pulse and throb around him, eager for more.

And the wave of euphoria that washes through me makes me sink into the mattress.

Only after the last of my shockwaves subside does Leo release the suction holding me inside his mouth. His finger eases out of me, making me ache for more.

Rising onto his knees as he lets my legs fall open, Leo studies me, his gaze intense. I reward him with a lazy smile, too intensely satisfied to keep my carefully made mask in place.

"Did you like that?" he teases, running a finger through my folds and eliciting another delicious shiver that makes me tremble.

"Yes," I breathe.

"You want me to make you come again?"

I nod, scarcely able to form words through the haze of my deep contentment.

He chuckles, and his hands push his boxers down over his hips, releasing the impressive erection I felt earlier. A pearl of precum coats the swollen tip, making my stomach tremble.

Lowering himself between my thighs once more, Leo covers me with his muscular frame, enveloping me in warmth as he aligns our bodies. One hand travels slowly up my side, raising goosebumps as he feels my curves.

His thumb brushes along the outside of my breast, and then his fingers guide my arm up over my head. Interlacing our fingers, Leo pins my hand above me. Then, he does the same sensual movement with my other arm.

My heart breaks into a sprint as I realize I'm trapped, his strong hands holding my arms in place, but as he leans in to claim my lips, it fills me with exhilaration. His chest brushes lightly against the taut nubs of my nipples, and his tongue tangles with mine in a tantalizing dance.

Then he shifts his hips, and I feel the press of his silken head as it slides between my folds to find my entrance. Pulse fluttering, I start to breathe heavily once again. The anticipation of having him inside me is laced with fear of the unknown.

What will it be like this time?

What man will Leo be tonight?

I long for the man who took my virginity, who handled me with such care. But I know he's not real. That man was a figment of my imagination, a daydream. One Leo played so very well.

But as Leo eases inside me now, his thick cock stretching me to my limit, he takes his time, savoring every euphoric second, and it's as close to the man I crave as I will ever get. Because he's soft and slow, allowing me to relish every inch as he enters me.

It doesn't hurt this time at all. In fact, the strength of my excitement overwhelms my senses, awakening a hunger inside me that I didn't know I possessed. And suddenly, I'm desperate for more.

Moaning, I roll my hips, and tingling euphoria ripples up my spine.

"Sexy little thing, aren't you?" Leo growls, his fingers tightening around mine as he starts to rock inside me.

And every time he presses into my depths, his hips shift forward to brush against my clit. It feels so intensely good, I can't hardly think. My back arches up off the bed as I squirm beneath him, unable to contain the fire that drives me.

Leo captures my lips, his tender affections growing impassioned as he picks up his pace. The pleasure that it releases makes me lose my mind. I don't care if it makes me crazy. Right now, I want Leo with every fiber of my body.

He fills me up so completely, giving me a deep sense of satisfaction as he presses deep inside me. And as he withdraws, tingling anticipation replaces that emptiness inside. I'm starting to recognize the feel of an orgasm as it builds in my body, making my muscles tremble with tension.

As Leo penetrates me again and again, his lips scarcely allowing me a moment of reprieve as he kisses me deeply, I feel myself reaching that peak where I'll soon topple over the edge. Toes curling against the mattress, I tighten my fingers around Leo's palms, bracing for the force of my release.

Leo's hips drive forward in rhythm with my rocking motion, intensifying the pleasure as we come together with greedy need. And when I feel as though my lungs will explode if I can't come up for air, he releases them.

Together, we pant, his lips hovering mere inches from mine as his warm breath washes across my skin. I close my eyes, lost in the euphoria of the moment. And the feel of his perfect, godlike body on top of me, claiming me, controlling me—it feels so dangerously good that I can't hold on.

I cry out as my release takes over my body, sending electric heat pounding through my veins. My walls clamp around Leo's impressive girth, throbbing and pulsing as I grip him like a vise. He grunts, and I open my eyes to find his expression intense, the tendons in his jaw popping as he grinds his teeth with effort.

"You're fucking sensational," he groans, his head sinking to rest against my pillow as his lips settle next to my ear.

He increases his pace, extracting every drop of pleasure from my body as my orgasm seems to build rather than fade. His labored breaths send zinging excitement up and down my spine, and though I'm still tingling with the bliss of my climax, I find myself quickly climbing to another.

"You're mine, Tia," he breathes, "and I intend to teach you just how good sex can be. I'll open your mind to a world no one else can show you. A world where pleasure is your oxygen and I'm your god."

The statement might sound arrogant, but I'm so lost in the haze of my euphoria that I don't even think to argue. I want him to show me everything he knows. I want to learn the sinful pleasures of being with a man.

If this is my reward for selling my soul to the devil, then I'm ready to live in hell.

"Come with me, *bella mia*," he commands, his thrusts driving me further into oblivion.

I feel him harden and swell inside me, stretching me to my limit. And as the first burst of hot cum pours inside me, I find my release. My lips part to release my cry of pleasure, but I'm so consumed by it that I can't make a sound.

My head swims as all my blood pounds through my core, making my clit ache with each fluttering twitch. Leo grunts, his hips jerking erratically as he releases burst after burst of his seed, finally relieving himself after a painful night of waiting.

And as we slow together, he settles lightly on top of me, his body covering me like a weighted blanket. Breathing heavily, our chests rise and fall in sync. I let my legs relax, my feet sliding across the soft sheets as I lie in a puddle of heavenly bliss.

Slowly, Leo eases out of me and rolls onto the bed beside me. I turn to look at him, mesmerized by his gorgeous masculinity. Every inch of him represents strength and power. He radiates authority. And when he touches me, it's like he effortlessly commands my body, playing with me like putty until he makes me sing.

One arm flung casually above his head, Leo turns to look at me, and a lazy smile stretches across his lips. But instead of saying anything, he reaches out to wrap his arm around me. And he pulls me to him, bringing me against his body in a shockingly tender embrace.

My cheek rests on his shoulder, my palm falling over his beating heart, and my leg naturally settles across his body, entwining us as he holds me close. And despite myself, I find the comfort of his arms so compelling, I can't pull away. Instead, I sink into the welcoming warmth of darkness as sleep overcomes me.

21

LEO

The sun hangs low in the sky as I stand inside one of the long-abandoned cabins near the edge of my property. My mind swirls with conflicting thoughts as I wait for my men to arrive. And Tia's face lingers behind my eyes, an unexpected presence that refuses to be ignored.

Despite the pressing matters at hand, the anticipation of seeing my new bride tugs at the edges of my focus. It's a problem I hadn't anticipated—a distraction that threatens to compromise my carefully honed discipline. Business comes first, above all else. It always has. But the thought of having Tia between the sheets once again has been dogging my mind all day.

I can't stop thinking about the intoxicating way she looked at me, the way she moved so sensually beneath me. Her smell lingers in the back of my mind, a subtle spicy citrus scent that makes my mouth water, like the bouquet of a fine gin.

The memory of her body wrapped around mine, makes me ache. And I know I can't let myself dwell on our night together if I'm going to have my shit together for this meeting.

I shove all thoughts of Tia impatiently to the back of my mind as ten Valencia men file through the front door and line up before me, several of my most trusted captains following them in, guns held lightly in hand. The Valencia family's inability to fall in line weighs heavily on my mind, a relentless undercurrent beneath the surface of my thoughts.

As the head of the Moretti family, I cannot afford to be lenient, especially not in the precarious world of organized crime. Loyalty is everything, and the Valencias' have breached the vow they made to us on more than one occasion since they bent the knee.

So, today is a test of whether they properly heard the message I delivered personally on my wedding day. I sent word for their members to be brought in for a reckoning—a reckoning that will determine whether they remain loyal allies or face the consequences of betrayal. Any proof that they're trying to steal from me today will require swift and decisive action.

The forgotten cabin I've chosen to conduct this grim business in bears the scars of past conflicts. Though its windows are still intact, the walls are splattered with dark stains, and the furniture is in disarray, several chairs broken from the number of interrogations that have taken place here.

It's a fitting backdrop for the confrontation that awaits, and a convenient location away from prying eyes and law enforcement that has been growing increasingly pricey to bribe lately—one of the many reasons I need to come to an understanding with Mayor Romney. If I can garner his cooperation, I won't be quite so hard-pressed to be discrete.

The Valencia members shift uncomfortably as they stand before me, avoiding my eyes as they hold their duffle bags full of collection money. A motley crew of men, they seem to bear the weight of their responsibility in the hard lines etched into their faces.

I stand at the center of the room, a silent observer of the unfolding drama. Loyalty is a delicate balance that requires trust, which can be easily shattered and challenging to rebuild. It's a lesson I aim to impart upon them today.

They wait quietly, a collective facade of fearful submission. I meet each gaze with a steely resolve, and once again, my thoughts flit momentarily to Tia—not far away in the main house on the far side of the property—before I pull myself back to the present. Focus is a luxury I can't afford to sacrifice.

"I think you all know why I brought you here for collections today," I state matter-of-factly. "Your don has proven unreliable when it comes to delivering the amount he's promised me every two weeks. Let's hope you all received the message I sent and you've become more... aligned with the choice to pay tribute rather than die."

No one looks up or says a word, a sure sign my message was delivered properly. Let's hope it was clear enough that I don't have to manage any more problems.

I signal to my men, who begin the process of collecting the earnings these Valencia men have accumulated. Using the table before me, they take one duffle bag at a time and count the money inside. The room is tense, the air charged with anticipation. My gaze moves from face to face, searching for any hint of guilt or deceit.

But if anyone thinks they're going to get away with something, it isn't obvious to me just yet.

As the bags of money are brought forward one by one, I calculate the expected sum in my mind. They had better hope their bags match what I know they owe us. The first few men present their earnings, and to my satisfaction, the numbers align with my expectations.

Perhaps my message on the day of my wedding reached them after all. Loyalty, I remind myself, is a currency more valuable than gold in our world. And though it can take proud men time to accept when they've been beaten, it seems that perhaps Don Valencia has finally given up his juvenile attempt to undermine me.

But just as I start to think this might be a day without violence, one of the men steps forward, his eyes intently avoiding mine as he hesitantly places his duffle bag on the table. A bead of sweat trickles down his temple, a telltale sign of unease. I watch him closely, my senses sharp, as he releases the bag of money that looks lighter than it should be.

Silence radiates through the space, and the Valencia men seem to hold a collective breath as they wait for my captain Drake to count the contents. He sets the bundles out on the table for everyone to see, a distinct difference from the way he handled the previous three bags.

He suspects the bag of being light as well.

My pulse quickens, the anticipation of confrontation crackling in the air as he pulls the last bundles from the bag and turns to me with a subtle shake of the head.

"This isn't the agreed-upon amount," I state, my voice cutting through the room like a blade as I take a slow step forward.

The man stammers, his excuses feeble attempts to mask the guilt that clings to him like a second skin. "W-We had some unexpected setbacks. I can have the rest for you next week—"

I raise a hand, cutting off his pathetic attempt at a compromise. It's the same excuse I've heard countless times before. "Your reasons for the missing money are not my concern. Loyalty is. Your family pledged allegiance to the Morettis, and once again, the Valencias have dishonored their vow."

The room hums with tension, the air thickening as I assess the gravity of the betrayal before me. Maintaining respect and obedience is a delicate dance, and these men have stumbled and tripped over their own deceit. I step forward, my gaze fixed on the traitor before me.

"I warned you what the consequences would be for stealing from me," I declare, the weight of my words settling like a shroud. "Betrayal demands payment."

"No, please," he begs, his eyes wide with panic as the sweat drips down his brow now, staining his shirt as it falls.

I give a nod, and my men, a silent chorus of enforcers, close in on the guilty man.

"Everyone outside," I order as the Valencia member is dragged through the back door and toward the trees surrounding the small cottage.

I step outside behind him, my men corralling the rest of the collection crew through the door after me so everyone can see what becomes of people who betray me. It seems that words alone are not enough.

"Put him on his knees," I command, pulling my gun from its holster beneath my suit jacket and cocking it.

The man struggles, trying to stand and flee despite the two men who grasp his arms forcefully, shoving his shoulders down until his knees hit the ground.

"Please," the man begs, tears spilling now as he shuffles toward me. "Please have mercy. I have a family. I won't—I'll get you the money today. All of it. Just give me another chance."

"So, you don't need another week to get the money you owe me?" I prod, looking at him haughtily. "Interesting."

"I can make it happen. Just please, please spare me."

"Did the two men who died before you not serve as a strong enough example?" I demand. "I'd hoped we might come to a quick, clear understanding. But it seems that a one-handed messenger was not convincing enough. So you'll have to help me drive the point home, I guess. It's nothing personal. But I want the men you came with today to see what I do to traitors. I assure you I don't give them second chances."

"Oh god, no. Please!" he howls as I lower my gun, aiming it right between his eyes.

Then I pull the trigger.

The punishment is swift and brutal—a reminder to all who witness what are the consequences of treachery. The shot echoes through the small clearing, sending the man's head snapping back. As his head lolls, a small hole dots the space between his eyebrows, a stream of crimson liquid trailing down his nose. The man's lifeless body slumps forward a moment later as my men release his arms.

In the deafening silence that follows, I hear a soft gasp. One that originates from the trees beyond the cabin. My eyes snap in that direction as I realize we might have a witness. Though who would be this far beyond the house, I don't know. We're on the edge of wilderness, miles from civilization in any direction.

Whoever it is must have followed us to end up on the outskirts of my land, right where I don't want them to be. My stomach drops as I realize they could easily have incriminating evidence that would destroy me.

And as I scan the trees in search of them, a flash of movement catches my eye. The hidden observer jumps up, turning to flee into the woods. And I don't get a good look at them before they vanish beyond my line of sight.

"Fuck," I hiss. "Finish the collections, and get rid of the body!" I snarl over my shoulder toward my men.

Then I go tearing after the witness before they can escape.

22

TIA

Late-morning sun filters past the heavy drapes that cascade down from the two-story windows lining one entire wall of the library. It casts a warm glow on the books and mahogany furniture. I sit, curled up on an overstuffed leather couch, reading. Or trying to, at least.

But my thoughts keep turning to Leo and how I found myself still wrapped in his arms when I woke this morning. The echo of our passionate night together lingers in my mind, making my pulse race through my veins.

And it raises a storm of troubling emotions within me.

Leo can be brutal, almost savage, in the way he behaves. But last night, he unveiled a side I hadn't anticipated—a level of tender concern that caught me off guard. Like how he came to check on me when I was throwing up and held my hair back after he realized how sick I was. Or the way he touched me in bed, his sole focus seeming to be on my pleasure. Even his readiness to grant me access to a car and unlimited time with my sisters.

I'm less certain today of my plans for revenge, less sure that Leo is entirely the monster I made him out to be in my head. Maybe, just maybe, I need time to understand him better.

For the first time, I find I'm not dreading what the future holds for me and the baby growing inside me. Perhaps we could find happiness in Leo's care. The night has left me in a state of confusion, questioning my assumptions and opening up the possibility that the alliance with my family might be a viable option.

As my father seemed to hope.

Sighing, I close my book. I must be going crazy.

Finding happiness with Leonardo Moretti? That can't possibly be a sane notion.

Worrying my lip, I wrestle with my thoughts, but no answer comes to me readily.

Digging into my pocket, I pull out my phone to call Maria. As my best friend and closest confidant, my younger sister is always the first person I talk to about things. And though I know I can't fully explain to her everything that's gone on between Leo and me, I still miss her and her sage advice appropriate to someone far beyond her years.

The phone rings, and finally, Maria's voice comes across the line. "Hey, Tia," she greets, her voice laced with curiosity. "How's married life? You kill that jerk of a husband yet? You calling for a getaway car?"

I snort in shock at her blunt delivery and pray there's no way Leo can tap my phone. "Maria!" I scold, all the same.

"I'm kidding. I'm kidding," she says dryly. "Mostly. But I miss you. How are you?"

"I'm okay," I respond, uncertainty evident in my tone.

"Well, that was convincing." Her tone drips sarcasm, and I can just picture her deadpan expression.

"I just really miss you too. Can you come over once you're done with your lessons today?"

Maria pauses, and when she speaks next, her voice is tinged with concern. "Of course I will. As long as I can get permission. You know how Father feels about the Morettis..." Her voice trails off as she seems to realize that I now fit under that umbrella. "Well, you know what I mean," she quickly recovers. "But, Tia, are you sure everything is okay?"

I take a deep, steadying breath before speaking. "I'm fine. Really. We can talk about it when you get here."

"Okay," she agrees. "I'll ask Father if I can stay for dinner."

That makes me smile, and my shoulders relax as I think about getting to spend some quality time with my sister. "That sounds great."

We exchange a few more words, and after hanging up, I'm left alone with my thoughts once more. Today, it's a challenging place to be left, and I'm not sure that sitting quietly is going to help me stay sane.

The day stretches before me, and I decide to walk the estate grounds until Maria arrives. Maybe the fresh air will clear my head.

"Shall we venture outside, little one?" I suggest to my tummy, resting my palm over it. "I agree. It's a beautiful day."

Rising from my chair, I slip my book back onto the shelf I took it from and head for the library's tall double doors. Thankfully, I'm already wearing a pair of joggers and tennies—the perk of being pregnant and trapped at home—so I won't have to change.

Instead, I head straight for the terrace that stretches from the back of the house.

The estate is vast, with well-manicured gardens and sprawling lawns. But I've already explored every inch of the gardens and arboretum. Today, my curiosity leads me deep into the woods surrounding the back of the house. They seem to stretch on for miles without another property in sight.

A person could get lost in them easily, except for the looming Allegheny Mountains that confirm which way is east and west.

The rustling leaves and distant bird songs provide a comforting backdrop to my inner turmoil. And I breathe freely as I pick up my pace, determined to cover some good ground before I have to return.

I cover several miles as I watch the sun make its slow procession across the sky, and as it dips toward the horizon, I know I'll need to head back soon if I'm going to beat Maria's arrival.

But just as I start to slow, hooking a left, something in the distance catches my eye. A cottage of sorts that looks fairly abandoned.

Is this still Moretti land?

I was under the impression that their estate was the last one that defined part of the borders of Piovosa's town limits before succumbing to the wilderness beyond. And though I don't want to intrude on anyone's land accidentally, the darkened windows draw me in, awakening my curiosity.

I creep closer, hoping to get a peek from the treeline that rings the small property. And as I walk a slow path around the perimeter, the distant sounds of a commotion reach my ears. Intrigued, I follow the noise past the corner of the small cottage.

As I pause near a towering red oak, my hands pressing against the rough bark as I hug its side, the scene that appears before me turns my blood to ice.

Leo stands with several Moretti men, their guns pointed at a group of prisoners. My heart pounds in my chest as I watch, hidden from view as I slip further behind the broad tree trunk.

The air vanishes from my lungs as Leo, cold and unyielding, issues orders to the men who haul one prisoner further from the cottage before forcing him onto his knees.

A sense of dread washes over me. I'm not naive. I know the world my family inhabits is steeped in shadows. My father is no stranger to the complexities of power and the lengths one must go to maintain it. Yet, in all his dealings, he never brought that darkness within the confines of our home.

To happen upon it now, while I was just walking in the woods, fills me with a deep sense of dread.

The ruthlessness of the scene is foreign to me, a perversion of the sanctuary I believed my new home to be. And the thought that it's happening so close to where I sleep sends a horrified shiver down my spine.

My heart pounds. Dread courses through my veins as I grapple with the reality that Leo—the man I was intimate with just last night, the man whose arms I woke up in this morning—is capable of such savagery.

He seems untroubled by the weight of his actions, oblivious to the monster he projects to the world. A fear settles over me as I realize I've been thrust into a world where the line between tenderness and brutality is thin, almost imperceptible.

My hands grow clammy with sweat as Leo continues the merciless display, unaware of my presence. He's in control, a master of his domain, and the prisoner shakes visibly, begging for his life as he weeps.

Leo's gun cocks with an audible click, and though I can't quite make out the words he says, he delivers them with a cold indifference —a haughty arrogance—that chills me to the bone. He lowers his gun, aiming it at the cowering man before him, and with a few last words, he pulls the trigger.

A bullet blasts through the man's head, sending blood and gore splattering across the ground behind him.

It strikes terror into me like I've never known before.

I've heard rumors of Leo's savage brutality, experienced a hint of his cruelty even, but watching its full force and effect with my own eyes is entirely different. The air is thick with the scent of fear, and I find myself frozen, a silent witness to his black world.

Leo's actions reveal a side of him that I had only glimpsed before. As the gunshot echoes through the forest, I gasp, stunned by his casual violence.

Leo's head turns sharply in my direction, his piercing gaze finding my hiding spot in an instant.

Panic grips me, and I spin to run, not bothering to be quiet in my desperation to flee. My footsteps echo through the woods, matching my heartbeat as I race as quickly as my feet will carry me.

I know he saw me, and I hear him shout something to his men before the sound of pounding feet breaks out behind me, alerting me to his pursuit. He's hot on my trail, and the trees that were once a sanctuary to me become a labyrinth closing in from all around.

As I run for my life, my mind races. I have no clue what I'm going to do. It's only a matter of time before he catches me.

Because despite my considerable head start, he's already closing the distance.

I weave through the trees, my breath ragged, the fear of the unknown propelling me forward. Leo's footsteps make a steady beat behind me, a relentless chase that fuels the panic gnawing at my insides.

The world blurs as I navigate the maze of greenery, branches snagging on my clothes and scratching my skin. My legs ache, and my lungs burn, but I can't afford to stop. I can't let him catch me now because I don't trust that he won't hurt me or even our unborn child.

Fear for the innocent life growing inside me drives me forward, pushing me past the limits of my physical abilities.

And still, with each passing moment, the distance between us narrows.

23

LEO

Adrenaline courses through my veins, a fiery surge that heightens my senses. My breaths come hard but measured, each one laced with the acrid taste of anger. I'm certain of one thing—whoever I'm chasing witnessed the execution I performed as a lesson to the Valencia men.

Otherwise, they wouldn't be running.

I am left with no choice but to pursue, to eliminate this threat to my carefully constructed world. Regardless of whether they're a servant who wandered out where they have no right to be or a spy ready to offer up proof of my murder to the authorities. I can't let them live.

The soft rustle of leaves as I brush past trees and bushes echoes in my rapid heartbeat. I move with a predator's determination, each step calculated, every muscle tense. The late-afternoon shadows play tricks on me, distorting the landscape, but I press on, fueled by fury and the need to protect my secrets.

They're fast, whoever it is. And fit by the distance they're capable of running at such a breakneck speed. But they have no chance of escaping me in my domain—despite their lengthy head start. I navigate the unmarked pathways between the trees with ease, the layout etched into my memory. I've lived in these woods my whole life. I know them like the back of my hand.

My quarry, however, betrays their unfamiliarity with their surroundings, stumbling blindly through the rough terrain. And their footsteps are growing more haggard as they finally start to slow from exhaustion. They're getting clumsy with fatigue.

I relish the thought of catching them, exposing their intrusion, and silencing them before they can unleash chaos on my life. I've worked too hard to let it all fall apart now.

As I close in, the terrain shifts, and I realize with a cold shiver that the intruder is heading straight for the gorge that defines the boundary line of Moretti land. The treacherous drop is a natural defense, a guardian that separates our haven from the untamed wilderness beyond.

The fleeing witness's reckless sprint toward the edge could only end in death. A cruel fate they seem oblivious to—or would prefer over ending up in my hands. I can't say that I blame them.

Half-tempted to let the gorge claim its victim, I continue my pursuit from a safe distance, ready to stop once they've taken the leap and removed themselves from the equation. Perhaps the cliffs will be the justice my anger seeks, sparing me the additional blood on my hands.

Because, despite my reputation for bloodlust, I don't enjoy killing people.

It's a necessity that comes with the job.

Resolved to let fate take its course, I hold a steady pace, finding some relief in the exertion of running several miles in pursuit of the snake who thought they could get the upper hand on me.

But the momentary peace evaporates in one horrifying instant.

Because, as the witness bursts into the clearing that starts mere yards from the cliff's edge, I finally see who it is I'm chasing.

Shock ripples through me as I recognize the familiar contours of her slender form, the long dark hair that whips behind her like a black silk ribbon.

It's Tia.

Panic grips my throat, choking me.

I have to do something—anything I can to stop her.

But she's too far ahead of me. I'll never reach her in time.

"Tia!" My voice cuts through the space between us, a desperate plea for her to stop.

The word carries the weight of my dread. And my stomach drops like lead when she doesn't slow or even hesitate. Instead, she turns her head, eyes wide as she looks back at me—away from the looming cliff edge.

For a fleeting moment, our gazes lock.

Panic and fear etch across Tia's delicate features, and it only seems to grow when she sees I'm the one pursuing her. The look in her eyes cuts like a knife. Still, if I could stop her with a word, I would. But it's clear now that she's terrified of me. Nothing I say is going to stop her.

And then it's too late.

The ground vanishes out from under her.

Her scream is shrill and bone-chilling.

And the void swallows her whole.

"No!" My hand reaches for her instinctually, though I'm too far away to reach her.

Horror seizes me, stiffening my limbs as I watch her disappear. My mind races, grappling with the unthinkable—the mother of my child plummeting to her death.

A scream claws at my throat, but I stifle it, the sound choked back by the enormity of the moment.

In an instant, I'm at the cliff's edge, flinging myself to the ground so I can peer far into the abyss. The low sun casts eerie shadows across the jagged rocks below, making the trees appear larger and more ominous than before.

But I see no sign of Tia. Panic gnaws at my insides, a feral fear clawing at the edges of my consciousness. She's just... gone.

"Tia!" I call again, my voice ragged with uncertainty.

The echo of her name bounces off the walls of the gorge, coming back to me in a mocking chorus. I never should have chased her. I should have let it be. But I was so hell-bent on catching whoever witnessed the execution that I didn't read the signs.

I didn't stop to think.

Of course, Tia would be out in the woods.

When is she ever where she's supposed to be? When does she ever do what she's supposed to? Naturally, it would be her wandering miles in the woods alone. She walked all the way from her home to my house party the night I met her, didn't she?

A sickening realization takes hold of me. I've lost her forever to the unforgiving rocks beneath me. It doesn't matter that I can't see her broken body. There's no way she survived the fall. The gorge is well over a hundred feet deep.

My mind races—a torrent of guilt, anger, and sorrow.

How did it come to this?

The pursuit of an intruder, a threat to my secrecy, has turned into a nightmare. I never intended for Tia to be in harm's way, and now the consequences of my actions loom over me like a specter.

Frantically, I scan the rocky terrain below, hoping against hope to catch a glimpse of her. The world narrows to the edges of the cliff, the abyss mocking me with its emptiness. Suspended between dread and denial, I'm unwilling to accept the truth.

The echoes of Tia's scream linger in the air, haunting me. As I kneel there, on the edge of a precipice, I grapple with a terrible realization that, despite my stubborn refusal to accept the marriage I was forced into, I care about Tia.

She's wormed her way into my heart despite my determination to hate her family—and her by proxy.

I held a treasure in my hands, just as her father claimed.

She was mine for the span of one perfect moment.

And now she's gone.

24

TIA

"Tia!" Leo's voice echoes from the cliff edge above, seeming to snap me out of my stunned state. *Was I unconscious for a moment after hitting the cliff wall?* The memory is fragmented, a blur of impact and disorientation.

I can't seem to find the air to answer him. I hit the side of the cliff with such force that it knocked the wind out of me completely, and now I dangle upside down, the blood rushing to my head and making it nearly impossible to catch my breath.

By some twist of fate or the watchful eyes of a guardian angel, when I turned to the sound of Leo's voice, my foot snagged in the roots of a long-dead tree. A tree that I see now, as it hangs over the edge of the cliff beside me.

I don't know if Leo called my name during the chase because he knew about the cliff and wanted to warn me or if he was just determined to catch up to me. And right now, I'm not sure I care. Because the fact that he got me to turn probably saved my life.

Trying to orient myself, I glance at the world below my head and instantly feel as though I'm going to throw up. A wave of vertigo hits me with alarming force, making the world spin and dip in a dizzying dance. Fresh panic surges through me as I realize just how far beneath me solid ground is.

I must be suspended over a hundred feet in the air, with nothing but a few roots securing me to the crumbling rocks of the cliffside. Forcing my eyes away from the terrifying sight far below, I look up at the rotting tree roots.

My tennie-clad foot is thoroughly tangled in them. As I sway in the breeze, a small shower of pebbles crumble away from the wall, tumbling down on me and coating me with gray dust.

Agony throbs in my leg, and I bite down on my lip to stifle a cry. My ankle appears to be an unwilling sacrifice I exchanged for my life. It's likely what took the brunt of my weight to stop me from plummeting to my death. And now it's buckling under the strain of holding me.

Beyond the roots of the tree, an overhang obscures the top of the cliff, leaving me stranded in a suspended reality. I have no clue how far I fell. And I shudder at the uncertainty of what it might take to find my way to safety.

"Tia!" Leo's voice is like a lifeline above.

His shout slices through my terror, and I can't help but feel a surge of relief. He's still looking for me. With a shaky voice, I call, "I'm down here!"

I hear shuffling, as if he's trying to find me from where he stands, but I'm too well hidden.

"How secure are you?"

"I'm stuck. My foot got caught in a tree root, so I'm just... hanging. Upside down. Please help me, Leo," I beg.

Tears sting my eyes as I realize it might be in his best interest to just leave me here to fall to my death. After all, he was likely chasing me with the intent to kill me in the first place. And the pause that follows makes me wonder if the same thought doesn't cross his mind.

"Hold on. We'll get you out of there."

His tone is sincere, his concern real, and I try to breathe to calm myself. Maybe I'm letting my imagination get the best of me. Gritting my teeth, I try to ignore the pain in my leg. Blood pounds in my ears, making my head feel painfully heavy as it clouds my thoughts.

A moment later, a torrent of curses comes to me from above.

"What?" I demand, fresh panic threatening to strangle me once again.

"I don't have any service," Leo growls, frustrated, and his admission hits me like a second blow. "Fucking phone," he mutters almost imperceptibly.

Tears well up, blurring my vision as my fear overcomes my composure.

Like an animal caught in a trap, I'm desperate to do anything I can think of to escape. And right now, I feel far too vulnerable just hanging upside down. With a grunt, I attempt a midair situp, reaching for the roots wrapped around my leg. But the jarring motion ripples dangerously up my leg. A sharp pain shoots through my ankle, forcing a cry from my lips.

"What's wrong?" Leo demands, his tone sharp with worry.

"I... tried to pull myself up," I grit through clenched teeth.

"Stay still, Tia. I'm coming down."

My heart skips a beat as I wonder how that could possibly be a good idea. *If he comes down, won't we both get stuck?*

But before I can unlock my jaw to say anything, Leo's fine Italian leather dress shoes appear along the cliffside. My stomach flip-flops as he free-climbs down to my level with shocking dexterity. Somehow, the term "free-climb" seems too casual for the perilous act he's performing, navigating the sheer face with an ease that makes my head spin.

His fluidity astounds me, his graceful descent momentarily distracting me from my predicament. His movements are like a dance against the craggy canvas, each foothold and handhold a deliberate step toward salvation. And the speed with which he does it belies an impressive confidence.

Within minutes, he settles onto a narrow ledge mere feet below my head. I couldn't see it before, and it looks just wide enough to support him. I try not to look past him to the terrifying drop below, but when I catch sight of his heel just inches away from the sheer drop, it makes me want to throw up all over again.

He turns to me, his hazel eyes assessing my situation in a matter of seconds, and a rush of gratitude floods my body to know I'm not entirely alone. Then he steps forward to the edge of the ledge.

Strong arms snake beneath my back, lifting me as he turns me upright at the same time.

Heady relief loosens the painful knot in my chest as my back finds his muscular chest, a rock more solid than the crumbling cliff we're clinging to. His hold allows my circulation to rebalance, the excess blood draining from my brain and leaving me lightheaded.

I grip his forearm like my life depends on it.

"I've gotcha," he assures me, one powerful arm like iron around my waist.

He digs in his pocket with the other hand. Then he flicks out a pocket knife, opening it in one fluid motion. Just the sight of the steel makes my heart flutter fearfully—an irrational reaction, considering he climbed down the side of a cliff to come help me.

"You carry a knife in your suit pocket?" I ask, my tone incredulous.

"We're clinging to a cliffside, and that's the question you want to ask?" he counters.

He leans forward, reaching up the length of my leg to saw at the rotting tree. With skillful precision, Leo cuts away the roots ensnaring my foot, freeing me from the precarious grip.

I gasp as my legs freefall for a moment, and my muscles tense instinctually. But Leo has me so securely in his embrace that I'm in no danger of falling. The warmth of his broad chest and the solid ground suddenly resting beneath me are reassuring, a stark contrast to the perilous spot I hung from moments ago.

The ledge is barely large enough to accommodate both of us, and I find myself grateful for Leo's solid presence. The proximity of the cliff's edge sends shivers down my spine. It's a fragile sanctuary, one I would love to get off of, but I don't see how. Unless you're Spider-Man, like Leo apparently is, there's no way up or down.

He sets me gently on my feet, his hold loosening slightly as he allows me to take my own weight. And for a moment, I'm uncertain whether the solid ground beneath me can hold both of us. But I try to stand on my own, wanting to give Leo as much freedom to maneuver as he might need.

The attempt to stand proves excruciating. A sharp cry escapes my lips as the pain in my ankle flares. I wobble dangerously as the weight of my body on my injured leg threatens to send me tumbling once again. Then Leo's there, his arm a reassuring presence as he grasps me firmly, stabilizing me once again.

"Thanks," I breathe, my heart hammering at the second close call I've had within a matter of minutes.

Rather than answering, Leo assesses the situation with a pragmatic calm. Closing his knife, he slips it back into his pocket. His eyes scan the overhang I fell from, the rotting tree that caught me, then they move to the sheer cliffside. "Do you know how to climb?"

"I mean, I've climbed trees before, but with this ankle... I don't know how far I'll get." My voice trails off, uncertainty clouding my words as I try not to cry.

Leo nods, a silent acknowledgment of the obstacles before us. Then, without hesitation, he starts to remove his shirt, tie, and belt. He does it one-handed, keeping the other firmly on my arm so I won't topple over the edge.

The urgency in his movements is a stark reminder that time is not our ally. And though I can stop to appreciate the muscles he's revealing to put his clothes to use, I'm just grateful he's willing to sacrifice the fine apparel to save my life.

He fashions a makeshift rope and ties it securely to the belt around my waist, then gives the contraption a tug to ensure the knots will hold. Leo's eyes meet mine, and the gravity of our situation hangs in the air between us.

"It's not a far climb—about ten feet," he assures me. "But you're going to have to help me. I don't trust my clothes to hold your weight if I have to haul you up the whole way."

I swallow hard, the reality of the climb ahead settling like a stone in my stomach. I nod. The rope of clothing, a lifeline that binds us together, is a fragile link in this precarious journey.

"I'll go up first," he continues. "Watch where I find foot and hand holds, and use the same ones as best you can."

"Okay," I breathe, trying to keep the panic from my voice.

Leo helps me turn until I can use the cliff wall to support my weight. Then, he begins the climb back up the rocky edge.

I watch with a mix of trepidation and determination, etching every movement into my memory as Leo navigates the cliffside with the same dexterity that brought him down to me. His back glistens with sweat, bringing his tattoo to life.

When Leo reaches the top, he turns to look at me. Kneeling, he looms over the edge, a silhouette against the evening sky. "Okay, Tia, your turn!" he calls, his voice calm and encouraging.

I draw in a steadying breath, focusing on the task at hand. Gingerly, I follow his path as Leo coaxes me along the same route he took. The makeshift rope keeps me anchored, allowing me to climb without relying on my injured leg. Each move is a calculated step toward safety, a collaboration of trust and survival.

The pain in my leg is a persistent reminder of my vulnerability, but Leo's presence above and the constant support of the lifeline encircling my waist fuels my determination. Sweat beads on my forehead as I inch my way upward, ignoring my ankle's protests.

The world narrows to the path before me, and each foothold becomes a success, a defiance of the abyss below. I never imagined I would one day be relying on Leonardo Moretti to keep me from plummeting to my death. But I'm suddenly immensely grateful that he's the person here with me now.

As I near the top, the taste of victory lingers on my tongue. My hands are almost within reach of the solid ground above. I look up to see Leo's intent gaze fixed upon me. With one hand, he holds the makeshift rope as he reaches out with the other, ready to grab me as soon as I'm within reach.

Spurred on, I climb higher, pulling myself up with all my strength. I'm almost there. My uninjured foot feels around to find its next foot hold, and I find purchase before my hurt leg can give out. Then, in an instant, I feel the treacherous support crumble beneath my weight.

A shriek rips from my throat as my fingers are unable to take the sudden force of my weight. Leo's eyes widen in fear, his lips parting, but I can't hear him over my terrified cry.

And I plummet toward my death once again.

25

LEO

Tia's eyes widen with terror as her grip slips, fingers losing purchase on the unforgiving surface of the cliff edge. Her scream stops my heart dead in its tracks as she begins to freefall.

Without thinking, I lunge forward, my hand shooting out to grasp her arm just in the nick of time. The force of her fall pulls me down, threatening to drag us both over the edge to our deaths. My torso slips precariously, my bare chest scraping across the coarse ground.

But I refuse to die like this.

Releasing the makeshift rope, I dig the heel of my free palm into the rocky ledge to stop my forward motion, my heart pounding in my chest.

"Leo!" Tia gasps, and I can feel her panic reverberating through her body.

"I've gotcha," I growl with effort. "I won't let go. But you've got to get a better grip if I'm going to pull you up."

Tia reaches with her free hand to clasp my wrist, strengthening the bond between us as I hold her suspended in the air. My joints groan in protest from the unreasonable force of stopping her fall, followed by the need to hold Tia with one arm.

She might be light, but it's still no walk in the park to keep her from falling now.

Gritting my teeth, I fortify myself, stabilizing my body as I shift my center of gravity.

Then, arms straining as I grip her wrist with bruising force, I use every ounce of my strength to pull her up. Adrenaline surges through me, heightening my senses, and with a burst of determination, I finally manage to haul her over the cliff edge and onto solid ground.

We collapse together, Tia falling on top of my body, her palms resting on my chest. She keeps them there, as if feeling that my heart's still beating—we're both alive. Our eyes connect for one long moment as we pant together, and Tia releases a breathy laugh that draws a smile to my lips.

Then she rolls to the side, collapsing backward to lie spread eagle onto the dry, rocky dirt beside me. Gasping for breath, we stare up at the sky, marveling at the fact that we're both still alive.

Turning my head, I look at Tia sprawled by my side. Her chest rises and falls with ragged desperation. The reality of how close we came to disaster sinks in, and a shiver runs down my spine. I never anticipated I would feel the depth of the anxiety that consumes me now at the gut-wrenching realization that I almost lost her.

I can't stand the thought.

My chest tightens, and suddenly, it's painful to breathe. To lose her—and the child she's carrying—would have been more than I could bear. My breath catches, and I turn my head away, pretending to survey the landscape to hide my turmoil.

It's Tia who breaks the silence eventually. Her voice is still shaky but awed as she sits up to look at me. "Where did you learn to climb like that?"

I glance at her, watching the shadows of the evening light play across her face, and I sit up as well. Turning to face her, I bend my legs and rest my arms on my knees. "Rock climbing is a hobby of mine," I confess, the words feeling strangely vulnerable. "I find free climbing therapeutic."

Her eyebrows shoot up in surprise, and she lets out an incredulous laugh. "Therapeutic? Hardly. I can't see anything calming about the possibility of falling to your death." She shakes her head in disbelief. Then her onyx eyes flash back to me with a new, sharp edge. "Though maybe, in your case, something extreme like that would be necessary. I imagine you must need a lot of therapy to cope with the amount of death that seems to surround you…"

I tense, the edges of my calm facade beginning to crack. "You weren't supposed to see that," I say darkly, dropping my eyes to my hands.

"Well, that clears it all up. Knowing I wasn't *supposed* to see it makes murder *so* much better." Her voice drips sarcasm, triggering my temper.

"Well, if you hadn't been snooping around, sticking your nose where it doesn't belong, maybe you wouldn't have nearly gotten yourself killed."

"Maybe you shouldn't have chased me!"

"You didn't seem too upset about it when I was climbing down to get you," I growl.

"That's not an excuse for killing a man."

"You wouldn't understand. What were you even doing that far out in the woods? If you'd stayed closer to the house, you could have continued living happily as the naive little princess you've grown up to be. Without a care in the world."

Tia's eyes narrow, and she snaps, "I'm not a little princess."

"You are if you think I'm doing anything that your father hasn't done a hundred times before." I shoot back, my voice laced with bitterness. "You have no clue what really happens in this town, do you? Don Guerra might be more subtle about it, but believe me, he's killed at least as many people as I have."

She scoffs, unimpressed by my argument. "Even if that were true, my father has had several decades more to rack up the body count you've accomplished in just a few short years." She boldly lifts her chin, eyeing me with haughty contempt. "You know, not every problem in life needs to be solved with a gun or a hammer, Leo. You seem intelligent enough to figure out the difference."

A surge of irritation courses through me, and I can't mask it in my next words. "Not every problem in life can be solved with diplomacy either, Tia."

Her eyes flash with defiance. "Maybe you do know the difference, then, and you just prefer to be a cold-blooded killer rather than a don who knows how to lead through respect."

"You can't have respect without fear," I counter.

"Yes, and I'm sure once we're all dead, you'll have an army of ghosts who respect you immensely," she says sarcastically.

Infuriated by her deliberate stubbornness, I hold my tongue before I say something I might regret.

"You didn't even blink, Leo." Her voice is hushed, breathy in her disappointment. "You took a man's life like it was nothing."

I stand abruptly, furious with Tia for rubbing my face in my ugly work when I just saved her life. For a moment, I contemplate leaving her there until I can collect myself. But the sun is setting quickly, and the longer I wait, the farther I'll have to carry her in the dark.

With a frustrated growl, I scoop her up unceremoniously, holding her securely in my arms.

"What do you think you're doing?" she squeals, squirming as she pushes fruitlessly against my bare chest. But her protests are easy to ignore.

"I don't imagine you can walk home," I reply, my tone cutting through the air like a knife.

She stops fighting me at that, and a tense quiet falls between us. Her protests are replaced by a brooding silence as I carry her toward home. The weight of her in my arms is both a physical and metaphorical burden, the echoes of our argument lingering in the air as I think about the violence she so detests me for.

And yet, she's willing to defend her father?

That makes her a hypocrite. Or she's lying to herself.

Either way, I don't like it.

What frustrates me further is the fact that I just saved her life. Not once, but multiple times. At no small risk to my own survival. But apparently, that counts for nothing compared to the traitor I executed to keep the rest of the Valencia men in line.

Not that I think any reason I give her will merit my actions in her eyes.

It baffles me to realize that just when I thought we might be finding a way to live with our arrangement, it turns out she wants nothing to do with me.

Fine.

We don't need to talk while I walk.

The landscape changes around us as we make our way back into the trees and toward home. I focus on the path ahead, determined not to let Tia's words get under my skin. But beneath the stoic exterior, her accusations gnaw at me, a seed of doubt taking root.

Tia breaks the silence once more, her voice softer this time. "Leo, why do you choose violence when there are other ways?"

I grit my teeth, the question cutting deeper than she realizes. "Sometimes, there's no other choice."

"You always have a choice," she murmurs, her eyes intent on my face.

I work my jaw as I struggle to keep my temper under tight wraps. "You should keep your mouth shut about what you don't understand."

She falls silent once more, her eyes shifting to her lap as her eyebrows buckle into a frown.

I carry her through the growing darkness, each step holding the weight of the unspoken words between us. Thankfully, Tia's light, easy to carry, and after over an hour of walking, the house starts to come into view.

Relief surges through me. Not because I'm struggling to hold her—I would be perfectly fine to carry her farther if need be. But she exerted herself quite strenuously *and* took a pretty terrible fall. Not to mention, her ankle definitely needs attending to.

As soon as we get to the house, I'm calling the doctor so I can ensure she and the baby are okay.

26

TIA

The bedroom is well-lit, the soft glow of the bedside lamp casting a warm hue across Leo's face. He sits silently beside me, lost in thought, his expression brooding. The air is heavy with tension as I recline on the bed, nervously fidgeting with the hem of my shirt as I try not to worry about my baby.

The events of the day replay in my mind like a broken record, each moment a jumble of fear and anxiety. *How did we go from waking up in each other's arms to this bottomless chasm of uncertainty between us?*

The door creaks open, and the doctor steps inside, his expression unreadable as he carries his medical equipment in with him. Leo stands, turning to face him as he moves out of the way. My heart pounds as I wait for the doctor to start the exam. Then his eyes meet mine, and soft reassurance settles onto his face.

"How are you feeling today, Signora Moretti?" he asks kindly, his familiar demeanor soothing when I'm already overwhelmed with stress.

He's the same doctor who's visited me about the pregnancy from the beginning, and today, I'm more than grateful that Leo and his father let me keep him on.

"I was fine until a few hours ago. But I had a pretty bad fall. I just want to know that my baby's okay." I rest my palm protectively over my abdomen, fighting to keep my trembling chin under control.

"Of course." Dr. Luca pats my hand comfortingly. Then he settles onto the bed beside me, hooking his stethoscope into his ears.

My eyes shift to Leo. My husband stands at the foot of the bed now, one arm lying across his chest, the other palm resting on his cheek in a look of disconcerted anxiety. It's an uncharacteristic display of emotion. I don't like seeing it now, when all our minds are on the welfare of the tiny life inside me.

The doctor first listens to my heart and lungs, checking my vitals and shining a light in my eyes. Then he moves on to the baby, retrieving a portable ultrasound machine from his bag. Slathering my stomach with clear goo, he runs the wand over my belly.

And for one terrifying moment, I don't hear anything.

"There they are," he says, a smile breaking across his face as the hummingbird thrum of my baby's heartbeat fills the room.

I gasp, tears stinging my eyes as relief washes through me. And when I look at Leo, I'm shocked by the wonder that takes over his proud features. His hand falls from his face, his eyes widening as he stares openly at my belly. Then he looks up to meet my eyes.

The deep emotion there rocks me to my core, and for the first time, I can see what it means to Leo to be a father. It shakes me deeply to realize the child I'm carrying is as significant to him as it is to me. He might not love me, but he already loves our baby.

Fighting to subdue the wave of emotion that threatens to consume me, I clear my throat. "Is she okay?" I breathe, my heart fluttering nervously. And to my astonishment, the baby's heartbeat increases, filling the room with energy as it matches mine.

Dr. Luca smiles knowingly. Finished with his inspection, he takes the wand away from my belly and offers me some Kleenex to clean myself up.

But before he can answer my question, Leo cuts in. "She?"

I blush, realizing my secret belief came to the surface due to my anxiety. "I don't actually know," I say shyly. "I just have a feeling."

"I can tell you the sex at twelve weeks if you'd like to know for sure," the doctor says.

"Does that mean the baby's okay?" Leo asks, practically hovering over us now.

Rather than answering Leo directly, Dr. Luca turns his soft eyes to me. "You and the baby are both fine. No signs of distress or complications, though it does look like you bumped your head," he says, his voice calm and measured. "No concussion, though."

Relief washes over me like a tidal wave, and I let out a breath I didn't realize I'd been holding. "Thank you, Doctor," I manage to say, my voice shaky. The weight of worry lifts from my shoulders.

"Will you check Tia's ankle, too, while you're here?" Leo asks, his tone gruffer than before. "She hurt it during the fall."

"I got caught up in some roots," I explain, leaving out the details of my tumble to avoid too many questions I won't have answers to.

The doctor shifts to examine my ankle, his fingers probing gently. I hiss as he finds a particularly tender spot, and to my right, Leo shifts uncomfortably—like he would rather not be in the room.

"It's a sprain, Signora Moretti. Nothing too serious. It shouldn't take much longer than a week to heal, but you'll need to take it easy for a while. I'll wrap it up for you, and I recommend using ice to reduce swelling. Rest is crucial. Keep weight off it as much as possible," the doctor advises as he wraps the tender joint. "And if the pain persists, don't hesitate to contact me."

I nod gratefully, and the doctor stands, putting his equipment back in his bags.

"Thank you, Doctor," Leo says curtly.

"Of course." Dr. Luca excuses himself, leaving Leo and me alone in the room.

The silence between us is stifling, and I can sense a storm brewing within my husband.

But before he can say whatever is on his mind, the door bursts open, and my sister Maria rushes in, eyes wide with worry.

"I saw the doctor leaving, and someone said you fell," she blurts out, her gaze flicking suspiciously between Leo and me. Then her eyes widen in astonishment as she takes in our collectively disheveled state.

Leo's still shirtless, a smattering of grit coating his fine muscles. He grumbles something about using a guest room to get cleaned up, then he heads for the exit, slamming the door unceremoniously behind him. Left alone with Maria, I release a breath and smile.

"Are you okay, Tia? Is the baby?" she asks, concern etched on her face as she helps me sit more comfortably on the bed.

I give her a small smile, grateful for her presence. "I'm fine, Maria. Just a sprained ankle. The baby's okay, too," I assure her, my voice tinged with exhaustion.

"Thank goodness," she gushes, pulling me close for a hug. "Can I help you wash up without letting that bandage get dirty?" she offers, pointing to the wrap the doctor just put on.

"That would be amazing," I confess, suddenly aware of the sweat and dust that clings to my body.

I give her instructions as to where the supplies would be, and she scurries about, collecting a bowl of warm water, a washcloth, and some fresh clothes. Then she settles onto the bed beside me once more.

As Maria helps me clean up, toweling me off without aggravating my injured ankle, a sense of normalcy returns. The familiarity of my sister's touch and the concern in her eyes offer a comforting contrast to the chaos that has unfolded today.

"So, tell me, what's been going on at home?" I ask lightly, not quite ready to dive into thoughts on my life when I've hardly had time to think them through myself since I called Maria earlier today.

Maria glances toward the door to make sure we're alone, and that subtle gesture is enough to tell me that I'm not going to like what I'm about to hear.

"Father's been pretty aggravated about the alliance this whole last week," Maria admits.

My heart drops into my stomach at the foreboding news. "Really? Why?"

Maria shakes her head. "You know Father. He doesn't talk about the business in front of us. But I did overhear him talking to Mother about how the Morettis are using it as an excuse to order Guerra men around. And they've been crossing our territory lines all over town."

"Has Father done anything about it?" I ask, worry tinging my tone as I think about what I witnessed in the woods today.

Could that happen to my family if my father gets too vocal?

Leo wouldn't flat-out murder an ally, would he? Not one who's the father of his wife, surely. Then again, I can't say that I really know Leo at all after today. It feels like every time I think I've found my footing around him, he pulls the rug out from under me.

"Well, Father spoke to Don Moretti, but I guess the don didn't seem overly concerned about doing something. He just said he would speak with his son." Maria shrugs, dunking the washcloth back into the quickly graying water and rinsing more rock dust from it. "Are you going to tell me what this is all about?" she asks, gesturing to the warm bowl of water she's using to help clean me up, then sweeping her arm to take me in as well.

I sigh, letting my shoulders settle as I wonder just how much I should tell her. In the end, Maria's my sister, and she's the only person I have to really talk to. And I need to talk to someone.

"Things have been… hard since I left home," I admit, not really wanting to get into the details of my wedding night with my sister. I'm still working through the conflicting emotions of what happened that night—how Leo took me on the patio for everyone to see, how I still found it arousing. It mortifies me to know I could come multiple times, even when he was so demeaning.

"Does he hurt you?" Maria demands, her tone fiercely protective.

"No," I insist. "I mean, I don't know. He makes me cry a lot, I guess. But it's not like I expected this to be easy, you know? And I didn't have much choice. In truth, though, in the little bit of time we've spent together, for most of it, he's been quite… nice," I confess, thinking about how he cared for me last night, both at dinner and after we got home. "He even apologized for what he's done to hurt me," I admit, considering our exchange in the garden once again.

Then I shake my head, dropping my eyes to my lap.

Finished cleaning me up, Maria sets the dirty bowl of water aside and comes to sit beside me, giving me her full attention. "But?" she prompts.

"But I just can't seem to trust him. Every time I think we might be heading in the right direction, Leo does something that throws me completely off balance."

Maria raises her eyebrows, her eyes patient as she waits for me to explain.

"I was out walking in the woods behind the house today," I say, then take a deep, fortifying breath as I prepare myself to say it out loud for the first time. "And I came across Leo with several of his men. They had several of Don Valencia's men rounded up, and... He executed someone today, Maria. I don't know why. Leo just... shot him." I breathe the last part, then glance nervously toward the door.

"Holy shit," she says, the cuss word catching me by surprise.

We don't normally curse, as Mother says it's not ladylike. But it's certainly fitting for the situation.

"Yeah. Which was terrifying. So I panicked and ran, and he came chasing after me."

Maria's face looks stricken this time.

"Of course, I had no idea where I was going, and I literally ran right off a cliff."

"You *what*?!" she shouts, jumping up from my bed.

"Shhh," I calm her urgently, glancing toward the door. I have no clue how much of this I would be allowed to tell her, and I don't want Leo to send her away.

She glances toward the door as well, then settles back onto the mattress beside me.

"Long story short, a bunch of tree roots saved my fall." Not wanting to stress her out further, I cut to the chase. "That's how I sprained my ankle. I got all tangled up, and it stopped me about ten feet from the top."

"Jesus. How did you get back up?"

"That's what's so confusing," I confess, my brows pressing into a frown. "Even after Leo chased me, he came down to help. He literally scaled a cliff wall, just free climbed it, to cut me free from the roots."

Maria releases a low whistle. "Well, I'm glad you're still alive. Do you think he intended to kill you? You know... before you fell?"

"I don't know," I murmur. The same question had been plaguing me for a while now. "But he seemed genuinely concerned about my welfare when the doctor was here. And after watching Leo during my ultrasound, I don't think he'll do anything to me as long as I'm carrying his child."

"That doesn't give me much peace of mind," Maria says dryly.

"Well, it gives me the time I need. I'm working on a plan that might remove the Morettis from the equation completely," I glance nervously toward the door yet again.

Maria sighs, as though she already suspected as much. "Just promise me you'll be careful, Tia. I can't bear the thought of something happening to you."

"I won't let anything happen to me or the baby," I assure her, holding her gaze. We sit in silence for a moment, the weight of the conversation settling over us.

"I've missed you, Tia," Maria says finally, giving me a soft smile.

"I've missed you too!" A pang of longing hits my chest, and I pull my sister into a hug. "You want me to call for some dinner?" I suggest.

"I'm starved," she agrees.

As we continue talking, I feel a renewed strength. Maria's support is a lifeline, a reminder of the love and bond that transcends the chaos surrounding us. But Leo lingers in the back of my mind, and I know I can't let my guard down. The resolve to take down the Moretti family strengthens within me, fueled by my love and responsibility for my family.

And I can't let any wayward feelings for Leo get in my way.

27

LEO

Standing in the guest room shower, I let the water cascade over me, washing away the dirt and grime from coming to Tia's rescue. And as I lean my palm against the cool rock wall of the shower, I consider my conversation with Tia. The one we had after I saved her life this afternoon.

She all but called me a cold-blooded killer.

And maybe that is what I've become.

It ended in a rather ugly argument. One I'm not proud of. After all my talk about appreciating a woman with opinions, when Tia spoke up today, I shut her down. Not my finest moment, I'll admit. I got so defensive, so prideful, that I refused to hear her out.

But now, for the first time, I'm starting to question my path as a conqueror. My father raised me to be the brutal strategist I've become. I thrive in the spotlight, eager to prove myself not only worthy of the Moretti name but capable of bringing our family to greater heights.

And yet, in the few months I've known Tia—hell, just in the few days since our wedding—she has challenged all of my priorities.

She seems to find my unquestionable strength distasteful, my ambition selfish, and despite my initial disregard for her, I find that I want her approval. I want to be more like the man Tia thinks I'm capable of being. And more than that, I want to be the kind of man my child can be proud of.

I hadn't realized it until today. Until I heard our baby's heartbeat, and Tia called our child a "she." But somehow, knowing that I could have a little girl makes me want to do better, to be better so the world I raise her in will be good enough for our little girl—or boy.

Sighing heavily, I turn off the flow of water and finger-comb my hair out of my face. Then I step out of the shower to quickly towel dry. This room is smaller than the one Tia and I occupy, but the furnishings are just as nice. And it works just fine.

I wanted to give Tia some time alone with her sister. Hopefully, that will help her calm down and see the big picture. Because I don't think she's facing the reality of how close she came to dying today. If she were, I doubt she'd be picking fights about who I may or may not have executed and why.

But that doesn't make her point any less valid.

After pulling on a fresh pair of clothes, I head back out to the main house in search of my father.

"Come in," he says as soon as I knock on his office door. "Ah, Leo. I just heard from Rasco that the Valencia collections took a few... unexpected turns today."

I nod.

"I doubt we'll have any more trouble with the Valencia family for a while. Did you catch the witness?"

Grinding my teeth, I resist the urge to keep the truth from my father. But it won't do any good. "It was Tia," I state flatly.

My father raises his eyebrows, his expression one of mild curiosity. "And?"

"She nearly killed herself trying to run away from me."

"Is she going to be a problem?" he asks more pointedly, seeming entirely disinterested with her survival.

I shake my head, keeping my face stoic.

In truth, I hadn't even broached the topic with Tia of keeping quiet about what she saw today. Because she's the daughter of a don. Regardless of her ideals, I know she understands the importance of keeping things close to the vest. And seeing as our families are allies now, regardless of how she feels about me, she won't betray her father. Therefore, she can't betray me.

"Good," my father says, turning his attention away from me. Then he seems to realize I haven't left the room. "Is there something else?"

"I've been thinking. Are such violent tactics strictly necessary now that we've brought the Guerra family into the fold? It seems that, with law enforcement breathing down our necks and no more rivals threatening to stand in our way, perhaps we can begin to garner more respect from the people in our domain."

My father studies me for a long minute, his gaze cool and speculative. "You're too young to be getting a weak stomach, Leo," he says dismissively. "It takes years to build a reputation that people fear. And that reputation is what will win you respect. You can't afford to be soft right now."

"I'm not being soft. We have the control we've sought. No one else is opposing us. Perhaps now, with a balance of fear and respect, we can start to run Piovosa, not just conquer it. We can use diplomacy and strengthen our alliances."

My father leans back in his chair, steepling his fingers in front of him. "You're talking about mind games and compromise. Save that for Mayor Romney. You're going to need it to win him over. But as far as I'm concerned, we only have one ally. The Guerras. And they have only earned that privilege because you were reckless enough to knock up Don Guerra's daughter. So, in my book, you've already given up our queen to take a mere pawn. Now is the time to reassert our power, not dabble in collaboration and hope for the best."

Clenching my jaw, I try not to let his accusation get to me. Even though he knows I used a condom, he's never going to let me live this one down. If all goes right in my plans, he's perfectly on board with thinking they're great. But as soon as shit hits the fan because of something entirely outside my control, he's all about pinning the blame on me.

"Diplomacy is what you use when you don't have the strength to crush your enemies. When it comes to the men who serve us, it will take an iron fist to ensure we maintain control. You can't afford to let your guard down or show any weakness. They'll sniff it out like a pack of wolves."

His words hang in the air, a heavy decree that settles over me like a suffocating shroud. "But what if there's another way? What if we could rule by inspiring respect and loyalty?"

My father scoffs, the sound echoing in the dim room. "Fear inspires loyalty, Leo. Kill a man in front of his brothers, and they'll be less likely to betray you. Respect, on the other hand, is a luxury. It's earned over time, not given freely. You earn it by taking power, by making sure everyone knows the consequences of crossing us."

He leans forward, eyes narrowing. "You can't afford to be soft, son. The world will chew you up and spit you out if you show any weakness. Remember your priorities. We're Morettis. We don't let emotions dictate our actions."

I clench my fists, the frustration bubbling over. My father's eyes drop to the subtle demonstration of my feelings. A smirk mars his lips, and he raises his eyebrows pointedly.

"From the looks of it, I'd say your pretty little bride has you wound up and wrapped around her finger. I would suggest you get ahold of yourself before your little misstep carries beyond this room. You don't want to lose everything you've worked so hard for over a feminine notion that one can rule with respect and loyalty."

Releasing the tension from my arms on a breath, I nod. Perhaps my father is right. After all, I couldn't have gotten this far without violence. But it was a pretty notion, getting to set aside the death and destruction to peaceably rule over the empire I've accrued.

"Yes, sir," I rasp.

"Good. Now, I would recommend finishing the task you started for the day. Collections have been made, but your men need debriefing and to know what happened with your spy. I would counsel you to consider if a story about your unruly wife is the best one to tell them... considering the conversation we just had. Mm?"

"Understood," I say flatly, then turn to head from my father's office.

As I walk down the hallway, I call Rasco and Johnny for an evening meeting.

28

TIA

Saying goodbye to Maria tonight was hard. It was so wonderful to talk to my sister once again. And now, my resolve is stronger than ever. I need to stick to my guns and play my cards right so I can bring the Morettis down. Even if my feelings for Leo are growing more tangled by the minute.

But someone needs to stop them. I need to find a way to destroy them—Leo in particular—to free my family from the alliance that sounds more and more like a farce.

Sitting on the edge of my bed, I slip into the lingerie I found in my dresser drawer—a bluish-gray satin slip with cream-colored lacing around the low neckline and hem—then wait for Leo to come home. He didn't come back from cleaning up in the guest room. And now it's well past dinner.

I wonder if he had to do some damage control after what happened this afternoon.

When the bedroom door clicks open gently, my eyes cast toward the clock on my nightstand—nearly 9 p.m. It's late.

Leo slips quietly inside, his gaze finding me for a moment before he turns his attention to undressing, stepping out of his shoes as he undoes his tie. "You're awake," he observes, the statement mild.

"I was waiting for you to come back," I say sweetly, clinging to my memories of last night and trying to push the image of Leo killing a man today from my mind.

But he doesn't seem to notice the suggestive tone in my voice. Instead, he offers a grunt and heads into the bathroom to brush his teeth. Sighing, I realize that I might have to get more deliberate if I'm going to convince him I want to move past our disagreement.

As far as I can tell, he's still put out about what I said.

The sink runs briefly, alerting me to the end of his cleaning, and I climb gingerly out of bed, aware that my muscles are starting to protest more audibly about my fall as they stiffen over time. It's a wonder I'm not covered in bruises. Yet.

Hobbling to the end of the bed, I cling to one of the posts, attempting to look seductive.

And when Leo walks through the doorway into the bedroom a moment later, he stops short. "What are you doing out of bed? You're supposed to be resting," he says, crossing the space between us to grasp my shoulders with surprisingly tender care.

"I didn't thank you properly for saving my life," I insist, my eyes widening innocently. I don't think I thanked him at all, actually, and at least addressing that wrong will help my act seem more convincing. "I want to make it up to you now. To show you just how deeply I appreciate your bravery."

"Tia," he warns as I sink onto my knees before him, my stomach knotting nervously.

I've never tried to do this before, and I don't quite know where to begin. Thankfully, he's already naked except for his boxer briefs—his preferred sleeping apparel.

Hooking my fingers inside his waistband, I call upon my best memories of how he did this last night. A shiver runs down my spine as I think of Leo removing my panties with his teeth. I'm not quite so bold. But I imagine I can fumble my way through this.

"Tia," he breathes this time, his objection transitioning into arousal as I wrap my fingers around his length. His cock doesn't look quite as intimidating now. But it immediately starts to swell, growing and hardening into what I've come to expect.

I swallow hard, suddenly unsure of how I'm supposed to fit his thick girth inside my mouth. I try anyway, stretching my lips wide to accommodate him.

Leo groans, his warm hand settling lightly on the crown of my head and stroking down the back of it to pet my hair. I press forward as I suck, taking more of him into my mouth.

"Easy with the teeth, *bella mia*," he rasps, his hips jerking.

I try again, one hand grasping his base as I ease forward over his hardening length.

"Fuck," Leo growls, his fingers tightening in my hair. He seems to thoroughly enjoy the demonstration of appreciation.

I hum, remembering how good it felt when he did that against my clit. Air hisses between his teeth as his cock twitches in my mouth. I'll take that as a good sign. Slowly, I start to get a feel for what to do. Guiding my head forward and back, I let his cock slide past my lips and as far into my mouth as my gag reflex will allow.

His hips form a soft rhythm to match my own, rocking forward and back. And despite the foreign feeling of his cock in my mouth, I feel the familiar heat of arousal pooling in my belly.

"God, you're sexy," Leo rasps, and when I look up the length of his gorgeous body, his eyes watch me with fiery need.

A shuddering breath leaves me as my anticipation escalates. I hadn't realized that pleasuring him like this would turn me on. But seeing the hunger in his eyes sets my skin on fire. My enthusiasm increasing, I take more of him in my mouth with each forward motion until his silken head starts to press against the back of my throat.

Leo groans, his fingers tangling in my hair as he presses gently against the back of my head, intensifying the penetration. I suck in a lungful of air as his cockhead begins to obstruct my breathing with every forward thrust.

Then, out of nowhere, I lose control of my gag reflex. I cough and sputter, pulling back so as not to accidentally bite down on him. His thick girth slips from between my lips, allowing me to suck in a lungful of air. Before I can regain my composure, Leo scoops me up into his arms.

It's effortless, like I weigh little more than a feather. And as he straightens, bringing my body close to his chest, he captures my lips in a fiery kiss. I kiss him back, placing one hand on the side of his cheek as I deepen my level of affection.

He carries me back to the bed and lays me down, taking extra care not to disrupt my ankle. Grasping the bottom of my grayish-blue satin slip, I pull it slowly up over my body and head. And when I reveal that I'm wearing nothing underneath, Leo's eyes light with passionate desire.

It's my first successful attempt at seduction, and my skin tingles with anticipation as he climbs onto the bed with me, crawling between my knees. His hips spread my thighs, and I sink back onto the soft sheets as he falls on top of me.

My ankle twinges slightly from the lightest weight, but before I can decide how to adjust my feet, Leo glances toward it—as if he could read my discomfort in my face. He lightly hooks my knee around his elbow, raising my leg to remove the weight from my injured foot.

Then he does the same with my other leg, and suddenly, I'm on full display, my hips at the ready as my legs spread wide.

"Hmm, I could get used to a view like this," he purrs.

Leaning in, he claims my lips as he bends me in half. I kiss him back fiercely, falling into the passion that swells between us. His thick erection presses against my sex, intensifying my need without even being inside me.

In the heat of the moment, I could easily fall for the tender compassion he shows.

But when I recall the image of the man pleading for his life and Leo's cold-blooded execution right after, I know that these small demonstrations of kindness don't excuse Leo from his sins.

That's not what tonight is about, however.

Tonight is about convincing Leo that I've let go of our differences.

That my gratitude for him saving my life overrides anything I might have said. And I'm so aroused that it won't be hard to demonstrate.

"Please, Leo," I breathe against his lips.

"Please what?" he murmurs, leaning in to kiss my neck.

"I want you."

He releases a soft breath that somehow conveys his own desire, and I feel his iron cock shift, sliding along my slit and pressing between my folds to find my entrance.

I moan as he pushes inside of me, this new angle intensifying the sheer size of him as he stretches me slowly and deliciously. I gasp, my fingers tangling in his seductive curls as I pull his lips to mine. And as he starts to rock inside me, I whimper, overcome with lusty desire.

"You're so wet," he rasps. "Did you like going down on me, Tia?"

"Yes," I breathe, heat blossoming across my skin at the admission.

Leo groans. "You are just the sexiest little minx." He nips playfully at my lower lip as he continues to press inside me and withdraw with special care not to disrupt my ankle.

"I just wanted to show you how thankful I am," I murmur, opening my eyes in round innocence. "I acted horribly ungrateful after you saved my life."

Leo releases a low chuckle even as he presses kisses behind my ear and along my jaw.

"So you decided to give me head? We'll have to argue more often," he teases, and it makes my heart skip a beat.

It shouldn't make me as happy as it does to hear he liked what I did.

But before I can say anything further, Leo reclaims my lips.

He's so slow and gentle. I can tell he's trying to be careful with me. And I wonder if he's worried about hurting me further or if hearing the baby's heartbeat has changed the way he sees me. Whatever it is, this Leo is a world away from the one who used me so roughly on our wedding night.

And despite myself—and my conviction to end his reign of terror—I can't help but relish the way he makes me feel. He builds my desire with deep, penetrating strokes, his cock sliding between my folds until he's buried inside me to the hilt. And each time he fills me up, his hips grind forward against my clit, lighting my soul on fire.

If this is what makeup sex is like, I think I rather like it.

My breaths come hard and fast as my pleasure builds to an intensity I can hardly contain, and I know I won't last much longer. I'm teetering dangerously close to the edge already.

"Come with me, Tia," Leo rasps, his voice strained with the heat of his arousal.

And it sends a jolt of anticipation through my body to know he's ready, too. My clit twitches dangerously, and I nod. Picking my head up off the pillow, I suck his lower lip between my teeth and give it a playful nip.

Leo grunts, his thrusts intensifying as he drives our pleasure home. I cry out, my back arching as I find my release, and my body tightens around his hard length, milking him as I urge him deeper inside me.

He obeys as if on instinct, shoving inside me to the hilt as his cock begins to twitch and throb. Warm wetness floods me, filling me with a deep and sinful satisfaction. And as the ripples of euphoria wash through me, I melt like a puddle in his arms.

We breathe heavily together, sharing the same air as Leo hovers above me, his hips pinning me to the bed. Then he eases my legs back onto the bed, taking special care of my injured ankle.

I can see a world of conflict behind Leo's eyes as he slides out of me, but when he presses a chaste kiss to my lips, I know that, whatever is troubling him, it's not directed at me.

Curious, I'm sorely tempted to ask him what's on his mind.

But before I can work up the courage, he pulls me into his arms, trapping my back against his chest as he spoons me. And after such a trying day, both emotionally and physically, I'm suddenly bone weary.

And as soon as my eyes slide closed, sleep whisks me away to a world of troubled dreams.

29

LEO

The mayor's front reception area is a grand room adorned with polished oak furniture and portraits of the town's illustrious leaders. I take a moment to adjust my tie, glancing at my reflection in the window. Confidence is key, and I can't afford any missteps.

Tia's charm and quick ability to win people over might have opened the door for me, but it's up to me to walk through it.

"He can see you now," his smiley young receptionist says to me and gestures to the door behind her desk.

"Thank you," I say, rising from my chair to pass her.

As I enter his office, Mayor Romney rises from his leather chair, a welcoming smile on his face. "Leo, good to see you. Please, have a seat."

I reciprocate the friendly expression and extend a firm handshake. "Thank you, Mayor. I appreciate you taking the time to meet with me."

"Not at all, my boy."

We settle into the plush chairs, and the meeting begins, Mayor Romney cutting straight to the point with little attempt at polite conversation. I suppose for a man in his position, he has little time to beat around the bush.

"So, you said you have some ideas to help with Piovosa's growth and infrastructure?" he says curiously.

"Yes. I think our location provides a rare opportunity to become something more than a throughway from the interstate not far south. Traffic has been growing in the last few years, but no one is stopping. Why?"

"Because we don't have the appeal of a city like Harrisburg or Philadelphia," he says knowingly.

"Yes, but not for lack of amenities. We have the hotels, the attractions, the entertainment. We're not just rich in beautiful nature but an art culture that could compete with many larger cities. So what makes us so unappealing?"

"Our reputation for violent crime," the mayor states, his eyebrow cocking ironically as his gaze turns pointed.

"Exactly, a reputation well earned from decades of a few reputable families taking advantage of their positions of power to manipulate the system. No one moves here because, regardless of where they land, they'll be caught in the middle of some territory dispute or unwittingly challenging the authority of one man's pride or another."

"I feel as though you're about to get to the point," the mayor says dryly.

Leaning forward so my elbows rest on my knees, I cut to the chase. "I believe in the potential for collaboration. Our town deserves the best, and I'm willing to offer my support to ensure that happens."

He arches an eyebrow, clearly skeptical. "Support? From someone like you? What would that look like?"

I take a deep breath, choosing my words carefully. "I have a proposal. My men have skills, resources, and a commitment to order. I've been investing heavily in trying to break the mold of several powerful families who are running our town solely to their benefit and liking. But it occurred to me that we could work together to achieve a more efficient system. I'm willing to bring my men into the fold, to work as an extension of your government, to ensure the safety and prosperity of this town."

Mayor Romney leans back in his chair, his fingers tapping rhythmically on the polished mahogany. "And what's in it for you, Leo?" His question is shrewd, cutting through my attempt to appeal to his more idyllic side.

I need to play my cards carefully. "I've been pouring considerable sums into maintaining the current state of affairs. If I can have a more direct say in law enforcement, it would not only benefit me but also ensure a more secure and orderly town. Think of it as a win-win."

He considers my words, his eyes never leaving mine. After what feels like an eternity, he nods. "An interesting proposition. I must admit my police force has long been incapable of putting an end to the back alley crime that plagues this town. But I need more than just words. I need to see tangible results to make me believe you can actually *help* protect Piovosa."

It's not a flat-out no, something I'd been prepared for. And I wait patiently as he seems to mull it over.

"We could have your men provide security for a few of our government events," the mayor suggests, leaning back in his chair. "It would be a great way to test the waters, build trust."

I nod, seizing the opportunity. "That sounds like a solid plan. Let's start with a test run."

The mayor's eyes narrow slightly as if he's gauging my sincerity. Considering this is a scheme to put a buffer between my own plans and the men who could lock me away if I'm not careful, it seems the mayor has a strong enough nose to sniff out suspicious activity. It's only a question of how well I can play my role.

"There's a charity ball the Friday after this coming one," he says after another long pause. "How about your men coordinate with the Piovosa police force to provide security for that? It would be a good chance for us to observe how well they handle the responsibility."

A charity ball? "Perfect." I maintain a composed expression as I accept the offer.

"And, of course, I would hope you and your lovely wife will be able to attend the event as my guests," he says, with an undercurrent of expectation.

"We would be honored," I agree, but a twinge of discomfort grips me when I remember Tia's twisted ankle.

The mayor seems to notice my hesitation. "Something wrong?" he asks, a glimmer of suspicion in his eyes.

"No, no, not at all," I say quickly. "It's just that, unfortunately, Tia met with a little accident. She twisted her ankle, and the doctor advised her to rest. So I'm not sure she'll be able to attend. It's a shame. I have no doubt she would have loved a charity ball. And it would have given me an excuse to dance with her again. Plus, I know how much she enjoys your family."

The mayor's suspicion intensifies, and I know that it, along with his hesitation to work with me, stems from my reputation for violence. Not that I can blame him. I've only earned this opportunity through the mayor's affection for Tia. From the looks of it, he suspects me of hurting her.

"That's terrible. I hope she's alright," he says pointedly, the undercurrent of tension growing.

I need to act quickly to salvage the situation and avoid the mayor suspecting I'm hiding something. Scrambling to recover our rapport, I assure him, "She's in good spirits. Just less than happy with being told to take it easy. My wife isn't one for idle bed rest."

The mayor humphs, though, from the glimmer in his eye, I know he's thinking about Tia's lively energy—the way she overcame a supposed bloody nose to finish dinner with his family just days ago. And the memory sparks an idea in my mind.

"Actually, why don't you all join us for dinner?" I suggest. "Tia can share her rather daring adventure, and you can put your mind at ease that she's recovering safely. I'm sure she would love the company while she's housebound as well."

After a moment's contemplation, Mayor Romney's expression softens, and he nods. "Dinner sounds like a wonderful idea. It would be good to catch up with Tia. The poor girl seems to have an uncommon amount of misfortune."

You have no idea, I think darkly as I consider how much of a misfortune meeting me has proven to be. Once upon a time, I didn't think twice about using Tia without concerning myself with the consequences she might face. Now, it seems that despite my best efforts to give her comfort and a sense of peace in her new role, she's determined to find trouble.

"We're available this evening," the mayor suggests, cutting into my train of thought. "Will that work?"

Likely, the short notice is his attempt to get ahead of any effort I might make to avoid looking guilty.

I nod, my smile unwavering. "Absolutely. I'll have my chef prepare something special. Consider it a small celebration for the start of this new partnership."

The mayor nods, but his expression still holds a hint of trepidation that hadn't been there when I first arrived. It would seem my success in this endeavor might rely more heavily on Tia than I ever could have imagined.

Hopefully, she's up for painting me in a good light tonight. And though she's shown me nothing but gratitude and dangerously enticing attention in the days since our fight, I can't help the feeling that she hasn't forgiven me for what she saw in the woods that day.

She hasn't brought it up, but I can see it in her eyes, as if the image of me pulling that trigger plays in her mind on repeat.

It feels a bit risky to be welcoming the mayor back into my home when such a heavy secret still weighs on Tia's mind. She could possibly destroy all the progress I've made—and throw me into a thicket of legal troubles—if she decides to let slip the reason she was running.

But based on the way Mayor Romney's attitude shifted when he heard Tia was hurt, I think it would be far riskier to let him sit on his suspicion any longer than is strictly necessary.

"I look forward to tonight, then," he agrees, rising from his chair to shake my hand once again.

It's a subtle gesture to indicate our meeting is over. And frankly,

I'm grateful because, without Tia present to diffuse the tension, I feel as though I'm walking on eggshells every time I speak.

Still, despite barely scraping by in a precarious conversation, I leave Mayor Romney's office with a newfound sense of accomplishment. I've managed to salvage a potentially disastrous situation.

Tia might be out of commission for a while when it comes to social events, but her charm and our invitation for dinner will keep suspicion at bay.

The chess pieces are moving in my favor, and I can't help but smile as I contemplate the upcoming moves in this delicate dance. It's a small step toward the chance to reshape the power dynamics in this town. And my plan puts Mayor Romney unknowingly at the center.

30

TIA

Sun streams through the heavy brocade curtains, casting a warm, golden glow across the room. I watch the dust particles dance in the sunlight, a distraction from the dull ache in my twisted ankle. The crutches lean against the bedside table, a constant reminder of my current state.

I've spent the majority of the past few days in bed, listening to the doctor's advice to take it easy. I haven't wanted to push my luck, mostly because of my anxiety over the trauma my baby might have suffered. But I've also been phenomenally stiff and sore from head to toe until this morning.

My ankle feels as weak and useless as when I sprained it, and the small lump at the base of my skull from hitting my head is still a little tender. But the rest of me is on the mend. Even the dark bruises that color my wrist don't hurt as bad this morning.

The distinct fingerprints from where Leo grabbed me to stop my fall raise conflicting emotions within me. I trace them delicately, mesmerized by the strength with which he held on. The sheer determination on his face as he pulled me to safety using one arm. It could almost be enough to prove he truly cares for me.

That day has been coming back to me in flashes of brilliant clarity

—the scenes like snapshots in my mind. The terror of looking down to find the jagged ground a hundred feet below me. Leo's arms lifting me effortlessly from my vulnerable state. His breath soft by my ear as he reached up to cut the roots tangled around my foot. His steady calm when he told me we would have to climb.

But what sticks with me most is the intense concentration on his face as he watched for an opportunity to pull me up, the fear in his eyes when I lost my footing right near the top of my climb. And the fierce desperation with which he saved me.

It shakes my confidence in my decision to take him down. And at the same time, I can't stop thinking about the man he killed in cold blood. That could be my father if the alliance between our families continues to grow more tense. I don't know how I'm supposed to trust Leo. In anything. Because he can be so incredibly tender at times. And utterly brutal at others.

But my family is depending on me, and that, more than anything, is what drives me from bed today. Collecting the crutches Luigi provided to give me a bit more freedom around the house, I tuck them under my armpits and head toward the door leading from our bedroom.

My twisted ankle hampers my movements, a cruel reminder of what took place after I fled from Leo's brutal scene at the cottage. That man, falling lifeless to the ground, blood staining the dirt around him. I can't shake the image from my mind. But with my current physical state, I'm confined, unable to explore what else might have taken place there. I can't gather evidence concerning his execution either.

So, instead, I'm confined to looking for any weaknesses Leo might have hidden somewhere around the house. He must have a few skeletons in his closet. And I know the best place to start.

His office.

He showed it to me casually the night I first met him, when he was giving me a tour around the house. And I haven't cared to explore it until now. But it seems the most likely place he would want to keep something locked away that he doesn't want me to find.

The halls are fairly quiet as usual, aside from my thumping three-legged walk. The servants move with silent intent, the Moretti men I pass only offering respectful nods on their way to do Don Moretti's bidding. I'm starting to get a concept of which men work more closely with the don, seeing as he seems to operate from the estate more often, whereas Leo is gone for the better part of every day.

Where normally, I might welcome the brief interactions and wish for more human connection, today, nervous tension makes me jumpy every time I hear footsteps. Still, I hobble around the house, determined to find something, anything, that will help me uncover a chink in Leo's armor.

With no small amount of effort or exertion, I finally arrive at the door to Leo's office. With bated breath, I look up and down the hallway to ensure no one's watching.

Then I reach tentatively to place my hand on the cool metal knob. I twist, but it doesn't budge. It's locked. It would seem it's off limits when he's not home, a fortress I can't breach without drawing attention to my intentions. And I can't risk alerting the staff to any suspicious activity.

I wipe my brow as a trickle of sweat makes its way down my temple. Hiking around the expansive floor plan is a lot more challenging on crutches. Worrying my lip, I debate where I might look next. I've already explored our bedroom from top to bottom with no success.

I wish I could talk it through more with my sister. Maria's support feels like my lifeline. During her last visit, we hatched a plan. Or at least we agreed that I would collect what information I can so we can figure out how best to hit Leo where it hurts.

But we agreed it wouldn't be safe to discuss sensitive matters over the phone, not when the walls have ears. So her visits are how we'll make our clandestine meetings. If we spend our time in the garden and keep a close eye out for eavesdroppers, we should be able to share information without risking our family's safety.

Still, that won't help me now.

I debate how reckless it might be to try exploring Don Moretti's office. I doubt I could get near it without a very valid reason for being there. But when no other places to look come to mind, I start to wander in that direction, trying to come up with some excuse to be in that part of the house.

"Tia, what are you doing out of bed?" Leo's tone is disapproving as it chases me down the hallway, and it makes my stomach lurch.

Slowly, I turn, wiping the anxiety from my face as I prepare to lie through my teeth.

Worry lines etch my husband's forehead as he strides toward me, leaving me surprisingly unstable.

And I stammer, searching for an excuse. "I was just... I needed some fresh air. What are you doing home so early?"

Leo's eyes narrow in suspicion, and ignoring my question completely, he closes the distance between us. He takes my crutches from beneath my arms and leans them against the wall. Then he effortlessly scoops me up in his arms. The unexpected gentleness contrasts sharply with his stern expression.

"What are you doing?" I demand, exasperation tinging my voice even as my arm wraps around his shoulders. And though I refuse to admit it, my body is immediately grateful that I'm off my feet. My ankle's throbbing miserably, and my armpits feel raw and chafed from the foreign mode of transportation.

"You're supposed to be taking it easy. Remember? Putting unnecessary strain on your ankle could prolong your recovery or endanger the baby."

The mention of the baby makes my stomach tighten. Maybe I did push myself a bit harder than I should have. As driven as I am to find how I might bring the Morettis down, I don't want to hurt our child in the process.

Obviously, I can't admit why I overexerted myself. I take a deep breath to release an exasperated growl. But in such close proximity to Leo and his intoxicatingly masculine cologne, I'm suddenly intensely aware of how sweaty I must smell.

"I can't lie around all day," I insist to distract myself. "I did that for the last two days, and I'm going to go crazy just staying in bed. Besides, the exercise helps with the stiffness."

Leo sighs as he carries me effortlessly back toward our room. And it reminds me distinctly of the impressive distance he carried me home the other day. The feeling of his arms around me makes my pulse flutter involuntarily.

"I understand, but your health and the baby's well-being are my priority. If you're stiff, we can schedule you for a massage or something."

"I'm a big girl, Leo. I know how to take care of myself," I insist.

"Tia, your ankle's swollen. You pushed yourself too far," he states flatly, closing the discussion.

Heat pools in my cheeks as I look toward my feet and realize he's right. My right ankle is nearly twice the size of my left, and it's an angry shade of red around the edges of my bandage.

"You need to stay in bed and ice it until our guests arrive for dinner," he commands, brooking no argument.

The mention of guests catches my attention. "Guests? Who's coming?"

Leo hesitates for a moment, the strain in his voice revealing more than he intends. "Mayor Romney and his family. I met with him today, and he was concerned when he heard you got hurt. I invited them to join us for dinner to put them at ease."

The realization hits me that this dinner must be important to him. I don't know what his business with the mayor might be, but the mayor's approval seems to hold some significance to Leo. I just can't quite put my finger on what it is. My mind races, trying to connect the dots, but the pieces of the puzzle remain elusive.

I force a smile, feigning enthusiasm. "That's thoughtful of you, Leo. I'll do my best to be presentable."

Placing me gently on the bed, Leo straightens, his eyes softening as he looks down at me. "Rest, Tia. I don't want you to strain yourself. They won't be here for a few more hours."

He turns and heads back toward the door, and my stomach knots inexplicably at the thought of him leaving.

"Where are you going?" I ask, feeling suddenly vulnerable.

He turns back to look at me, his gray-green eyes lighting with surprise, and I wonder if he can't hear the anxiety in my voice. "I was going to get you some ice. And your crutches."

Fresh heat blossoms in my cheeks. "Oh. Right. Thank you."

Leo chuckles, the sound low and somehow soothing. "You're welcome."

As Leo leaves the room, closing the door behind him, I'm left alone with my thoughts. The room feels suffocating, the weight of secrecy pressing down on me. I need to find a way to uncover Leo's secrets without jeopardizing our family, but it makes things so much harder when he's playing nice.

I hate it. This uncertainty.

I can't deny the facts—Leo has manipulated me multiple times, abused my trust, and used our relationship to prove his strength and lack of mercy to the people he wants to crush. But when he's sweet, it never fails to disarm me.

Maybe it's because it feels so genuine. That hint of disapproval and exasperation is just enough to make me believe he truly cares. And that makes the truth of his indifference that much harder to bear.

31

LEO

"Just let me help you take a shower," I insist as Tia wobbles on her one good foot, her hand clasping the glass as she tries to lean her crutches close enough to the shower entry.

"I'm fine," she says, reaching for the stone bench that sits along the far wall.

But it's too far of a stretch, and she pitches forward with a gasp, her hands shifting to catch her fall. I step forward, closing the distance between us as I catch her just below her breasts, trying to avoid putting pressure on her stomach.

"Why are you so fucking stubborn?" I demand, picking her up and setting her gently onto the bench.

"I'm not stubborn," she objects, her cheeks coloring.

I give her a flat look, then pull my shirt up over my head and toss it onto the bathroom floor. Undoing my pants, I toss them and my boxers into the same pile, then turn on the water and wait for it to get warm.

Once it's the right temperature, I take Tia's hand, interlocking our fingers so I can better balance her, then I guide her carefully to her feet. She leans heavily on my arm as she moves beneath the stream, her shoulder blade pressing against my chest as she lets the water rinse her clean.

Reaching with my free hand, I grab her loofa and hold it beneath the liquid soap. With my thumb, I squirt some onto the mesh ball, then I bring it to her back to lightly scrub circles across her creamy skin.

Tia scoops her hair out of the way, revealing a patch of goosebumps along her shoulders and neck. I smile, silently enjoying the way her body responds to me. When she glances over her shoulder, her look is shy but knowing.

To my surprise, she lets me scrub every inch of her, her eyes fluttering closed as I lightly circle her breasts and make my way up her inner thighs. We rinse her clean, then I guide her back onto the seat so she can shampoo her hair.

It's rather sexy watching her massage the suds into her scalp and down her long, luscious locks. And this time, when I help her stand, she seems much more willing to accept my help.

I turn her to face me this time, unashamed by my arousal, as I grasp her hips and hold her firmly against me, supporting her weight while leaving her hands free. She leans back, putting her hair beneath the heavy stream of water and running her fingers through her hair to wash the soap from her scalp.

The view is more than a little pleasing as her pert nipples harden, and I get an eyeful of the delicate curves of her body. She really is fit, an understated kind of athletic that I hadn't really considered before.

"Do you run?" I ask, suddenly curious.

Tia laughs. "Why? Do you think I would have gotten away if that cliff hadn't stopped me?"

"Not a chance," I growl, enjoying her playful response. "But you are fast."

"Well, I should think so after having to chase four younger sisters around all the time."

Tia reaches for the conditioner, balancing on her one foot. She works that into her hair as well, our bodies causing delicious friction as I hold her close. Then she leans back into the stream of water once more.

"All set?" I ask as she straightens, wiping her face clean of water.

"Yes, thank you." Her voice is almost apologetic, as though she regrets arguing with me in the beginning. But I know better than to expect her to say as much.

Leaning around her, I turn off the faucet. Then I scoop her into my arms. She doesn't fight me this time. Instead, her arm falls naturally around my shoulders as I step backward out of the shower, careful not to hit the glass with her feet.

"Grab a towel," I say, leaning so it's within reach.

Tia grins as she obeys, grabbing both towels and pulling them onto her lap. And as I carry her into the bedroom, she unfolds one to wrap it around my shoulders.

"So thoughtful." I press a kiss to her lips, then set her gently on the bed.

She smiles up at me as she dries off where she sits. I towel off beside her, then wrap the terry cloth around my waist.

"You feeling daring?" I joke, heading toward the closet with the intent of picking out her clothes.

Laughing, she starts to towel dry her hair. "Do your worst—but..."

Her face flushes as I pause in the doorway, turning to meet her eyes.

"Maybe pick something with long sleeves." Tia raises her wrist tentatively, revealing the dark ring of fingerprints from where I grabbed her to catch her fall.

My stomach knots, knowing that I hurt her, even if I didn't have much choice. I nod, disappearing into the closet a moment later. When I come out, Tia is wearing her towel around her body like a mini dress, her foot up on the bed as she attempts to rewrap her ace bandage.

From the grimace that mars her full lips, it's not going well.

"Does the concept of asking for help completely elude you?" I demand, only half joking as I toss the long-sleeve burgundy dress I picked out for her onto the bed.

She pauses in her efforts, looking up at me with an almost bashful face. "I feel so helpless," she groans.

But when I settle onto the bed next to her, she willingly relinquishes her half-wrapped foot. "Do you mind?" she asks tentatively.

I give her a half smile and cradle her calf, then glance up to meet her eyes. "Now, was that so hard?"

Smiling softly, Tia leans back onto her palms. "I guess not."

"Good. Then try it more often." Focusing on the wrap, I loop it slowly beneath her heel and then back up around her ankle, trying to mimic the way Dr. Luca wrapped it. "There. Can I help you get dressed?" I offer, fully expecting her to turn me down.

"I haven't picked out my panties yet," she says, glancing toward her dresser drawers.

"Perfect." I flash her a wicked smile, then I start to take her dress off its hanger.

"What do you mean, 'perfect'? I am not about to go through dinner with the mayor and his family, without panties, in *that* dress," she insists.

"Why not?" I lift it, admiring the short, flowing layers of the gauzy skirt.

"Leo," she scolds, leveling me with a deadly serious gaze. "If you can't dress me properly, then I'll just have to dress myself."

Stepping toward her, I capture Tia's chin with my fingers, tipping her face until she's looking up at me. "I'll let you get away with wearing panties this time," I murmur. "Because you're hurt. But I promise you, you won't get away with it forever."

Tia's breath catches, and her cheeks flush a beautiful shade of pink, making me smile with satisfaction. I release her then, and her eyes follow me as I head to her dresser and pick out a pair of panties and a bra, then I bring them back over.

She dresses easily enough, giving me a fantastic show when she removes her towel to don the lingerie I picked out. After, I carry her to her vanity chair, leaving her to her makeup while I get dressed.

Rather than dry her hair and style it down, as Tia often does, tonight she pulls it up into an elegant ballet bun atop her head.

"Shall I carry you to dinner?" I offer, not entirely put out by having an excuse to hold her in my arms once again.

Tia smiles. "While I very much enjoy making you carry me everywhere, I don't think it would be the most dignified way to welcome our guests," she points out. "Especially considering the length of my dress."

"I'm starting to get the impression that you don't approve of my fashion sense," I quip.

She laughs, the sound warm and melodic, and it warms my chest. "I assure you, that's not the case. Just maybe your more... creative ideas. Imagine if I'd said yes to both. I'd be flashing our two new friends and their children before they've even had a drink to calm their nerves."

With a Cheshire grin, I hand Tia her crutches. "I assure you I would have saved that pleasure exclusively for myself."

Holding the door for my wife, I follow her out into the hall, and with her slow and slightly laborious progress, we make it to the entry just in time for Luigi to open the door for our guests.

"Welcome," Tia says graciously, her lips spreading in a wide smile as the four Romney family members step inside.

Leah and Hannah scan the grandiose entry with wide eyes and open mouths, seeming taken by the opulence that they're experiencing for the first time.

"I *told* you she was a princess," Hannah whispers to her sister. "She lives in a castle."

Tia's eyes meet mine as she covers her smile with her fingers, and I can't help but chuckle.

"Thank you for joining us this evening," I say as Signora Romney gives Tia a gentle but affectionate hug. "I hope you're hungry."

"Famished," Mayor Romney says, patting his robust belly.

"I thought we might enjoy dinner on the terrace, if that sounds nice," I offer. "As my wife would tell it, she might just lose her mind if she has to stay inside any longer."

They laugh, agreeing that the beautiful summer night and the soft glow that lingers on the horizon would make a perfect ambiance.

"How are you, Tia?" Signora Romney asks, her voice concerned as we all walk past the mirrored wall separating the entry from the ballroom. "Luke told me you took a fall and sprained your ankle?"

"Oh, just wait until you hear the story," Tia says, her tone emphatic. She rolls her eyes as if in exasperation with herself. "But I'm doing much better now. The doctor thought I might be well within a week or so."

"If she rests and stops overexerting herself," I say pointedly. "Signora Romney, I'm hoping I might enlist your help in talking some sense into her. Today, when I got home, she'd worked herself into a sweat wandering around the house."

"Running from something, my dear?" Mayor Romney jokes, but I can't help noticing the slight edge that comes with it. He's prying for any sign that she's in danger.

But Tia laughs, the sound disarming any suspicion. "Yes, running from boredom. I'll tell you, on a cold winter's day, I could curl up with a good book for hours. But condemn me to bed for days straight during a beautiful summer like this? I don't think so."

Reaching the terrace beyond the ballroom, I pull out the nearest chair for Tia, and she settles into it gratefully. Before anyone can say a word about it, Leah and Hannah pick the chairs on either side of her.

"I'm so sorry," Signora says, her hands going to her cheeks as she sees I've been ousted from my seat beside my wife by her two daughters.

"It's quite alright," I say, taking the seat across from her, next to Leah. "I can't say I blame them."

"Not to mention he's been hovering over me since I hurt my ankle," Tia says, her tone somehow both affectionate and exasperated.

"I'm glad to hear he's taking such care of you," the mayor says, and once again, I'm grateful to Tia for knowing exactly how to paint me in a flattering light.

"Wine?" I offer the couple, and they accept with friendly smiles.

A moment later, the hors d'oeuvres arrive, all foods I've confirmed with the kitchen have been acceptable to Tia's palate.

Foods that won't leave her sprinting—or hobbling—for the bathroom.

"So, tell us, Tia, what's the story behind your ankle?" Signora Romney insists as we sit and sip wine.

Despite my trust in Tia's expertise to say the right thing in challenging situations, anxiety still grips me as I stress over whether Tia might let something slip.

But Tia does an impressive job of skipping past any incriminating information from the very start as she describes the event. "So, there I am, running near the far end of the Moretti property, only this estate is so monstrous and enormous that, despite my best efforts to learn the land, I still can't find my way half the time. And I hadn't realized there was a cliff nearby."

Signora Romney gasps, covering her mouth with her hand as her eyes grow wide.

"Yeah, exactly," Tia says, validating her fears. "I was running headlong toward it, but with the lighting, I didn't see it was a drop-off. And Leo's too far behind me, so when he calls me, I can't tell what he's trying to say. Then, all of a sudden, the ground just vanishes from beneath my feet."

"How far did you fall?" Signora Romney asks with bated breath.

"Well, we reckon I only fell about ten feet. But I assure you, that cliff was over a hundred feet high." Tia pauses, letting that sink in for a moment. Then, she finishes the explanation to relieve the suspense. "See, when Leo called to me, I turned and must have snagged a tree root with my foot. It tripped me. And it also saved my life."

She glances my way, her eyes softening as she smiles. "Well, it at least stopped my fall. It was Leo's quick thinking and bravery that really saved me. He scaled the cliff to come get me. Helped cut me free of the roots that I got my foot tangled in. Helped me climb back up despite my injured ankle."

The mayor and his wife prove a rapt audience as Tia describes my heroic efforts to save her in great detail, describing the numerous times she thought she was going to plunge to her death only for me to rescue her time and again.

It's a brilliant story, one that showcases me as the knight in shining armor. By the end of it, I could almost believe I'm a hero. Only I know the truth of why she was running in the first place.

At the end of her story, Tia receives a round of applause followed by immense relief from the mayor and his wife.

"I'm just so grateful to know that you're okay. After such a close call..." Signora Romney is almost overcome with emotion, her eyes shining with unshed tears as she reaches across her daughter's plate to give Tia's hand a warm squeeze.

"Thank you. Me too." Tia gives a breathy smile, her face relaxing after getting through the strenuous retelling of an experience that is clearly still fresh in her physical memory.

And it seems like we might just be out of the woods when it comes to tiptoeing around the condemning facts.

"Why were you running in the first place?" Mayor Romney asks, his question like a punch to the gut.

The table falls silent for a beat, and when Tia meets my eyes, I'm sure all my carefully laid plans are about to unravel with this one loose thread.

32

TIA

The table falls deathly silent, and when my gaze travels instinctively to Leo, I can see it in his eyes—he's put everything on the line here.

For whatever reason, he does not want the mayor to know about the blatant murder he performed in the woods—despite his apparent comfort with most people knowing about his violent grab for power.

I could teach him a valuable lesson here and now: destroy whatever relationship he's trying to build with the mayor, possibly even get him arrested for murder. *But what are the odds that the mayor would be able to prove Leo's guilt?*

And besides, saying anything now wouldn't bring Leo to his knees. It might hurt him. It might create a significant roadblock in whatever his goals are with the mayor, but it wouldn't destroy him. Anything short of that will only come back to hurt me, my family, and my unborn baby.

I need to wait for the opportune moment.

Even if it kills me to be patient.

Quickly doing my best to recover, I give another incredulous laugh as I tear my eyes from Leo's before their stricken expression can send me into a full panic. "You're not going to believe me," I confess to buy myself time to come up with an elaborate lie.

Then it hits me, and I boldly meet the mayor's inquisitive eyes. "Leo and I were enjoying a picnic together in the woods when this black bear waltzed right into camp. No fear, no shame. I, of course, panicked and ran. Of course, knowing the hazard in the direction I was running, Leo came after me. But I was just so terrified, I couldn't stop myself until it was too late."

The mayor releases a low whistle, and for a moment, I worry that I overdid my tale. It won't do us any good if he can see through my lie.

"You must be one of the bravest men I've ever met," the mayor's wife confesses.

And to my immense relief, the mayor agrees, his support emphatic. "What happened to the bear?" he asks then, his eyes shifting between me and Leo.

At this point, Leo cuts in—thankfully, as I'm running out of steam on my story, my confidence balancing on a knife's edge. But his confidence smooths the rough edges of my fabrication with expert ease. "The bear honestly seemed more interested in the picnic than either of us. He didn't follow when I went running after Tia. He must have just seen the picnic basket as a good free lunch. The food was gone by the time I went back to collect it the next day."

"Well, it looks like you're finally getting that picnic, eh?" the mayor asks jovially as our meal arrives.

The rich smell of stuffed shells fills the air, and I glance at Leo gratefully. It's one of the few dishes I can't seem to tire of now that I'm pregnant. And it works wonders at keeping my stomach calm and happy.

He gives me a playful wink, and butterflies erupt in my stomach as the unexpected gesture takes me completely off guard. Why I would find a wink so entirely sexy, I can't say. But I'm suddenly warm with giddiness.

When the conversation shifts to a more casual exchange, I turn my attention to little Leah and Hannah. They ask me a hundred and one questions about the castle I live in and if the silverware ever starts to sing and dance.

It makes me smile, their excitement on the same level as if they were visiting Disney World for the first time. And their giggles fill the room as they talk about wanting to find a prince charming just like I have. It melts my heart and, at the same time, makes me intensely aware of how different perception can be from reality.

And though Signora Romney tries to rein them in, their enthusiasm is unrelenting.

By the end of the evening, my cheeks hurt from smiling so much —in a very good way. I genuinely adore the Romney family.

"Honey, don't you think it's time we put the children to bed?" Signora Romney suggests lightly, placing her hand on her husband's arm.

He glances at his watch, and his eyes widen. "Is that the time? Yes, I think we might have overstayed our welcome. We'll let Signora Moretti get her rest as well," he says, giving me a warm smile.

"Believe me, I've appreciated the distraction," I assure him.

"Ah, speaking of distractions, before we go, I wanted to reiterate the invitation I gave your husband earlier today. We completely understand if you can't attend, but Alicia and I would love it if you could come to our charity event the weekend after this coming one— as our honored guests." The mayor places his hand over his heart in what I've come to learn is his signature gesture of heartfelt sincerity.

"Oh, I would love that!" I say, glancing at Leo to be certain. And when he smiles, I turn my attention back to the mayor. "We'll be there. Even if I have to attend on crutches," I promise.

"Wonderful. We'll send you a proper invitation shortly," he beams.

We all rise, the mayor collecting one sleepy daughter as Signora Romney gathers up the other. They walk slowly, keeping pace with me despite my stunted speed. And as Alicia and I walk in companionable silence, I listen to the mayor as he speaks with Leo.

"I look forward to working with you," he says as we reach the entryway.

And though I don't know what working relationship they must have agreed upon, I can see the significance in their partnership. This is a big deal for Leo—something he's been working toward for some time now.

"Thank you for a wonderful evening," Signora Romney says, offering me a smile as she holds her sleeping daughter.

"Get home safe," I insist as she and the mayor tiptoe through the door.

Leo and I wait at the door until they're all packed into their SUV, and the mayor pulls away.

As soon as their tail lights mosey down the drive, Leo turns to me, his eyes warm as he steps close and cradles my face between his palms.

Then he leans in to kiss me passionately.

It's soft and sensual, his lips gentle as they part mine so his tongue can trace them in the most tantalizing way. I positively melt, though I can't lean into him as I would like to because the crutches make an awkward third wheel.

When he finally draws back, I breathe, "What was that for?"

"You never cease to amaze me," he murmurs, his hazel eyes warm in a way that takes my breath away. "You're brilliant, and I'm starting to see what your father meant when he said I now possess one of Earth's greatest gifts."

Stunned by his statement, I don't quite know what to say. "Is that all my father said?" I ask, shocked that he would say something so affectionate—especially after how terribly I failed our family.

"Well, he also said I can either cherish my gift as it should be cherished, or I can squander it and learn too late about the consequences."

My heart hammers against my ribs as I try to process my father's words. But Leo's far too close—and after that kiss, I can no longer think straight.

"Now more than ever," he murmurs, his voice alluring, "I'm convinced I should cherish you as the gift you're proving to be."

My breath catches at the shockingly romantic statement. My lips part as if to say something, but I can't think of the words.

Leo doesn't seem to mind, however. He simply takes my crutches from me with a daring smile. "I think you've done more than enough walking for the day," he insists, then he picks me up like a bride, carrying both me and my crutches back to our bedroom.

I can't find it in me to object; I'm so immensely grateful to be off my feet and cradled in Leo's strong arms.

But something doesn't sit right with me about my father's statement. It gives me an odd sense of foreboding. And for the first time, I find I'm thinking twice about his insistence that I make this marriage work with Leo.

At the time, when my parents sat me down and told me how critical it was to marry him, I felt slightly abandoned, like the fate of my family rested entirely on my shoulders. If I didn't sacrifice my happiness, then I might be killing us all.

Maybe that was true. Maybe my choice to marry Leo saved my family.

But it makes me nervous to think my father could be using me as a distraction. While I've been determined to hatch my own plan to destroy Leo, he might have used my pregnancy and marriage as a window of opportunity.

I'm willing to risk a lot for my family, but with a baby to think of, it's not just my welfare that I need to look out for now. And while my father's words could seem so loyal and loving, I wonder if they might not have a darker meaning.

Was I just a lamb led to slaughter?

Perhaps I've been too naive from the start. Perhaps, while I'd hoped I might mend the damage I caused, hope was already lost. Maybe I was dead to my parents the moment Leo dropped me on their front porch.

If so, my father's words could spell ruin. Not just for me and Leo. But also my baby.

33

LEO

Tia's cheek rests lightly against my shoulder, her body a comforting weight in my arms as I carry her through the doorway and into our bedroom. She's quiet enough, I almost wonder if she's fallen asleep in my arms.

And the feel of her closeness, the fresh citrusy scent of her body wash, and the memory of her charming laughter tonight fills me with a warmth—a happiness—that I'm not quite sure what to do with. No woman has ever made me feel this way before.

I take her straight to bed, placing her on the soft sheets, and her deep onyx eyes meet mine with silent gratitude.

"Thanks for carrying me so much," she murmurs.

"You're welcome." My lips tilt into a crooked smile, and rather than leaving her to get ready for bed, I kick off my shoes and join her on our king-sized mattress.

I know I can come across as abrasive and short-tempered at times, and I would never deny that I'm difficult. But after such an impromptu dinner tonight that Tia met with flawless grace and charm, I'm determined to show her the appreciation she deserves for saving my ass with the mayor. Because I know that without her boastful description of my heroics, her ability to look past all the harm I've caused her, and recognize the good in me, I never could have won him over.

Even still, I sense our relationship hangs by a threat, one that Tia spun into existence with sheer determination and surprising willingness.

Propping myself on one elbow, I peer down at my striking raven-haired bride, and she looks up at me with fathomless emotion in her eyes. When I lower my lips to kiss her passionately, her eyelids flutter closed, and I press my lips to hers with all the tenderness I feel for her at this moment.

Tia sighs sweetly, the sound so delicate and feminine that it makes my body ache for her—not in a lustful, ravenous way, but with an almost painful urge to protect her. Cradling her cheek with my palm, I stroke the pad of my thumb across her silken skin as our tongues dance together in a delicious dance.

And when Tia's hand finds mine, cradling it against her face, I want to never stop kissing her. Her fingers brush lightly across the back of my hand and trace up my wrist to my elbow, where my cuffs are rolled to, then she trails a soft line back down to my knuckles.

Pulling back, I give her a soft smile and catch her delicate pianist's fingers. Then I brush a kiss across them before resting them lightly on her belly. A jolt of anticipation snaps through me. The simple gesture brings into sharp focus the fact that Tia and I are having a child together. That our child is growing safe and warm beneath her palm.

And it fills me with wonder.

"You're magnificent," I breathe, tracing a finger along her jawline and down her throat, following the line of her collarbone and then sternum until I reach the gauzy red fabric of her dress.

Tia's breath catches, her breasts rising, and I lean in to press a kiss to the swell of one.

"God, Leo, you're driving me crazy," she breathes, her chest rising and falling more rapidly now.

"Oh?" I tease, quirking an eyebrow as I move down the bed to be near her feet. Then I take her uninjured ankle and lift it to press soft kisses in a trail up her leg. "How about now?"

Tia moans, her head tipping back as I reach her thigh and suck the smooth skin lightly between my teeth.

"Yes," she whispers.

I can't wait to find out how wet she is for me. But tonight, I intend to take my time and properly worship her body. Hands gliding up her pale thighs, I guide the flowing layers of her skirt up inch by inch.

And all the while, my lips creep higher up her inner thigh.

Tia gasps as I reach the peak and brush my nose across her lace-clad slit, inhaling her intoxicating scent at the same time.

"I could eat you up," I growl, peering up the length of her body to meet her eyes.

Her expression is agonized with longing, and I smile. Then I turn my attention to slowly undressing her. Starting with her hair, I reach up to the dark knot sitting high on her head. I find the band holding it in place and gently pull it until the bun unravels, sending her hair cascading across the pillow in silken waves.

Tia runs her fingers along her scalp, loosening the strands from their tight updo.

Meanwhile, I turn my attention to her dress. Gripping the layers of her skirt, I guide the stretchy fabric up over her ribs, her breasts, her shoulders. Tia sits up, raising her arms to allow the dress to come up over her head, the sleeves turning inside out as they come off last.

And that's where I start my sacrament once again. Clasping her palm, I press kisses to the purple fingerprints that mar her delicate wrist. Tia watches me, the fingers of her free hand combing into my curls as she soaks up the attention like a starving man who's just been given a hearty meal.

I smile softly against her skin, relishing the way she looks at me with fire in her eyes. The heat of intense desire. A shiver ripples through her body when my lips find the sensitive spot at the crook of her elbow, and goosebumps rise across her flesh.

Humming appreciatively, I suck the skin between my lips and stroke it with my tongue. She moans softly, her hips shifting on the bed, and I know I'm turning her on. With a last soft kiss, I release her arm to return my attention to her lips. As I kiss her, I reach behind her to unclasp her bra with one hand.

Guiding her back onto the bed, I hover over her as I claim her lips, kissing her deeply. At the same time, I lift the tantalizing lace cups from her breasts and toss her bra aside. And when I palm her breast, Tia's back arches, pressing the soft flesh between my fingers.

I caress her with all the tenderness swelling in my heart, and Tia seems to blossom under the attention, her body shifting and undulating in the sexiest of dances as her excitement makes it impossible to hold still.

Her fingers find the buttons of my shirt as I kiss her, kneading her breast and rolling her taut nipple beneath my thumb at the same time. She starts to undress me, undoing my shirt one button at a time, careful not to disturb my sensual attention.

When the flaps fall open, she pushes the fabric back over my shoulders, showing me what she wants. Impatient to keep my attention on Tia, I rise to shake my arms free of the fabric and toss it aside. Then I fall on top of her once more, my lips finding her throat this time.

Air hisses between her teeth as Tia inhales sharply, and her breasts swell upward, pressing against my bare chest. I groan at the astounding softness of her body, like rose petals of the creamiest variety. And I can't get enough of her.

My hand travels down her curves, exploring her figure. Then my lips follow moments later. I want to kiss every inch of her, to show her just how much I care. How clearly I see her now. How intensely I want her. How achingly grateful I am that she's still here. Alive. In my arms.

And as I lavish her supple skin with my lips, my hands massage and knead her body into putty. Tia's firm stomach tenses and stretches as I kiss a trail over her navel. I pause, my palms on either side of her waist as I consider the sacred life she's carrying.

"*Ciao, piccola. Non vedo l'ora di incontrarti,*" I murmur, speaking to our baby like it's a secret. But seeing as Tia knows Italian along with three other languages, I'm confident she knows what I said: *Hi, baby. I can not wait to meet you.*

And when I glance up between my wife's perfect mounds of flesh, her eyes shine with tender emotion. Her fingers comb into my hair, brushing the curls from my forehead, and I smile, pressing another kiss to her belly.

Then, I continue lower.

Fingers hooking around the waist of her panties, I slowly ease them over her hips and down her legs. Then I kiss my way up the inside of her other leg this time, paying extra mind to be gentle with her injured ankle.

"Oh god, Leo," she breathes, her head falling back onto her pillow as my tongue finally strokes the seam of her pussy.

Tangy arousal already slicks her sweet folds, and I savor it, knowing she's so excited by the way I touch her. Fingers pressing gently into her hips, I hold her steady as I lick her slit again and again. Tia trembles beneath my hands, her body responding to me with the sexiest of subtle movements.

And when I wrap my lips around her clit, she cries out. Her fingers curl around the sheets as her breasts press toward the ceiling. My cock throbs against the seam of my pants as I relish the way she squirms, seeming unable to control her body with the intensity of her passion.

Circling her clit with my tongue, I bring one hand between her thighs and press two fingers inside of her. Tia shudders, her walls clamping around me as I curl slightly inside her, stroking her G-spot.

Panting, Tia bucks, her thighs twitching as she works to keep them open wide enough to accommodate me. I can feel she's close by the way her clit twitches against my tongue. And I suck gently at the same time as I finger her.

Screaming my name, Tia finds her release, and having my name on her lips in the throes of passion fills me with a deep, overpowering craving to hear it again. I continue to suck and finger Tia as her walls spasm and her clit pulses.

And only after she collapses onto the bed with a huff of relief do I release her. Rising, I wipe her juices from my chin with my palm, my gaze burning into Tia's as I yearn to be inside her an ungodly amount.

Her teeth trap her lower lip as she follows my hands with her eyes, watching with anticipation as I unbuckle my belt and then unbutton and unzip my slacks. I remove them and my boxers in one go. Then I climb between her thighs, resting my arms on either side of her as I hover on top of her.

Tia lifts her head up off the pillow, claiming my lips without hesitation, and I groan when her hands travel down my back with a feather-light touch. Cock twitching to be inside her, I ease forward and find her entrance.

A soft breath rushes from Tia's mouth into mine as I fill her slowly, easing inside her until I'm buried to the hilt. And for the first time, I'm not taking my pleasure by soaking up the power of owning Tia's body—of knowing how to make her squirm with need. This sex somehow feels more meaningful. Like it's not lust driving my arousal but a far deeper emotion.

As I move inside Tia, my focus is on pleasing her, and the deeper level of intimacy rocks me to my core. I've never experienced this with a woman before. It's almost as if it opens a new door of emotion inside me, a protective concern for Tia that unlocks a chivalrous desire I'm entirely unfamiliar with.

It's the closest I've come to making love to a woman.

And while I have no inkling of what being in love is like, I'm starting to wonder if I might not be in danger of falling for Tia.

We breathe heavily together, and still, I can't stop kissing her.

Until a slow smile spreads across her lips.

"What?" I murmur, drawing back just far enough to meet her eyes.

"You taste tangy," she admits, her creamy skin flushing beautifully.

I chuckle, low and soft. "You like it?"

Tia nods, her blush intensifying.

"Good," I growl. "Because I find the thought of you tasting your arousal on my lips entirely too sexy."

The air leaves her on a gasp, and Tia combs her fingers into my hair, bringing me closer so she can kiss me with sinful sweetness. I groan as my cock throbs from the way her tongue strokes greedily between my teeth. And though I want to make Tia come all night long, I don't know that I can last much longer with how erotically she kisses me.

"Oh god, I'm going to come," Tia murmurs against my lips just moments later.

It's a whispered confession only I get to know, and it launches me into a frenzied desire.

"Say my name, Tia," I command, rolling my hips to penetrate her deeply.

"Leo," she moans, her head tipping back as her fingers tighten in my hair.

I grunt as my release slams through me with such powerful force it leaves me almost lightheaded. Pushing deep inside Tia, I pour my seed into her with throbbing bursts. Her pussy tightens around my hard length in response. Her walls milk me eagerly as she holds me buried in her addictive depths.

I break our kiss as my lungs begin to burn and lean my forehead against hers as we pant together, our pulsing climax in perfect sync. And Tia shudders with the final aftershock before melting into a puddle of blissful relaxation beneath me.

"Holy hell, Leo," she breathes as I ease out of her and collapse onto the bed at her side.

"Yeah," I agree on an exhale, trying to wrap my mind around the intensity of our connection.

I stretch my arm toward Tia, and she wordlessly accepts the offer, rolling onto her side as she snuggles closer, resting her cheek on my chest. Her hair tickles my shoulder as it brushes lightly across my skin, raising goosebumps across my flesh. And I turn my head to press a kiss on Tia's forehead.

"What would your dream in life be?" I ask after several peaceful moments of silence. "If you could do anything, I mean."

Leaning up on an elbow, Tia turns to face me, her dark eyes penetrating. Then, after a slight hesitation, she says almost shyly, "I want to see the world. I hardly even know the town we live in. I've lived such a sheltered life, but I've read enough books to know there's a whole big world to explore, and I wish I were free to see it."

A pang of guilt lances through me as I realize that, not only is this the first time I've asked something really personal of Tia, but I also stole her one real opportunity to have the adventure she seeks. Because I postponed our honeymoon without any intention of taking her at a future time.

Inspired to do something meaningful for her, I find fresh conviction to right that wrong. Because this is one time I actually can fix what I've done. "I'll take you on the adventure of a lifetime someday," I promise.

Capturing her chin between my finger and thumb, I sit up to seal the promise with a kiss.

34

TIA

"You're getting around pretty well on those crutches," Maria observes as we make our way slowly down the steps to the flower garden.

I laugh. "Thanks. It still feels like I'm moving at a snail's pace, but I've gotten the hang of it now."

"How much longer until you get to start walking?" Stooping to admire a collection of zinnias, she plucks one and brings it to her nose.

"Dr. Luca will be out again on Tuesday to check on my progress. But the swelling is gone, and it really feels much better. I'm just using crutches because I'm pretty sure Leo's tasked the help with watching to ensure I use them until I'm given permission by a medical professional to stop."

Maria nods her understanding as she lightly strokes the petals of the flower she picked, brushing them with her fingertips. "How have you been otherwise? Any issues with the bump on your head?"

"Oh, no. That was gone within a day or so of the accident."

Maria glances left and right before dropping her voice to a whisper. "Have you... spoken with your husband more about that day? What you saw?"

I shake my head. "The one time I questioned him about it, we got into an argument. I don't think he and I will ever see eye to eye on what he did."

"And you haven't gotten any more... details?"

"He's not dumb enough to let something useful slip. And it's not like I could get back to where it happened." I glance around nervously, anxious that someone might be in the garden with us, making me jumpy.

Then Maria giggles, pulling my eyes back to her. "I can just imagine you hobbling around, three-legged in the woods. If anyone would try it, that would be you."

I snort. "Now you're starting to sound like Leo. He accused me of being stubborn the other night. Can you believe that?"

"Whaaat?" she asks with false disbelief.

"Oh, hush," I scold, bracing on my crutch to swat her shoulder.

"Oh, come on, Tia. You can't deny that one. Don't you remember the time you stayed on the piano bench *for hours*, refusing to get up because you didn't want me to keep playing *Chopsticks* wrong?"

"It wasn't just wrong, it was *horrible*," I insist. "You were just pounding the keys haphazardly, with no rhyme or reason."

"Yeah. Chopsticks," my sister says as if they're one and the same. "Point being, you couldn't just let me have my fun. You wanted it done the right way."

"That's not stubborn. I was doing the world a favor."

"And now you're stubbornly refusing to acknowledge my point," she says dryly.

This time, I can't deny it, and I laugh. "Fine, maybe I can be stubborn sometimes. But I'll refuse to admit it to Leo."

Maria giggles. "While I feel obligated to point out that's just another example to prove his case, I fully support your decision."

Laughing, I shake my head, letting my eyes fall to the gravel pathway we're covering slowly but surely.

"I miss having you around all the time," Maria confesses sadly, her humor falling away as she grows nostalgic.

"I miss being with you all," I agree, my smile slipping from my face.

"Anna, Vienna, and Sofia told me to tell you hi, by the way. I think they might cry if you don't invite them soon."

My heart twinges to think they might feel I've abandoned them. "Oh, please tell them I want them to come! And that I miss them. I just wasn't sure Mother would think they're old enough to… visit me without supervision. You know, after…"

Maria nods. "I don't think she will. But I'm sure it would mean a lot to them to get an invite. And I'll offer to keep an eye on them, in case that helps. Who knows? Stranger miracles have happened."

Without thinking about it, my hand falls onto my belly, and Maria's eyes follow the motion. "You still getting sick every day?"

"I've actually made it two whole days without throwing up," I say proudly.

"Well, that's good. I can't imagine hobbling to the bathroom on crutches has been very convenient at all," she jokes.

I laugh, shaking my head. "No, but I've learned the timing better now. I know the signs and can get to the bathroom before it's an emergency."

"A new accomplishment to put on your resume." Maria's eyes twinkle as she smiles at me.

"Yes, that will go at the top of the list," I assure her solemnly.

We laugh together, and as we near the far end of the garden, we settle onto the bench there. Casually scanning the space around us, we check to make sure we're completely alone. Then Maria turns to me with a new sense of purpose.

"Have you found anything we can use against the Morettis?" she asks, her voice dipping to barely above a whisper.

My heart skips a beat as I think about what little information I've gathered. "Well, Leo seems pretty insistent on forming a good relationship with the mayor, and for some reason, he's needed me to make that happen. I get the feeling that Mayor Romney was reluctant to interact with him or establish a relationship of any kind. But we've had dinner with the mayor and his family a few times now, and this last time, the mayor invited us to his charity event next weekend."

Maria's eyebrows raise. "That could give us something to work with. I mean, I don't know what exactly, but at least you have an idea of some connection that matters to Leo."

I nod. "He and the mayor seem to have come to an agreement that the Morettis will do some form of security for the event? I don't know. Leo's been rather vague on the details, and I don't want to show too much interest and raise his suspicion. I was hoping I might find another opportunity to visit with the mayor and his wife sometime this week. See if I can't get them to open up more about the details."

Maria perks up. "Maybe we can work with that—I'll think on it," she assures me.

And despite my convictions, a twinge of guilt hits me. I don't like plotting against Leo, regardless of what he's done to me. But it's not really about me. It's about my family and Leo's willingness to use violence to his benefit. My conscience won't just let me stand by and do nothing.

"Should I talk to Father...?" Maria's question trails off as her eyes grow round at something behind me, and my hands break into a cold sweat at the sudden anxiety behind the guarded look.

"Ladies."

My heart stops at the sound of Leo's familiar baritone, his rich voice like a nail in my coffin. Turning quickly where I sit, I look up at him, worried that he must have overheard our conversation before he appeared around the hedges.

"Leo," I gasp, trying my best not to look guilty. "You're home early."

A dashing smile spreads across his face. "And by the look of it, I've given you a fright."

"She's been ridiculously jumpy all morning," Maria steps in smoothly, lying like she was born to it. "Must be the pregnancy hormones."

"Maria!" I scold, turning back to my sister so I can collect myself.

She smiles at me, giving a one-shoulder shrug. "What? I've heard it's a thing."

"Well then, that must explain it," Leo teases, his voice dry.

I turn to look at him once more, searching for any evidence that he knows what we were talking about, but his gaze is inscrutable.

With a cordial smile, his eyes leave mine to find Maria's. "I hate to ask it, but might I steal your sister away earlier than expected? I have a... surprise for her."

The color drains from Maria's face slightly, and her eyes dart to mine, the hint of fear glimmering behind her well-composed features. It's a silent question. *Should she leave me alone with my husband? Or does he know?*

"We can make up for the lost time when I see you next," I offer, patting Maria's hand reassuringly, giving her a subtle indication that I'll be alright.

Regardless of whether he overheard me or not, I'm confident Leo won't hurt me while I'm carrying his child. Not after the transformation I've witnessed over the past week. However he might feel about me and our marriage, I'm confident in one thing at least. He loves our child—even before he's met her.

"Okay," Maria agrees hesitantly. She stands from the bench and bends to give me a light peck on the cheek. "Call me later?"

"Of course," I say, knowing that will put her mind at ease.

She gives my fingers a light squeeze before heading back down the garden path toward the house. Only when she's safely out of sight do I turn to face Leo, fully addressing my nerves for the first time as I consider the likely possibility that he might have overheard our schemes.

I brace, ready for the full force of his fury. Instead, my husband gives me a wicked smile, then puts his fingers to his lips and gives a sharp whistle that makes my heart skip a beat.

"What...?" I glance past his shoulder as the maid named Trudy steps around the wall of shrubbery, holding a beautiful evening gown.

Made of a deep hunter-green satin, the dress appears to be a draped collar wrap ruched cami dress, a deep slit running up one side. It's far more scandalous than any dress I've ever worn before, but it's breathtaking.

"What's this for?" I breathe, rocking forward on my crutches to run my fingers down the silky fabric.

"Are you up for an adventure?" he asks playfully. And the glint in his eyes makes my stomach quiver.

Excited that I might be getting outside the walls of my prison for an evening, I beam. "Where are we going?"

"You'll just have to wait and see." Taking my crutches out from under my arms, he passes them to Trudy. Then he picks me up in the hold I've grown quite familiar with over the past several days.

"I think I'm going to have to relearn how to walk after so many days of being carried around like a queen," I say cheekily, but inside, guilt gnaws at my stomach to know that while Leo was planning a surprise for me, I was plotting a very different kind of surprise for him.

"Would you prefer I let you do it yourself?" he asks, though his tone assures me he won't be letting me out of his arms.

"No, actually, I was just contemplating how I might convince you to provide this service indefinitely," I joke to cover the tumult of emotions that plague me.

He laughs, the sound low and enticing. And without an answer, he carries me back toward the house.

35

LEO

Putting together an adventure worthy of Tia proved rather challenging on such short notice and with her ankle making movement that much more difficult. But I want to do something nice for her, even if I can't take her much farther than our own backyard just yet.

And though I fully intend to make good on my promise to take her on a true adventure, this will have to do for now.

"Ready?" I ask as Tia checks her image in the mirror one last time.

She turns to me, a grin stretching across her lips. "Ready," she agrees, holding her arms straight, her wrists cocked in a look of girlish excitement.

She looks ravishing in the new dress I picked out for her, one I hoped might make her feel both sexy and sophisticated, just like she is. The satin clings to her curves in the most flattering way. The thin straps and low neck reveal a tantalizing amount of her cleavage anytime she leans forward. And the slit that runs to nearly the top of her left thigh entices me to turn this into an evening spent right here in our bedroom.

But rather than giving in to temptation, I lift Tia into my arms.

Her teasing words from earlier brings a smile to my face. And I love the fact that she's growing more comfortable with accepting my help.

"What are you smiling about?" she asks suspiciously, narrowing her eyes.

"Oh, nothing. Just, from this vantage point, I can see what you're wearing beneath your dress," I tease.

"No, you can't!" she gasps, pulling rather aggressively at the edges of the slit.

"No, I can't," I agree. "I just wanted to see how you would react."

"Yeah, well, you nearly convinced me to change," she warns darkly.

I chuckle. "Like I'd give you the opportunity now that I've got you at my mercy."

Tia shivers delicately in my arms, making my pulse quicken. Luigi opens the front door for me a moment later, offering a polite nod as we depart. At the foot of the stairs, my canary-yellow Ferrari convertible sits waiting, the top off, and the passenger door is already open so I can set Tia inside. It looks brand new now, all the bullet holes expertly repaired.

I glance at Tia from the corner of my eye, curious if she might not be upset by the reminder of our first night together. But if it bothers her, she doesn't show it. Instead, as I set her gently into the passenger seat, she smiles up at me, her look pointed as she adjusts her dress to smooth it lower.

I laugh darkly, loving her feisty behavior.

"Now, do I get to know where we're going?" Tia asks as I slip behind the wheel and close my door.

"I thought we might take a drive around town," I suggest. "Do a bit of sightseeing."

Her confession that she hardly knows the town of Piovosa makes me want to introduce her to it, to expand her horizons. Because after spending more time with her in the bedroom, I've come to realize I enjoy showing Tia something she's never experienced before.

It doesn't take long to make it into the center of town, and I drive slowly so she can fully appreciate the gothic architecture and the old-timey feel of the town center. I point things out to her as we go—the best restaurants around town, the businesses that are under the protection of my family, and now hers.

When she grasps the top of her door and turns to admire the grand opera house, I pull up to the curb.

"Have you ever been to a show?" I ask.

"Yes, but it's been years. We stopped going when..." Tia's voice trails off.

Her eyes dart in my direction before turning back to the proud stone structure, its columns giving the front entrance a Roman pantheon-type feel.

"When what?" I press, suddenly intensely curious.

"W-Well, when the conflict between our families began to escalate. I think my father believed it best to keep me and my sisters hidden from sight so we wouldn't become a tempting target..."

My gut twists as I realize why Tia would hesitate to finish her sentence. In short, I'm the reason she stopped going to the theater. My conquest began five years ago, the start of what many have dubbed my reign of terror.

"Well, we'll have to rectify that," I state, fighting my discomfort as I realize just how many ways I've hurt Tia without even trying. "Perhaps, now that our families have been united, we can all attend a performance together sometime."

"Really?" Tia turns to settle back into her seat, her face lighting up as she meets my eyes fully.

I smile, shaking my head. "Always with the note of disbelief."

Tia flushes as she gives me a shy smile. "I would love that," she murmurs.

"Good." Pulling away from the curb, I head to our next stop.

Somewhere along the line, I've come to realize that the innocent enthusiasm with which Tia approaches life is far more appealing than I realized on the night I met her. And while I've always been drawn to her more fiery, rebellious side, my attraction to her only seems to intensify when I accidentally land on something that reveals her vulnerability.

It's a strange, new attraction but one that makes me increasingly more curious about the deeper emotions that run beneath Tia's impressively still, composed exterior.

Pulling up in front of Pascal's, one of my family's favorite upscale restaurants that has resided under our protection for years, I park near the side entrance. It's a showy place with phenomenal food, but I don't make Tia get out of the car.

Not this time. I'll wait to show her off when she won't have to limp to our table on crutches.

Tonight, I want to give her a taste of life without letting her overstrain her ankle—which I know she'll do given the slightest chance.

"Pascal's?" she asks, reading the sign before turning to me.

"The best French restaurant you're going to find outside of New York City," I assure her.

"Sounds fun," she agrees, her hand taking her door handle to pop it open.

But before she can get out, a server dressed in black slacks, a white dress shirt, and a red bowtie, his long apron stretching past his knees, scurries through the side door, heading straight for our car.

"Sorry for the delay, Signor Moretti," he says breathlessly, handing me two large to-go bags of food.

"It's quite alright, Sebastian. Have a fine evening." I lean over the back of my chair, setting the food on the seat behind me, then turn to find Tia looking at me.

Her gaze is scrutinizing, her head cocked slightly.

"What?" I ask.

"It's nothing. Just..."

I wait, refusing to head on to our next stop until she tells me.

"It seems you know everybody's name—the men you work with, the help around your house. Even the servers who deliver your food," she says, gesturing pointedly to the young server as he vanishes back inside. "It's... impressive. And it shows you care."

I smile, torn between telling her the truth of the matter and letting her think better of me. And though I find I quite like Tia envisioning me as a better man than I am, I don't want to pretend with her. "One of the fastest ways to earn a person's trust is to use their name when speaking with them," I confess. It's a tactic I've used countless times, a skill I honed from very early in life.

"Oh. Right," Tia says, her eyes cast down to her lap.

"Does that disappoint you?" I ask softly, feeling the emotion radiating from her.

"No," she says quickly, her gaze snapping up to mine. "I don't know. I just... You're so skillful at reading people. At knowing how to get them to do what you want. Sometimes, I wonder if..."

"I'm manipulating you," I guess, understanding dawning on me as I realize she's far more perceptive about my actions than I had realized.

Though in Tia's case, I'm coming to terms with the fact that I don't want to play with her, to solely make her do what I want. I'm intrigued by her, and I want to see just what she might accomplish when left to her own devices.

Tia nods, her eyes falling to her lap once again, and I reach across the console to trap her chin between my thumb and finger. Gently turning her head, I make her look me in the eye.

"I'm done manipulating you, Tia," I vow. "I know I've hurt you, and I know that an apology can't fix the pain I've caused. I can't excuse the fact either. But what I can do, honestly and with every genuine bone in my body, is try to make up for my careless mistakes. Because I believe we might be better suited for each other than I could ever have hoped for. I think we might have a chance of making this a real relationship, a true partnership. And that's what I want."

Taking a deep, shuddering breath, Tia releases it in one powerful huff. Then she smiles. "I want that too," she agrees.

A smile breaks across my face, and I lean across the console to claim Tia's lips in a soft, chaste kiss. "Good. Because I have more plans for you tonight."

She grins as I put my car in reverse and head out once again.

This time, we drive past her father's house as we head out of town. Sitting up, she watches as the dark silhouettes of trees race by, forming a thick black wall.

"Now, where are we going?" she asks, her voice hovering somewhere between giddy and nervous.

"It's a surprise," I state, following the curving New England road farther into the mountains.

Finally, we reach the turnoff to the lookout point where I intend to bring her. The road is steep, carrying us up to the mountainside. Then I pull into the flat parking lot, whipping the steering wheel until we're facing back toward Piovosa.

Beneath us, the town looks like a field of fireflies alight with glowing bulbs. Nestled against the far mountain range, it's almost quaint, idyllic. But the sunset is what makes Tia gasp. The brilliant hues of pink, orange, and gold kiss the mountain tops, casting dark purple shadows on the world below.

"It's beautiful," Tia breathes, her voice rapt, her eyes glued to the beautiful scene.

"Have you ever seen home from this perspective before?" I ask, studying the enchanting wonder on her face. Her lips are parted slightly, her brown eyes round with deep emotion.

She shakes her head, her hands resting lightly on the dash as she scoots forward. "It's so... peaceful," she observes.

"Amazing how a little distance can give a person such a different impression," I note.

Then I clear my throat and reach behind me for the food before I say something that might ruin the moment.

"I hope you don't mind. I stuck with a few safer options on the menu. I figured if you like Pascal's, I can take you for a true in-house experience once we're confident you won't have any... issues."

Tia laughs, her eyes dancing as she turns to see what I have to offer. "I think you mean once I won't start throwing up at the slightest smell that offends me," she jokes.

"Precisely." I grin and pass her a fork along with the container of ratatouille.

"Mmm," this smells amazing," she says warmly, accepting the dish and taking a tentative bite. "Oh my god. It tastes even better," she groans, slumping as her eyes close so she can relish the flavor.

Reaching for the beef bourguignon next, I remove the stew's lid and try a spoonful. Just as flavorful as I recall. We share the dishes back and forth, breaking into a loaf of homemade French bread as well. And from her moans of satisfaction, I can tell that Pascal's is a hit.

"So, what do you have planned next?" Tia asks, her head leaning contentedly against the headrest behind her. She tilts her head to face me without lifting it.

The sun's soft glow finally fades behind the mountain. Our empty food containers rest on the seat behind us, and it's just about time for my grand finale. But I need to stall for just a few more minutes.

"Who says I have anything else planned?" I tease. "Wasn't this enough?"

Tia sits straighter, her cheeks pooling visibly with color even in the dim light. "It's been incredible," she assures me. "I only thought... since we're all dressed up..."

I chuckle. "I assure you, buying that dress has been entirely for my own benefit."

It's not entirely a lie. I don't have some fancy gala to take her to tonight. But I didn't want to make our first date feel too casual. I already cut corners to avoid making her hobble around on crutches all night.

Tia rolls her eyes, but the laugh that immediately follows confirms that she's still flattered—even if I only made her dress up for my pleasure.

"You'll have another opportunity to show it off," I assure her.

"I don't doubt it," she says.

"Well then, shall we go?"

"Sure," she agrees, settling contentedly back in her seat.

I turn on the car, and the lights cast an ethereal glow on the viewpoint parking lot. But rather than heading for home, like Tia expects, I simply turn the car around. Now, it's facing the trees behind us.

And the massive white tarp I had installed before them.

"What are you doing?" Tia frowns as I throw the car in park once more.

Then, her eyes dart to the trees as the projector comes to life, casting a film on our makeshift drive-in movie theater. Her jaw drops, and for a moment, she watches in stunned silence as the world around us fills with the sound of the movie's opening credits.

"How did you do this?" she breathes, turning to look at me.

"I just pulled a few strings," I say, shrugging nonchalantly.

"You did this all for me?" Her tone is incredulous, bordering on denial.

"Is that so hard to believe?" I sit up and rest my elbow on the console between us as I lean toward her.

But she doesn't answer, her eyes darting back to the screen.

"I hope it's not underwhelming. It was the best adventure I could put together on short notice. I'll give you the real deal once you can walk again," I promise.

And when Tia's eyes meet mine once again, they shine with deep gratitude. "It's wonderful," she murmurs, leaning in.

Then, her lips press against mine in a grateful sweep.

36

TIA

The spark that dances between our lips is as alluring as the first time Leo kissed me. And for a moment, all I can think of is how much I want him. The meaning behind Leo's gesture is so powerful. I'm overwhelmed by the romantic date he planned for me, touched by the effort he's gone to.

He didn't need to do it.

I'm bound to him whether I like it or not because divorce isn't an option in my world. I'm Leo's *literally* until death does us part. So he could treat me however he pleased, and I would have no say in the matter.

And that makes his gesture more meaningful than I ever could have imagined.

But as the movie starts to play, I force myself to turn and watch it. To fully appreciate the lengths he went to in order to make this night a magical one. He already launched it out of the ballpark. Because he clearly cared enough about what I said the other night to take it to heart.

And he's not just *telling* me he'll take me on an adventure someday.

He's doing it.

I grin as the movie's name flashes across the screen. *Treasure Island.* Glancing from the corner of my eye, I can see Leo's pearly smile as he grins mischievously. Somehow, the gesture seems meant for me, though his eyes are turned toward the screen.

Heart melting, I focus my attention on the opening scene. Then, his hand crosses the car's center line to take mine. My stomach flutters with inexplicable nerves, and I suddenly feel like that same seventeen-year-old girl again. The one who fell hard and fast for her family's worst enemy, a man she'd received countless warnings about.

It's terrifying.

It's a bit too similar to the very real and memorable sensation of actually falling—right off the edge of a cliff.

And yet, I can't seem to help this any more than I could when I literally fell.

Can I trust Leo to save me this time? To pull me back to safety like he did that day?

I don't know if I'm brave enough to risk it.

But after the night he's given me, I'm closer than I ever thought I would be.

I'm intensely aware of the electricity that buzzes between us, a spark that ignited with our kiss and only seems to be growing stronger in the dark solitude of our private theater. It crackles in the air and leaves me intensely aware of Leo's body.

I wish, suddenly, that the console wasn't between us, stopping me from coming closer.

Instead, I soak up the warmth of Leo's hand, aware of the cool air that envelops my shoulders—how it contrasts with the heat of his flesh. Closing my eyes for a moment, I try to recenter myself, to focus on the treat he went to so much trouble to put together.

When I open my eyes, I find it slightly more bearable to sit silently beside him, with nearly a foot between us.

Then, as if suddenly reaching the end of his patience, Leo removes his hand from mine. My stomach knots at the abrupt change, and I try to mask my disappointment as I turn to look at him. But he offers no explanation.

Instead, he opens his car door, stepping out onto the gravel that crunches beneath his fine Italian shoes. He rounds the back of the car, and a moment later, my door pops open.

"Are we going somewhere?" I ask, confusion lacing my tone, and I glance nervously out at the dark beyond.

Then Leo bends down, his face dangerously close to mine as he adjusts my seat, moving it as far back as he can before reclining it.

"What are you doing?" Baffled, I turn to watch him.

"Scooch," he insists, slipping into the car beside me a moment later.

Stunned, I sit up as he settles onto my seat, closing the door behind him. Then he pulls me close, my back against his chest, his arm around my waist as we snuggle. Despite the confined space, it's oddly comfortable.

Leo's warmth envelops me, relaxing my muscles as I melt into him. And I can't help but wonder if he didn't pluck my thoughts from my head. Because I had just been regretting the barrier that made it so I couldn't do exactly this.

Worming closer to him, I rest my head on his shoulder, more content than I have any right to be. And I settle in to watch the movie once again. I'm familiar enough with the story that it's easy to slip back into what's happening despite the distraction.

Leo's free hand rests idly on my thigh, his thumb drawing a feathery circle on the bare skin the slit has exposed. And despite myself, I can't help but think of the small surprise I have waiting for him.

Glancing up at his face, I'm momentarily mesmerized by how gorgeous he is. The sharp line of his jaw and full lips, the perfect amount of five-o'clock shadow that makes him look both manly and dignified. It's a wonderful contrast to the haphazard curls that seem to fall across his forehead with a mind of their own.

I love the way his curls fade into a clean haircut; the brilliant contrast is somehow a perfect representation of his personality. So sharp and sophisticated, and yet soft and carefree all at once.

As if sensing my eyes on him, Leo shifts his gaze from the screen.

And when he looks at me, that unspoken spark between us lights a fire deep in my belly. His eyes flick down to my lips, and my tongue darts out instinctually to wet them.

In an instant, it feels as though the oxygen has been sucked from the air around me. My heart flutters. My lips part in search of air, and still, I can hardly breathe.

Leo's eyes blaze with an intensity that makes me feel as if I were the only other person alive in the world. Shivers race across my skin as his hand leaves my thigh to brush the pad of his thumb gently across my full lower lip.

In a flash of heat, his touch releases my frozen lungs.

I exhale, the air passing shakily through my lips. And when Leo leans in—slowly, inch by inch—I crave his kiss more than my next breath.

It feels as though an eternity passes before our lips meet.

Then they do, and it's as if the world is set on fire. Leo's fingers comb back into my hair as he cradles the back of my head, holding me to him. And as his tongue darts out to deepen the kiss, mine does as well. It's soft, tender, a kiss filled with emotion.

Sparks of anticipation flicker across my skin, raising goosebumps in their wake. I shiver as it races along my spine.

Breaking our kiss, Leo peers into my eyes. "Are you cold?" he murmurs, his warm hand moving down my neck and arm, trying to wipe the tiny bumps from existence.

"No," I breathe.

It's not a lie. My skin might be cool, exposed to the late evening air, but my body is on fire.

Too impatient to wait for his lips to return, I grasp the back of his strong neck and pull him to me once again. Leo responds eagerly, his arms tightening around my waist as he holds me close.

And though I've kissed him a hundred times before, this time, it feels different.

Tonight, it's charged with emotion. My attraction to him is undeniable. I can scarcely understand the magnetism that draws me toward him. But when his lips meet mine, it's as if he's telling me he intends to lay the world at my feet.

But is it me? Are my emotions the only thing making this moment feel so meaningful?

I can no longer tell.

I'm scared to think that I'm out here on this ledge all by myself.

And scarier still is the possibility that Leo's standing on this precipice with me.

Because I've spent so long thinking of ways I could bring him down, now would be the worst time imaginable for our feelings to fall into place.

My head is a tornado of conflict.

But my body is driven by a single-minded purpose.

And as my pulse races through my veins, I guide my leg over Leo's, drawing closer, though I scarcely know to what end. Leo hums, the sound like a rumbling purr, and it releases butterflies in my stomach.

Trailing his fingers up from my calf, he explores my smooth leg, his touch light and tantalizing. He moves slowly inward, toward the warmth between my thighs. My breath hitches, my excitement rising to the breaking point as he takes his time.

His hand vanishes beneath my dress, making me throb as he explores a part of me that only he has had.

Then his fingers find the smooth, bare flesh at the summit of my legs.

"Fuck, Tia," he breathes, sending a heady dose of adrenaline flooding through my body. "You're not wearing any panties."

I smile against his lips, kissing him sweetly before shaking my head. "I thought I'd give you a little surprise as well," I tease, nipping his lower lip playfully.

Leo exhales heavily, pulling back to meet my eyes, and in his hazel gaze, I see an inferno raging. "How are you so fucking perfect?" he demands.

Then his lips are crushing mine, consuming me in a ravenous kiss.

I tremble with the sudden onslaught of pleasure, and Leo's fingers dip between my folds, stroking the sensitive, silky flesh. I gasp, the heat in my belly roaring to life at his touch. Feeling daring, I lift the curving hem of my dress, freeing my legs.

And I turn to sling one over his, straddling Leo as I settle onto his lap.

"Your ankle," he objects, his hands gripping my hips as if to take my weight.

"I'm fine, Leo," I promise, wrapping my arms around his shoulders as I twine my fingers in his hair.

Conceding to the moment, he wraps his arms around me, his hands splaying to feel my curves as he pulls me close. And he kisses me with such passion that it makes my toes curl.

Breathless, I lean back to catch my breath, my hands falling on his shoulders as I look deep into his eyes. "I want you," I murmur. "I want you so badly it hurts."

"I'm yours," he rasps, his voice hoarse with some unspoken emotion. "Wherever, however, whenever you what. I'm crazy for you, Tia."

The words blast through me like dynamite, shattering the world around me, the ground that felt so stable beneath my feet. I don't know what to say. Those words were what I'd hoped he would say to me the last time I found myself in the passenger seat of Leo's signature yellow car.

Instead, he tossed me to the curb, depositing me at my father's feet, ruined and brokenhearted.

How can I trust him now?

But I want to. Every bone in my body aches to believe Leo. And despite my better sense, I fall into the moment, allowing myself to believe the pretty picture he's painted—at least for tonight.

I capture his lips once again, kissing him deeply as my hands run down his firm pecs to find the buttons of his dress shirt. I undo them one by one, exposing the soft, dark hair that peppers his chest.

Throwing the panels wide open, I run my hands down his muscular body, relishing the feel of his stone-carved chest; the rippling movement of his well-defined abs as they tense beneath my fingertips.

Leo exhales audibly, the sound telling me he likes the way I touch him. And when my fingers land on his belt, he squeezes my hips in silent encouragement. I've never done something so bold and daring.

To initiate sex out in the open, where anyone could stumble upon us. It awakes in me that same anxiety as when Leo carried me onto our patio the night of our wedding. And at the same time, a heady exhilaration overwhelms me.

This time, I'm in command. He's letting me choose how far I want to take this.

And in the quiet parking lot, with only Leo and me in sight, I can't deny I want to try it.

I've never had the wild, reckless rites of passage described so prettily in books. My one attempt went so completely sideways that I was certain I would never do anything so stupid ever again.

But when I'm with Leo, I can't seem to help myself. He makes me feel alive.

Fingers fumbling with his belt buckle, I wet my suddenly dry lips. My breaths come shallow and fast now, my heart pounding a mile a minute. And when I finally release the button of his slacks and lower the zipper, I feel as though my heart might burst.

With a cool calm that only accentuates my nerves, Leo lifts his hips slightly to push his pants down. My core tightens as his thick cock springs free, standing to attention before me. A bead of precum graces the tip, making my stomach quiver.

As he settles back onto the seat, his hands finding my hips once again, I grasp his impressive erection and brush the pad of my thumb across his silken head, spreading the slick moisture.

Leo groans, his fingers pressing into my flesh, and when I look up, his jaw is clenched, the tendons flexing beneath his skin. I bite my lip, suddenly unsure of what to do next. I want him inside of me, but I don't exactly know how to take control. To be on top.

In theory, I get the concept, but now that I'm faced with the task, I feel my confidence slipping away.

"I..." I hesitate, worried I'm going to ruin the moment.

"Would you rather not?" he asks, his voice strained yet somehow boundlessly patient.

I shake my head. Then, I realize he might take that to mean I don't want to. Bucking up my courage, I swallow hard and force the words from my lips. "I want to, but I've... never done this before."

"My sweet, innocent girl," Leo releases on a heavy breath. And he sits up, bringing our lips closer as he cups my cheek with one palm. "That's nothing to be embarrassed about." He kisses me, the gesture soothing my anxiety. "I love teaching you... and knowing that I'm the only one who gets to satisfy you."

My breath hitches at the erotic nature of his confession. I can scarcely believe that of all the husbands in the world, I get a man who knows just how to satiate my desires. Nodding, I look down once again to stroke his impressive erection, and my core quivers with fresh anticipation.

Strong hands lift my hips, guiding me over his hard length. "Guide me to your entrance, *bella mia*," he murmurs against my lips.

I do as he says, shuddering at the euphoric feel of his silken head sliding between my folds. And when his cockhead finds my entrance, I feel an intense, aching desire to have him inside me.

As if sensing my need, Leo slowly guides my hips down on top of him. I moan at the glorious sensation of him filling me.

"Now roll your hips," he commands, showing me with his hands as he moves me gently.

It feels so good, I can hardly stand it. Somehow, the confined space of the Ferrari makes it feel even more intimate, the subtle motion awakening countless nerves inside my body. Wrapping my arms around his shoulders, I do as Leo said, shifting my hips until I'm rocking on top of him.

"Oh god," I gasp, overwhelmed by the sudden and intense stimulation.

Leo's lips find the hollow of my throat, and he kisses the tender flesh, sucking it lightly against his mouth. His hands roam up my back, his palms sliding across the soft satin of my dress, and the thin fabric makes me feel almost naked as the heat radiates from his body into mine.

It doesn't matter that we've only just started. I'm so turned on, I'm moments from coming.

The heady combination of our public exhibition, combined with the intimate closeness enforced upon us by the car, mingles with the charged tension brought on by the romantic evening and Leo's dangerously meaningful words.

I can feel it even in his touch, the tenderness that I craved so desperately on our wedding night.

This is what it means to become one with someone.

"Come for me, Tia," Leo breathes against my skin.

And my body can't seem to disobey him. I gasp as my walls clench around his hard length, my clit throbbing with the need for release. A wave of euphoria washes through me, and as it reaches the fire burning in my core, tingling electricity ripples out from the spot, chasing a million different lines as it sets my body alight.

Leo groans, his hands taking control of my movement as my strength leaves me in the wake of my release. And as he presses deep inside me, my pussy spasms, gripping him with each throbbing pulse.

I pant, my breaths ripping from me like sobs as the ecstasy makes the world around us vanish. Only Leo fills my mind and body, leaving me a burning ball of desire amongst the stars above.

Collapsing forward, I brace heavily against Leo's shoulders as I kiss him deeply, eager to reward him for the bliss that continues to dance through my body. His tongue strokes between my teeth, tasting me deeply as his hips rise beneath me, pushing further inside me.

And though I'm still riding the aftershocks of my first orgasm, I can feel a second one beginning to build in its wake. Leo's hands knead the supple flesh of my ass, even as he supports and guides my hips in a sensual ride.

Every time he presses into me, I feel as though we might just set the world on fire. Our passion burns white-hot, melting my insides.

"God, I could do this all night," Leo rasps against my lips, his voice strained with need.

Nodding, I tangle my fingers into his curls once again. "You feel so good," I breathe, though the words hardly do it justice.

Leo groans, the sound almost agonized, and it makes my core tighten deliciously.

"Fuck, Tia."

Leo's pace intensifies, as does mine. My need drives me forward, taking control of my body as my hips rock with newfound confidence —like they've suddenly taken on a life of their own. I grind down on Leo, my clit throbbing as it's crushed against him. And I know it's only a matter of seconds before I come again.

I've never done anything so intensely erotic, and it makes the pleasure that much sweeter.

Leo grunts, the sound alerting me to his impending release, and a moment later, he growls, "I'm gonna come."

I beat him to the punch by a fraction of a second, and I bite my lip to muffle the scream of pleasure that threatens to burst from my lips. Letting my head fall back, I press my eyes closed as my second orgasm rips through me like a tornado. Spurred on by the tantalizing sensation of Leo filling me with hot cum, I can't seem to control myself.

My hips rock forward aggressively, taking Leo deep inside my body as I grind down on top of him. And as my pussy throbs, my clit fluttering, I feel a deep sense of satisfaction at my accomplishment.

Breathing heavily, I slow to a stop, settling onto Leo's lap as I let my arms fall around his neck. Leaning forward, I press my forehead to his, soaking up the deep intimacy of the moment. And in a flash, I realize that this connection between us is going to obliterate my plans.

How can I betray Leo now, when I'm falling for him so hopelessly?

37

TIA

With each passing morning, the war waging within me intensifies as my ankle gradually heals. Sitting in one of the library's bay windows, I soak up the sun's rays as I stare out at the vast grounds of the Moretti estate.

It's a beautiful day, not a cloud in the sky. And the grass is a brilliant emerald green that contrasts the dark woods beyond. In the distance, I can see each peak of the Allegheny Mountains. It reminds me of the stunning view Leo showed me of our tiny town nestled in the valley below.

And as my thoughts circle around to my husband once more—like they have countless times this morning—I feel desperately torn.

The key to Leo's downfall is within my reach. I know it. I have dirt on him that could shatter the mayor's trust. I could expose Leo's violent tendencies and dismantle the façade he's carefully built—though I still don't understand the bigger picture that makes Mayor Romney so crucial to my husband's success.

But the more time I spend with Leo, the harder it becomes to see the monster I know lurks within. Despite the violence he's unleashed upon our town and the personal torment he's subjected me to, something is changing.

Leo is changing—I think.

And it confounds me.

Piovosa, once a rich tapestry woven by the old Italian families who founded the town, now bears the scars of Leo's conquest. His bloodlust and eagerness to upend tradition have torn through the fabric of our community. Or so my father has said.

And after witnessing Leo's violence firsthand, I understand the destruction he is capable of. Yet, a strange metamorphosis is occurring. Leo, the tyrant, has been showing me a softer side, making it increasingly difficult for me to view him solely as the ruthless conqueror I once believed him to be.

Not to mention, our drive around the streets of Piovosa makes me question who, besides the powerful families that so recently reigned, Leo's ambitions are hurting. Because the streets looked far more peaceful than I'd envisioned, the buildings were entirely intact. Even the server who brought our dinner out to us seemed perfectly at ease with my husband.

It feels as though everything I thought I knew has been cast in a strange and disturbing new light.

Are my pregnancy hormones playing tricks on my mind and weakening my resolve? Or is Leo genuinely changing? These questions echo in my thoughts as I navigate this precarious dance between vengeance and an unforeseen empathy.

"There you are!" Maria's voice echoes from the vaulted ceiling of the library, drawing me from my reverie.

I turn from the window to find her striding toward me, a smile on her face.

"How did it come as no surprise when your butler told me this is where I'd find you?"

I laugh, turning and dropping my feet to the floor as I stand. "You're early," I say affectionately.

"I skipped out on my last class of the day," she jokes. "No, I guess Mr. Whitley had to take his son to the doctor for an ear infection."

"Oh, poor Sammie," I say, my shoulders dropping.

"Yeah, sounds like he's on the mend, though. It's just a check-up to ensure the antibiotics are working properly."

"Well, that's good," I say, pulling my sister in for a hug.

"Speaking of doctors, where are your crutches?" Maria demands, her voice sounding impressively parental. I wonder if my absence from the house has required her to take up the role of oldest sister.

"I've been a grudgingly obedient patient. He said I don't have to use them as long as I listen to my body and don't push it too far."

"Yay! That's awesome."

"My arms are grateful," I acknowledge with a smile.

"Does this mean we should stay inside?" she offers.

"Of course not. I'll be fine going as far as the garden. There are plenty of benches where we can rest if I need to."

"Okay." Maria looks dubious, but when I link arms with her, she follows, her energy lifting once again.

"So, how's the family? Did you tell our sisters how much I miss them and wish they would come visit?"

"I did." Maria gives me a toothy smile as we exit the library, strolling casually down the hall. "They were overjoyed to receive an invitation. And believe it or not... Father agreed to let me bring them next week."

I stop short, turning to my sister. "You're joking."

"Nope." Maria pops her *p* for emphasis. "Actually, it seems as though things are calming down between our family and the Morettis."

"How so?"

Maria shrugs. "Well, Father's not going blue in the face ranting about *that damn Moretti heir* anymore. And according to Maury"—one of our many cousins in the family business—"Leo gave him and a few other Guerras fairly high positions in his new operation."

"New operation?" I ask, a red flag going up in my mind.

"Yeah, that business with the mayor you were telling me about. I guess things are expanding so rapidly that the Morettis are putting our alliance to better use."

I release a low whistle, reeling slightly from the drastic shift in such a short span of time. "I wonder what changed Leo's mind. Last time we spoke, it seemed like the alliance was more of an excuse for the Morettis to trample all over us..."

The subtle remark hinting at where my loyalties truly lie makes me think twice, and I realize that things aren't so black and white as I had seen them before. It makes me uncomfortable to think of it as "us and them." Not with Leo on the far side of the line.

"Well, rumor has it that Leonardo Moretti's new bride has turned him soft," Maria whispers conspiratorially, leaning in as her hold tightens around my arm. "But we both know *that's* a lie."

"Maria, hush," I scold, picking up the pace until we're outside the ballroom and walking across the fountain-laden terrace.

Still, I'm glad to hear that things between Leo and my father have grown more amicable. Maria's comment would hint that Leo's taken off his boxing gloves, and it sounds like our father might be more willing to maintain the peace I bartered than I had given him credit for.

It brings me a great sense of relief. Maybe my concerns over Father's words to Leo were misguided. Maybe he only said them out of genuine concern over marrying me off to a man who had hurt me before. Maybe he was just trying to protect me.

Maria and I walk in silence until we reach the garden, and as our feet crunch along the path, she glances at me with a concerned gaze.

"How have you been? Really?" she asks, her voice soft, inviting me to open up about the horrors I must have witnessed since our last visit.

But I have nothing weighing on my mind except the conflict of whether I have it in me to betray Leo anymore.

"Honestly?" I say, turning to face my sister. "I'm the happiest I've ever been in my life."

Emotion tightens my throat, and tears sting the back of my eyes. I laugh it off, trying to release my sudden weepiness.

"You're serious," Maria observes in wonder.

I nod, then loop my arm through my sister's once more as we

continue walking. "Maybe I'm just deluded. But since the day of my fall, it feels as though Leo's... changing."

"Well, it's not completely unheard of," Maria acknowledges. "People change, Tia. Sometimes, for the better. But that's a pretty massive shift in the few weeks since you got married. Can you trust it?"

The notion of change hangs in the air, and I consider her question silently for several seconds. "I don't know yet," I confess finally. "All I know is that Leo's shown me more care and consideration—more tenderness than I've ever known before." And he hasn't asked for anything in return.

That's what confuses me most. I could understand Leo better when he treated me nicely before asking me to play the good wife when he invited Mayor Romney over for dinner. But somewhere along the way, Leo stopped treating me like a pawn in his game.

Does that mean he sees me as a more valuable piece? Or has he stopped playing with me altogether?

I can't tell. I don't know how long I can trust his kindness to last. But I'm dangerously close to hoping he means it this time. That his feelings are real—not just for our unborn child, but for me as well.

As we talk, the prospect of forgiving Leo—actually letting go of the ugly past between us—begins to take root. The idea that he might be transforming, that the man I once saw as a conqueror could be evolving into something else, gains traction. And my heart flutters at the thought that I somehow stumbled upon true happiness.

If my father can let go of past grievances after so many years, can't I?

"Maybe it's time I set aside my anger," I murmur, the words carrying the weight of uncertainty.

Maria smiles, a sisterly understanding passing between us. "If you've genuinely found a way to be happy in your marriage, Tia, then there couldn't be a better time."

I laugh, the stress and anxiety lifting from my shoulders and leaving me as light as a feather. It's a risk, I know, letting go of my anger, my thirst for revenge that I've clung to like a shield since the plan first came into my head. But if Leo's actually changing, then perhaps I should give him one last chance.

"Wow," Maria says, stopping in her tracks.

"What?" I turn to face her, the smile falling from my lips.

"It's just... you really do seem happy. I've been so worried for you these past few weeks—having to live in the same house with a man who hurt you so badly, forced to marry him for the good of the family. I just can't believe how relieved I am that you really seem okay."

Maria sniffles, and for the first time, I see the deep concern that she's been hiding from me, her herculean effort to stay strong as my single lifeline back to our family.

"Oh, Maria," I breathe, pulling my little sister into my arms. "No one could ask for a better sister than you." Fighting to keep myself together, I cling to her with all my might, pouring every ounce of my love for her into the embrace.

Maria gives a teary laugh, squeezing me back. "I'm pretty sure I'm the lucky one," she insists. "But, Tia, really, I want you to know how happy I am for you. I hope Leo can live up to what it will take to deserve you."

I laugh, giving Maria one last squeeze before releasing her. Then I take her hand as we keep walking.

"I never expected it to happen like this," I admit, a wry smile playing on my lips as we stroll around a gurgling fountain.

"Life has a way of surprising us, doesn't it?" Maria acknowledges. "Man, I can't believe I'm going to be an aunt!"

"You're just now realizing this?" I tease.

"No!" Maria objects. "It just didn't feel right to get excited about it until now."

Her confession makes my heart twinge, and I wrap my arm around my sweet sister, grateful to have her as my closest, most loyal friend.

But her mention of the baby gives me another reason to be grateful for my newfound sense of peace. Until now, I hadn't allowed myself to think too hard about how Leo's downfall would leave our child fatherless. And for the first time, I can contemplate the possibility of this new future for myself and my child.

The journey toward reconciliation may be fraught with uncertainty, but I am no longer convinced that Leo is the irredeemable monster I once believed him to be. He might not be perfect—far from it. But if he's willing to change, if he's capable of the good I've seen in him over the past week, then maybe he deserves a second chance.

Perhaps forgiveness, not revenge, is the key to healing the wounds that run so deep.

38

LEO

"What do you think?" Tia asks, drawing my attention as she gives a twirl, showing off her elegant black evening gown.

Its A-line cut and corset bodice mold to her trim waist and draw the eyes to the keyhole in the gauzy fabric just above her breasts. The tulle then dips sharply to the right, forming a ruched one-shoulder strap.

More black tulle flares out from her waist in feather-light layers that accentuate her hips before trailing to the floor. A subtle shimmer in the lower layers mimics the glitter of a starry night. As Tia settles into a pose, her forward leg reveals a tantalizing side slit that reaches halfway up her thigh.

"Perfect," I say warmly, my voice low and predatory as I prowl toward her.

Tia smiles as I pull her into my arms, holding her firmly against me.

"I'll let the mayor know we'll be staying in tonight," I tease. Kissing her, I halt her objection as I silently tell her exactly what I would do with her if she'd let me.

"Leo!" she scolds, pushing playfully at my shoulders. "We said we would go, and you're not about to get away with depriving me of a night out. This is my first time wearing heels since my fall, and I intend to savor the full use of my legs again."

"Does this mean you intend to dance?"

"Well, it is a ball, isn't it?" she insists.

I barely danced with her on our wedding day. I'd been too busy making my point to Don Guerra to appreciate the value of that missed opportunity. And I intend to rectify my error tonight.

"I think we better get a move on, then," I state, pressing one last kiss to Tia's lips before releasing my beautiful bride.

She's gone all out tonight, her hair done up in an intricate display of ringlets that cascade from the loose knot that sits like a crown on her head. Her makeup is heavier than usual as she made it into a smokey eye with a hint of glitter that matches her dress. And her lips are a luscious shade of crimson, making her look dangerously like the seductress she's proven to be beneath her innocent facade.

Offering her my elbow, I lead her from the room. It fills me with relief and pride to see her walking confidently in her strappy high heels tonight. While Tia's been as stubborn as a mule about her pain over the past week, I was starting to worry her injury might be more severe than she was willing to acknowledge. But it seems the doctor was correct about her needed recovery time.

And if I'm perfectly honest, it brings me an impressive boost in confidence to have Tia in full health and by my side.

In the entryway, we convene with my father, all of us intending to ride together to the charity event that's the talk of the town. I'm relying on his silent presence to ensure things go off without a hitch.

While I'm to be the charming and respectable face of the Moretti family as Mayor Romney's honored guest, my father will handle any hiccups, should they arise. My best men are already in place, stationed at the town hall and debriefed on their duties, though the reason behind it, I've kept close to the vest. Only my father, Johnny, and Rasco know what's really at stake tonight.

This contract with the mayor demands discretion, and with my need to put trust in the Guerra family before they're truly vetted, I think it best if only those I trust with my life are privy to the details.

As we arrive at the town hall, I wait for my door to be opened, then step out of the car onto the red carpet, offering Tia my hand. Placing her delicate fingers on my palm, she uses me to steady herself as she alights from the car as if it were a carriage and she's the belle of the ball.

She smiles at me, her teeth white against the dark crimson of her lipstick, and my pulse quickens with pride to know she's the woman I'll have on my arm tonight.

"I'll see you both again at some point," my father acknowledges, straightening his jacket as he gives me, then Tia a curt nod. Preceding us up the steps, he pauses to shake the mayor's hand before vanishing inside.

"What's he in such a hurry about?" Tia asks, her eyes following him as we take a more casual pace up the stairs.

"He'll be overseeing the security we've been hired to perform while I get the night off to spend with my lovely wife," I state, pressing a kiss to her knuckles before tucking her hand securely around my elbow once again.

Tia hums happily, her smile growing. "How did she ever get so lucky?"

"Tia, you're back on your feet!" the mayor booms jovially, cutting our banter short.

Turning her radiant smile on the unsuspecting politician, Tia laughs. "Thank goodness. I was starting to think my arms might fall off by the time my ankle healed."

She and Signora Romney exchange air kisses to the cheek, the older woman giving Tia's forearms an affectionate squeeze. At the same time, Mayor Romney takes my hand in a firm grasp.

"I trust your men have everything in order?" the mayor asks, his voice dipping lower as he takes on a businesslike tone.

"I've employed my best men for the evening. I assure you, they won't let us down."

Mayor Romney releases a deep breath. "Good. Several of these auction pieces are very pricey, and I want to ensure they're in good hands."

"You have nothing to worry about," I assure him.

"Well then, please enjoy the night. Bid on an item if you see anything that appeals to you. It will go to a good cause, after all." He gives Tia a wink.

With a respectful nod to our hosts, I place my hand on the small of Tia's back, and we both head inside. The front room is bustling with activity, guests talking and laughing as they stand in their finest dresses and jewels.

My men stand as silent sentries around the room, moving slowly as they assess the attendees, their gazes sharp and alert but passive. Impressively respectable as a security detail—which shouldn't surprise me, considering their background of training.

"Should we check out the auction?" I offer, gesturing toward the sign that points us down a hallway to the room where the items are on display.

"Definitely," Tia agrees. Her heels tap lightly on the wood floor as we make our way past several gathered groups.

It doesn't escape my attention that many eyes shift to follow Tia as she walks through the room, men's gazes appreciative, almost covetous until they see me just a half step behind her. As soon as our eyes meet, they quickly avert their gaze.

This room is heavily guarded, with an attendant for each item as well as several more of my men with eyes on the open space. Each auction piece is enclosed in a glass case with a spotlight shining down on it in a flattering display.

"See anything you like?" I ask, leaning close to Tia's ear as we meander past the first few cases.

"They're all beautiful," she murmurs, admiring the rare pieces of jewelry and oil paintings, even a violin claiming to have belonged to Fritz Kreisler.

"Do you play?" I ask, teasing as I point to the elegant string instrument.

Tia breathes a laugh. "Not well. I'm more of a pianist."

"You're joking," I state, straightening.

She turns to me. "No. Why?"

I chuckle, taking Tia's hand and bringing her delicate fingers closer to eye level. "I've always thought you had the hands of a pianist. But I never thought to ask if you played."

Tia smiles coyly. "You have much to learn about me, Signor Moretti."

"And I intend to discover all your secrets in time," I tease.

The smile falls from Tia's lips, and then it returns so quickly, I almost wonder if I imagined it. But when she turns to keep studying the auction items, I sense there's something to my observation. *Is Tia keeping secrets from me?*

A sliver of doubt wiggles its way inside my chest, though I try and stamp it out. She's never done anything to break my trust. It would hardly be fair of me to condemn her over a look. And perhaps I'm reading too far into it. After all, there are some parts of who I am that I would rather she not know about, some less flattering facts that I'm sure Tia would not approve of if she found out.

"What about this?" I suggest, stopping in front of a metalwork rose sculpture.

The flower is so accurate; its petals curled to the point where it hovers near decay. A single fallen petal lies on the cut glass beneath it, the flower drooping toward it as if saddened by the loss.

"It's beautiful. But where would we put it?" Tia asks.

"Wherever you like."

She glances up at me sharply, deep emotion in her eyes. Then her lips curl into a breathtaking smile. "Let's make a bid."

I gesture for her to do the honors, and she leans over the table, scribbling our information into the next available slot. Her hand pauses over the bid amount, and I playfully take the pen from her fingers.

"Let's have a little fun, shall we?" I suggest. "After all, it's for charity." I put in a sum well over the value of the item, exponentially more than the previous bid.

Tia gapes at me. "You're joking."

I shrug. "I don't see why we can't splurge when it goes to a good cause."

Her face softens, and Tia leans up onto her toes to press a kiss to my cheek. "You're a rare man, Leonardo Moretti," she murmurs.

I take her hand in response, kissing her palm. "Shall we go see what the party's all about?"

Smiling, Tia nods, and we leave the action room to head toward the main hall. The ball seems to be in full swing, with a decadent buffet for people to enjoy food and music that floods the room with a lively tune. Couples move gracefully around the dance floor, spinning and twirling in a swirl of elegant, flowing skirts and crisp tuxedos.

"Mother, Father," Tia says, stopping short as her parents approach us through the crowd.

"Tia." Signora Guerra steps forward to pull her daughter into a warm embrace, and I take a moment to appreciate the sign of affection before turning to extend my hand toward Don Guerra.

"Excellent turnout tonight, don't you think?" he says, his eyes scanning the crowd.

"Hopefully, that means high bids for the charity auction," I say, and with a quick glance, I share a knowing smile with my wife.

"Undoubtedly," he agrees.

"It's wonderful to see you," Signora Guerra says, cupping her daughter's cheek. "You look well. Healthy. Maria said you took quite the fall."

"I'm fine. Just a light sprain, but it healed," she assures her mom.

Doing my best to keep the frown from my face, I'm intrigued that Tia's parents seem to not have spoken to their daughter anytime recently. From Don Guerra's word of advice at our wedding, I would have assumed them much closer. Then again, there are plenty of reasons their relationship could be on shakier ground right now.

But if I'm the reason their relationship is strained, I'll do my best to help mend fences where I can.

"We would love to have you—and the rest of your daughters, of course—over for dinner sometime soon," I offer, charming Tia's mother with a smile.

"That sounds wonderful," she agrees. "Right, Giuseppe?"

"Of course, a gracious invitation."

We exchange a few more pleasantries before the Guerras excuse themselves to head to the buffet table, and I turn my attention back to Tia.

"What do you say? Will you honor me with a dance?" I suggest.

Tia's eyes light up. "If you're lucky, I might just be willing to dance with you twice."

Chuckling, I guide my bride onto the dance floor, finding an open spot as the band pauses between songs. Then, as the music starts once more, I take up a ballroom frame and guide Tia into a foxtrot.

Tia smiles, her arm resting lightly on top of mine as she grasps my shoulder with one hand and clasps my palm with the other. Her neck arches elegantly to the side as she moves with flawless grace across the floor.

It brings me back to our first dance, how calm and poised she was from the very start of the day, how regally she'd carried herself. My wife is a wonder, a treasure I can scarcely believe I was lucky enough to have fallen into my lap. All because she waltzed into my house one night looking for an adventure.

Then, in an instant, the magic of the moment is shattered.

Gunshots ring through the open ballroom, the sound distant, as if coming from down the hall. But the sharp cracks are unmistakable. As are the panicked screams that follow.

The band falls silent, all eyes shifting toward the door, and Tia stumbles into me. Clinging to my arms, she leans against my chest as a frightened gasp rushes past her lips. And I instinctively wrap an arm protectively around her shoulder.

The violent shots come to an abrupt stop, and for one single, suspended moment, it's as if the world has gone completely silent. Then, a deep voice bellows down the hall.

Fuck. That's Johnny. Something's definitely wrong.

"Tia, find your father and hide," I command, pushing her gently toward the buffet table as I turn to make a beeline for the ballroom door.

Frustrated that my men haven't managed to keep the conflict quiet and furious that we have something to deal with at all when tonight is supposed to solidify my relationship with the mayor, I intend to crush the disturbance before it can get any further out of hand.

39

TIA

Despite Leo's orders—and the clear danger waiting in the direction he's headed—I race after him, following him from the ballroom and down the hall toward the auction room. Because I can't stop the terrible sinking feeling in my gut.

My father's energy was off tonight. He barely looked at me when we spoke. His gaze was distracted, his mind clearly somewhere else. And as soon as I reach the doorway of the auction room, my suspicions are confirmed.

Several of my cousins and many of my father's men—men I've known since I was a little girl—are now in the custody of Leo's men.

Maria must have told Father about the deal Leo made with the mayor—and the significance of tonight's event. I shared the information with my sister in confidence, when I was still trying to formulate a plan to destroy the Moretti family. But in her fear for my safety, my sister must have thought it best to pass my thoughts on to my father.

And apparently, he took the information and ran with it. He chose tonight as the opportune moment to betray Leo—just as I had originally intended to do. Like father, like daughter. Only my father didn't trust me enough to tell me about his plan.

And suddenly, I'm faced with picking sides when I desperately do not want to have to choose.

"What the fuck is going on here?" Leo growls, his presence intimidating as he seems to grow larger, more bearlike in his fury.

I hover just beyond the door's threshold, suddenly scared to enter at the expressions of fierce violence on the men's faces.

"The Guerras thought it'd be a good idea to come in guns a-blazing during the charity event and heist the auction items," one man growls, a man I think I've heard Leo address as Johnny once before. "Idiots didn't even try to be subtle."

The tendons in Leo's jaw pop as he clenches his teeth in fury. "Does Don Guerra know about your imbecilic plan?" he demands, pinning his gaze on my cousin Maury. "You do realize he's a guest at tonight's event. You can't possibly think this will shed a positive light on your family. And what gives you the right to use the two brain cells that make up your intelligence to come up with a plan anyhow? You work for me now, Maury. Or did you forget? You don't get to so much as sneeze without my permission. So, what the fuck are you doing here tonight?"

I've never seen Leo so angry. Even when he shot that Valencia man in the woods, he did it with a chilling calm. This new rage is something to behold, and it makes me tremble deep in my bones.

But like a true Guerra, Maury's too stubborn to back down from a fight. He just sneers, clearly oblivious to what's at stake. "You play such a big man, but you have no idea what kind of game you've set in motion. The Guerras are a powerful family that has ruled this town for centuries. You can't just waltz in and expect us to step aside because of one wedding."

My heart stops at the scathing words, and suddenly, my understanding of the entire situation shifts. Not just the standoff but everything. My pregnancy. The wedding. The tension between our two families, which seemed to vanish overnight.

My father never intended to follow through with the alliance. He sold me to the Morettis with every intention of using the temporary peace to lay his trap.

Why else would Maury have such clear disdain for Leo's authority?

Leo's back stiffens, his countenance shifting in an instant to the cool, apathetic man I witnessed outside the cabin in the woods. My blood turns to ice as a sense of foreboding takes hold of me.

"Perhaps a wedding won't stop you, but after the right number of Guerra men die, I'm sure I can bring your family to heel just like the rest," Leo states coldly, his voice entirely too calm all of a sudden.

The transformation is what terrifies me most. Like he's flipped a switch, shutting off the emotion that has made him seem so incredibly human this past week. And with horror, I realize just how close my cousin is to delivering his own death sentence.

My stomach plummets as Leo reaches for something in his suit jacket, and I recognize the distinct sound of a gun cocking a moment later.

In sheer panic, I don't stop to think. Sprinting across the room, I fling myself in front of Maury. "No, Leo, please. He's my cousin," I beg, my heart hammering in my throat.

"Get out of the way, Tia," Leo growls, his hazel eyes like iron as they stare past me at my kneeling kin.

And though I'm terrified, I can't bring myself to do as he says. Thick tears flood my eyes, spilling down my cheeks as I start to cry. "Please, Leo, show mercy!" I sob. "If you have a drop of love for me in your heart, don't kill my family. I'll do anything."

For a moment, I see a flicker of doubt in his eyes. A conflict that makes him hesitate.

Then his iron will wins out. "You might be my wife, but you get no say in this business. In my line of work, betrayal is the ultimate sin. And your family just proved how useless their vow of loyalty is. Now, they get to pay the price."

Trembling from head to toe, I force myself to stand my ground, praying I can think of something to save Maury while I use my body as a shield. Because I'm fairly confident that, even in his fury, Leo won't shoot me when I'm carrying his child.

But before I can come up with a single idea, my eyes shift to the suddenly occupied doorway. My father enters with Mayor Romney at his side. A look of thunderous fury takes over the mayor's usually kind features as he takes in the sight—Leo's men holding what appear to be unarmed members of the Guerra family at gunpoint.

"What is the meaning of this?" Mayor Romney demands.

Leo turns slowly, seeming to come back to himself as he lowers his gun. And from his expression, I can see all his plans come crashing down around him as he realizes his efforts have failed.

"You see, Honorable Mayor," my father says smoothly, his silken tone like a knife to my gut. "I told you he was nothing more than a violent brute. He's not to be trusted."

"Says the man who sold off his daughter on the pretense of forming an alliance," Leo growls. "You don't just dishonor your word. You betrayed your own daughter just to get revenge on me."

"Is that so?" my father sneers, his gaze condemning as he finally turns it on me. "But you see, Leo, Tia probably knows better than any of us about the business of vows and betrayal. After all, she's the one who told me about your desperate deal with the mayor. She's the one who informed me about the importance of this event. How your men would need to prove themselves as legitimate security. And why? I can only imagine it would be to convince the mayor that he should entrust Piovosa's security to you. And once you gained control of the law, who could possibly stop your reign of terror then?"

The room falls deathly silent, and the blood drains from my face as my father deposits me squarely in the line of fire. I have nothing to defend myself. And he just announced Leo's plans to the world, exposing him in front of the mayor. I don't see how Leo will recover.

But my father's not done twisting the knife. "You failed, Leo, and it doesn't matter what you do now. You're done. All your efforts to impress the mayor are for nothing, especially when you're so clearly willing to take an innocent, unarmed man's life right here in the middle of a charity event."

It's a cruel truth, and yet, I can't help but feel like my father's betrayal is so much worse. He used me, led me like a lamb to slaughter. *And for what?*

By the Maury's reckoning, it was just another move in some dark, twisted game.

But as I meet Leo's penetrating gaze, all I can think about is the utter betrayal in his eyes. And suddenly, I know without a shadow of a doubt that I made a terrible mistake.

I picked the wrong side.

And now it's too late.

CAN'T GET ENOUGH of Leo and Tia? Click here to gain instant access to a bonus scene from Leo's POV!

Ready for the end of Leo and Tia's love saga? Click here to get, Vicious Redemption, the final chapter of this love saga.

My worst enemy **turned out to be the only one I can trust…**

Until I betrayed him.

Leonardo Moretti showed me my first glimpse of freedom.

And in exchange, I gave him my virginity.

Then he broke my heart.

And left me with proof of our transgression.

His baby, growing inside me.

I took his name to protect my family—and our child.

And I vowed to get revenge on the monster who used me.

I never expected to fall in love with the merciless mafia heir.

When my father breaks the alliance between our families, he leaves me exposed, vulnerable.

And his betrayal forces me to choose between my family and my husband.

But now Leo knows about my plans to ruin him.

And he might never forgive me.

Have I condemned myself and the innocent life growing inside me by putting my faith in the wrong man?

Or can I save us with a vicious act of redemption?

Ready to start reading? Download Vicious Redemption here now!

Or click to join my Playhouse reader group on Facebook for updates on Vicious Redemption. Plus, gain access to exclusive content, giveaways and more!

Made in the USA
Monee, IL
22 October 2024